THE
ISLAND

Catherine Cooper is a journalist specializing in luxury travel, hotels and skiing who writes regularly for national newspapers and magazines. She lives near the Pyrenees in the South of France with her family, cats and chickens. Her debut, *The Chalet*, was a top 5 *Sunday Times* bestseller. *The Island* is her fourth novel.

@catherinecooper
@catherinecooperjournalist

By Catherine Cooper

THE
ISLAND

CATHERINE COOPER

HarperCollins*Publishers*

HarperCollins*Publishers* Ltd
1 London Bridge Street,
London SE1 9GF
www.harpercollins.co.uk

HarperCollins*Publishers*
Macken House,
39/40 Mayor Street Upper,
Dublin 1
D01 C9W8

First published by HarperCollins*Publishers* 2023
1

A catalogue record for this book is available from the British Library

ISBN: 978-0-00-849732-3 (PB)

Typeset in Sabon LT Std by
Palimpsest Book Production Limited, Falkirk, Stirlingshire

Printed and bound in the UK using 100% renewable electricity
at CPI Group (UK) Ltd

For all the journalists, PRs and influencers
I've spent time with on many fantastic press trips
over the years, for the generous hoteliers and tourist
boards who have hosted me. I hope I am more
Malia than Claire.

A Poison Tree

BY WILLIAM BLAKE

I was angry with my friend;
I told my wrath, my wrath did end.
I was angry with my foe:
I told it not, my wrath did grow.

And I waterd it in fears,
Night & morning with my tears:
And I sunned it with smiles,
And with soft deceitful wiles.

And it grew both day and night.
Till it bore an apple bright.
And my foe beheld it shine,
And he knew that it was mine.

And into my garden stole,
When the night had veild the pole;
In the morning glad I see;
My foe outstretched beneath the tree.

'All the papers are signed?' The solicitor is formal and expressionless. As if this is the kind of thing he deals with every day.

The woman, nervous and excited, nods. 'Yes. Everything is ready. We can't wait to take our baby home.' She takes her husband's hand and squeezes it.

'And you fully understand the terms of the NDA? The non-disclosure agreement?' he continues. 'There will be extremely serious consequences if it is broken. My client who, as you know, will remain anonymous, is a very powerful man. If you have any questions or any doubts, now is the time to voice them.'

She shakes her head. 'No doubts. You can rely on us. This child is everything we've ever wanted. We will be discreet. We won't do anything to risk the authorities intervening.'

The solicitor nods. 'Very good.' He hands over a file of documents. 'Here are some new identity papers I've procured for the baby, and a passport. As agreed, you will live a quiet life, in a new part of the country, not drawing attention to yourself or to the child, nor revealing the adoption at any point.'

The woman takes the file, her hand shaking. 'Thank you. We understand.'

'Right. In that case, I think that completes the formalities. If you are ready, I'll call the nurse to bring the infant.'

May, 1990

A cheer goes up as the opening of Black Box's 'Ride on Time' blares out of the speakers somewhere out in the ballroom at Tentingdon Hall, a seventeenth-century pile in the Berkshire countryside. This grand baronial estate which, in the past, has played host to historically significant balls with guests including prime ministers and members of the royal family, is today heaving with teenage bodies who have each paid twenty pounds for the privilege of being here.

A girl in a cocktail dress – especially bought for the occasion – is lying on the cold, hard ground, motionless, among discarded paper towels and worse. Her face is grey, her lips are blue and she smells of vomit.

Her friend is kneeling on the smeared white porcelain tiles, her taffeta skirt trailing on the wet and sticky floor, but she is far too upset and stressed to notice. She's crying so hard it sounds like hiccups. Her hair is in a complicated-looking plait but it has started to come loose and some of the bits are frizzing away from her face, almost like a halo.

'Wake up! Wake up!' she is shouting. Screaming. She looks up and stares wildly at the people who are starting to gather. 'Why won't she wake up?' she screams at no one in particular.

Other girls are coming out of the cubicles now and standing by the sinks, watching, their hands up to their mouths, wide-eyed, helpless, with no idea what to do.

'Should we call an ambulance?' one of them asks breathlessly, but her words are lost under the screams of the girl who is now hitting her friend on the floor in a panic, perhaps more violently than is helpful, shouting in an attempt to rouse her. Her face is covered in black rivulets of mascara tears.

'Wake up!' she is still yelling, uselessly. 'Wake up!'

No one is very sober.

The door flies open and a boy bursts in, staring aghast at the girl who is now shaking her prone friend by the shoulders.

'She's dead!' she screams. 'I think she's dead!'

Present
DAY ONE – Saturday, 7 p.m.

Malia

I'm so excited. I've never been anywhere like this before.

I love my room. In fact, it isn't really a room at all, it's an entire villa – an overwater bungalow. I have my own private pool, something called a catamaran net, which is like a massive hammock in a frame which hangs over the water, giant beanbags to laze on as well as loungers, a hot tub, an outdoor shower and even a slide which goes directly down to the water, all of this, just for me. And that's only the terrace, before you even go inside.

'Is everything to your liking, Miss Malia?' the uniformed butler asks. She is wearing smart black shorts and a black polo shirt with the Ketenangan resort's logo, a turtle embroidered in gold.

'Oh yes, it's amazing,' I reply. She nods, and pauses for a second, before adding, 'In that case, I'll leave you to get settled in. My name is Adhara, and I will be your personal butler during your stay. If you need anything at all, you can call me using this panel.' She points at something that looks like an iPad fixed to the wall, and another which is on a glass-topped coffee table. There are just two buttons – one with a picture of a bell, and the other with an icon like an old-fashioned telephone. 'You can press the one with the bell to ask me for whatever you need by text, or if you'd rather speak to me, you tap the picture of the telephone.'

I nod. 'But if I want to call reception, or room service, or something like that?'

She gives an enigmatic smile. 'Whatever you need, I will arrange for you. We don't have a reception desk as such, and I will relay anything you would like to the kitchen, bar or concierge myself. We feel that keeps things simpler for our guests, which is of the utmost importance. Here at Ketenangan, we offer an entirely personalized service. I hope, that during the course of your stay, I will come to get to know your likes and hope to anticipate your every desire, even before you've asked. That is our ultimate aim here.'

'OK,' I say, not sure whether to be delighted or a little creeped out. I'm not used to this kind of personal attention. 'Thank you.'

'Is there anything I can help with at the moment? Would you like me to unpack for you?'

I shake my head. 'No, thank you. I'd rather do that myself. But thank you anyway.'

'As you wish.'

She gives a nod and leaves the room.

My battered suitcase has already been placed on a luggage stand inside the dressing room and looks entirely out of place in the opulence of my surroundings. I don't know if Adhara thought I was being strange not wanting her to unpack but, I dunno. I felt weird about a stranger touching my underwear, and there a few things in my case that I wouldn't necessarily want her to see. I open the case and take out my selfie-stick before heading out to the terrace.

It was a long flight and I'm not looking my best, but I can sort all that out with filters later. Plus I'm trying to build my brand, such that it is, on not being perfect. Everywoman. My thighs are dimpled, my hair is prone to frizz, and I don't have the kind of boobs that allow me to wear skimpy tops or go braless, but my followers like that. I'm like them.

Though right now, for the next few days at least, I'm barely like them at all. I'm in an amazing place which I'd never be able to afford to visit in a million years. I can't imagine many people of my age would. Or indeed, many ordinary people at all.

I stand by the low rope barrier at the edge of the terrace with the sea behind me and spend the next ten minutes taking photos, some with the phone held high, some face height (almost never from below because that makes me look jowly), left, right, grinning, an enigmatic smile (I don't do duck face, it's not me), hat on, hat off, various permutations. People think being an influencer is easy, but it isn't. I might still be building up my following, but I put a lot of effort into my work.

Once the pictures are on the phone, I flop down on the huge beanbag and start scrolling through, immediately deleting the ones which are quite clearly simply wrong.

My phone pings – it's a WhatsApp from Araminta, the PR who invited me on this trip which she organized to promote the resort.

Meet in the bar in ten minutes for drinks with the hotel owners!

I don't want to be late but also, I want to get my first picture posted. Araminta was quite specific about how many pictures and stories I must post and how much engagement is expected from my followers during the trip, and I want to get off to a good start.

This is the first trip I've been on as an influencer, way more luxurious and lavish than anything I've been offered before, and I very much hope it will be the first of many. Up until now, the only collaborations I've done (as in, times where I have been offered the chance to try out something for free) have been with local restaurants, spas and a few slightly obscure clothing and jewellery brands. I have certainly never before been flown halfway across the world to spend time in an ultra-exclusive resort. So I am very keen to make the most of it, but also to make a good impression, gain followers and hopefully be invited on more trips like this one.

Even though the images aren't perfect, I eventually find one where I look quite cute peering up from beneath the brim of my straw sunhat with the azure sea sparkling behind me, add the Juno filter and type: Just arrived at Ketenangan in the Maldives! Bit jetlagged but WOW check out the sea! Can't wait to give you a room tour but am off now to meet the owners! More later! xxxxx. And then I add a series of hashtags which are known to promote the best engagement, most of which I have pre-stored in my phone especially for this trip to cut and paste onto posts.

I'm still a little bit bemused by the fact that I am here at all. There are plenty of influencers with way more followers than me, and those who specialize in luxury travel.

I don't entirely understand why I have been invited. But whatever. They must have their reasons. I'm going to stop doubting myself, make the most of it and enjoy it.

The bar is in the main overwater building, with a long wooden walkway across the water leading to the twenty bungalows, which are, in turn, each joined individually to a central point by small footbridges. The floor of the bar is glass and I can actually see colourful fish swimming about underneath. I reach to get my phone from my bag to video them for my story, but then I notice that no one else has their phone out and I'm not sure if fiddling with my phone would look rude or be inappropriate, so instead I make a silent note to myself to remember to do it later. I take a seat on one of the plush stools and a stunning waitress appears in front of me almost instantly with a silver tray of champagne-filled flutes. She looks familiar – maybe she is one of the stewards from an early series of *Below Deck*? I must find out. The rest of the group is already at the bar and most of them look like their eyes are glazing over as Araminta chats away. It's been a very long day, and she seems to be the only one of us who isn't completely flagging. I guess she's used to long-haul travel, or perhaps it's simply that it's her job to be upbeat when she's hosting journalists even when she doesn't feel up to it. She's probably a decade or even two older than me but has seemingly boundless energy.

'Ah!' she says as a middle-aged man with floppy blond hair enters the bar. 'Excellent. Here's Henry Cadwallader, one of the hotel owners.'

I'd already googled Henry before the trip. If anything, though, Henry is much better looking in real life than in his online pictures – a bit like Hugh Grant in that film about weddings and funerals my mum made me watch with her years ago, only older, probably about fifty. His voice is similar too – posh and plummy. Not like anyone I know.

He perches on a stool and takes a glass of champagne from the maybe-*Below-Deck* waitress who approaches him and then glides away so elegantly you barely notice she's moving at all.

'Good evening to you all,' he says. 'And thank you so much for coming. I hope you had a pleasant journey and are all happy with your rooms?'

'Oh, yes, everything went very smoothly and the rooms are beautiful!' Araminta gushes. 'Now, let me introduce everyone Henry . . .'

I tune out as she introduces everyone as I'd also already looked up all the names on the group email which Araminta sent with the itinerary and know who everyone is. Claire Dixon, freelance journalist for the last ten years or so, worked on staff for various magazines in Dubai and Australia before that. Rob Hall, general *bon viveur* and sometime journalist, who wrote acerbic columns for lad mags back in the nineties and then one of the nationals until he got sacked for writing something a little too close to the bone. These days he mainly works as a wine importer but still does the odd article here and there as far as I could see. River (like Cher or Madonna, doesn't need a surname), an influencer like me but with many more followers, been doing it a lot longer and more successfully than me. Lucy Fox, travel editor for a broadsheet newspaper, worked for the same paper for around twenty years, been its travel editor for ten.

They're all sipping their champagne and helping themselves to canapés as if they are totally at ease in this kind of environment. I'm sure it must only be me who feels like a fish out of water.

An imposter.

'Malia? What do you think?' Henry asks as I tune back in.

I look up at him and blush – those piercing blue eyes seeming to bore through me.

My champagne goes down the wrong way as I start to formulate some kind of reply and I start coughing. Araminta rushes over and starts slapping me on the back and the waitress rushes over as I spill my champagne into my lap.

'So sorry,' I splutter as she fusses and dabs. I look back up at Henry. 'Thank you for inviting me here,' I say. 'It's a beautiful place.'

If he notices that I haven't answered his question, because I didn't hear what it was, he doesn't say so. But then men like that are always brought up with immaculate manners, as my mum always used to tell me. It's bred into them from an early age. Not the kind of thing you can easily learn, or fake.

'Please don't apologize,' he says. 'All that matters is that you're OK?'

I nod, embarrassed.

'Great,' he continues, smoothly. 'Now, I'm sure you're all tired after your journey, so if it's OK with you, we've arranged a simple buffet supper for this evening. That way you can all eat with the minimum of fuss and then get to bed, as I'm sure you're dying to.'

The 'simple buffet supper' turns out to be nothing like I've seen before – huge platters of oysters glistening on crushed ice, a pyramid of jumbo pink prawns, a large dish of real caviar (I only know that's what it is because the tins are displayed alongside it), carpaccio of Wagyu beef, served by a uniformed man who explains its provenance from massaged cows with a carefully controlled diet, thinly sliced grilled vegetables mixed into a salad, little glasses and exquisite pots of things labelled with exotic names, many of which I've never heard of, and a dessert buffet of enormous meringues, macarons and tartlets, plus a show chef who is spinning sugar into little baskets to fill with tropical fruit and delicately whipped cream as we watch.

We are seated around a circular table which is accessed via a few steps down and recessed into the ground so that fish are actually swimming around the walls. There is, apparently, also a restaurant which is fully underwater which we will be visiting later in the trip. Between being somewhat overwhelmed by the surroundings, the opulence of the food and the fact that I now haven't slept for something like twenty-four hours, I'm finding it pretty hard to concentrate. But I am determined to be on my best behaviour and try to look interested in Henry's spiel.

'This is our fifth hotel in the chain,' he is saying. 'And while they are all exceptional in their own ways, we think this one is possibly our most special yet. We called it Ketenangan, which means tranquillity. Before we acquired the island, there was nothing here at all except for some wild plants, jatropha trees and a turtle colony. It's extremely difficult to be granted permission to develop uninhabited islands here as hotels, especially, and quite rightly, when there is wildlife involved, so we had a lot of hoops to jump through which took several years. Plus, we are lucky enough to be located in an atoll which, until now, has been entirely undeveloped. Eventually we managed to persuade the powers that be of our commitment to protecting the endangered colony of green turtles here, and to providing employment for local people, and we got the go-ahead. The turtle sanctuary was actually in place well before the hotel, which was part of the agreement.'

I notice that Claire, Rob and Lucy are taking notes in the little Moleskine notebooks which were left in our rooms alongside slim gold pens with small turtles dangling off in our pack of welcome gifts, and I feel a stab of alarm as I wonder if I'm not doing everything I should be doing. I take out my phone and press the record button, placing it on the table somewhat ostentatiously to make clear what I'm doing. Hopefully that will be considered appropriate.

'The island is entirely solar-powered and carbon-neutral. It's also one of the furthest from its neighbouring islands in the archipelago, and, with just twenty villas, it's one of the smallest Maldivian resorts. There are three staff members to every guest, assuring the best service at all times. Our resident chef is Michelin-starred, plus we plan to invite other celebrated chefs for residencies – you'll learn more about that tomorrow,' he adds. 'All the products used in the spa are organic and produced in the islands. Access for guests is by seaplane as a boat journey would be too long, and we are now the furthest resort from the mainland, which we like to think gives us an extra air of exclusivity. Plus, it as good as guarantees that none of our guests is unnecessarily

14

disturbed by any form of transport. We expect our clients will come here for the tranquillity promised in the name of the resort, and that's exactly what we hope to offer them.'

He pauses, as if to emphasize the peace and quiet, and indeed all that can be heard for those few seconds is the gentle lapping of the ocean.

'We considered not installing internet at all, and becoming a digital-detox retreat,' he continues, 'however, our market research found that most of the high-net-worth individuals who we want to attract would likely be put off by a lack of internet. We were unable to install a cable for ecological reasons, so instead, we have a satellite, carefully positioned to cause minimum visual impact.

'Everything is sourced as locally as possible, and almost everything we use here on Ketenangan is recyclable and sustainable. Anything which *can't* be recycled on site despite our best efforts is taken off the island, and, at not inconsiderable expense, recycled elsewhere or disposed of ethically. We also employ a full-time marine biologist to keep a check on the turtles and ensure that nothing we are doing is disrupting their lives, and also to oversee a breeding programme. In turn he welcomes volunteers from around the world, prioritizing those from disadvantaged communities. You'll be meeting him during your trip. We are very proud of what we've created here, and hope that our guests love the island as much as we do.'

Rob, Claire and Lucy are still scribbling away. River appears to be simply listening attentively and as far as

I can tell, everyone seems to think that's OK. Even so, I glance at my phone ostentatiously to check it is still recording and concentrate on looking interested, even though I'm so exhausted it's a struggle to keep my eyes open.

'The accommodation on the island is arranged so that guests can have total privacy if that is what they require,' Henry continues, 'which is often the case with some of our clients such as celebrities, politicians, world leaders, you get the gist. If you so choose, you can come here, order room service, and see literally no one during your stay apart from your butler. For this reason, and because we are such a small resort, there is no CCTV.'

'Ideal for criminals on the run too then,' Rob says, with a grin, looking up from his notebook. It's the first point at which Henry has been interrupted and for a second he looks a little taken aback before recomposing himself.

'Ha ha! Very funny,' he says, running his hands through his hair. 'Yes, complete privacy and discretion is assured here, whoever you are. Though you are our first guests here, and I would hope, no criminals among you,' he adds with a wink. A nervous laugh ripples through the group.

'Anyway, I'll try not to ramble on too long, but there are a few more things I want to say before leaving you all to get some well-deserved rest. While we expect many guests come to stay with us simply to "fly and flop", as they somewhat unattractively say in the trade, we also offer plenty of options for those who want more from their time with us, and who would like to explore this beautiful area further. We are planning a dive trip for you tomorrow, and other activities available on the island, some of which you will be sampling over the next few days, include quad biking, parascending and water-skiing. There are also gentler pastimes such as meeting the local turtles, stingrays and other wildlife, as well as spa treatments, paddleboarding, kayaking, and much more.

'We have developed an itinerary for you, but if you would like to arrange any additional activities at all, please do let myself or your butler know.'

He smiles and clasps his hands together. 'I'll be in resort and available throughout your trip, along with our hotel manager Mohammed who you will meet tomorrow. We look forward to your feedback, as you are our very first guests! And if there are any immediate questions now, of course I would be very happy to help.'

'Anyone?' Araminta asks brightly. Everyone looks like they are falling asleep.

'In all honesty, I'm pretty knackered and I'd like to get to bed,' says Claire, sharply, slamming her notebook shut somewhat pointedly. 'Are all the activities obligatory?'

'Nothing is obligatory,' Henry says, 'but the itinerary has been carefully planned to show you the best we can offer.'

Claire nods. 'OK. If it's all the same to you, I'll see how I feel in the morning about the diving. It's a pretty early start. Night all.'

DAY TWO – Sunday, 8 a.m.

Malia

There is a discreet knock at the door and Adhara enters.

'Good morning, Miss Malia,' she says. 'I took the liberty of bringing breakfast to your room as you had a long day yesterday – we thought you might appreciate a little longer in bed.'

I ease myself up in the giant bed and Adhara places the large wooden tray on the bed. The tray has little bean bags on each side so that it sits comfortably over my knees without even tilting. Clever.

I pull the Egyptian cotton sheet higher – I feel quite self-conscious being in bed with someone I don't know in my room – but Adhara seems completely unfazed by it.

'That's very thoughtful,' I say. 'Thank you.' I vaguely remember something about breakfast in bed being on the itinerary now, but I kind of wish I'd been more prepared. Showered and dressed. It's been a long time since anyone has seen me in bed and I'm not sure I'm entirely comfortable with it.

On the tray is a smashed avocado on wholemeal toast, Greek yoghurt with honey and blueberries, freshly squeezed orange juice and a latte in an ornate glass. It looks almost like an espresso martini.

'Gosh, all my favourite things!' I say. 'How did you know?'

Adhara smiles. 'The team will have checked your social media accounts before you arrived so that we can get a sense of what pleases you. I know posting on social media is your job, so they will have a very accurate picture. It's a standard service for all our guests, but for some we can find more information than others.'

'Wow,' I say, not sure whether to be impressed or feel like I'm being stalked.

'If you have everything you need, I'll leave you to enjoy your breakfast?' Adhara adds.

'It all looks lovely. Thank you.'

They have clearly done their research. Each item on my tray is exactly the kind of thing I am always posting on my feed, only these ones are much better versions than I am used to. The yogurt has flowers sprinkled on top of it. I assume they're edible? Surely they wouldn't put anything that couldn't be eaten in the food? The latte in the cocktail glass has a picture of a turtle drawn into the foam. The toast has the crusts cut off and there isn't a single speck of brown or skin in the avocado.

And the orange juice is served in a delicate crystal glass and unless it's simply the light, there are flecks of glitter floating on the top.

I pick up my phone and take some photos. The coffee will probably grow cold as I do so but it's important to get this exactly right. I ease myself out from under the tray and carry it out to the terrace. It would be nice to get some pictures with the sea in the background. I can hashtag it #breakfastalfresco or something like that. I will need to research the best tags to use.

Once I have finished my photos, I eat the breakfast. It's delicious.

While I drink the juice, I scroll through my messages. It's the usual stuff on Insta, 'Luv you!' 'Stunning!' etc. I reply to a handful and click hearts on others. Some influencers have people to do this for them, it's rumoured, but I'm very far from being at that level.

Yet. But if I'm now being invited on trips like this, who knows what might happen in the future? It's all very exciting, and I'm determined to make the most of it.

May, 1990

Xander

Henry takes a last drag of his Marlboro Red and drops it in the near-empty champagne glass next to him. The butt hisses and dies. He claps me on the shoulder. 'Good turnout tonight, Xander, well done,' he says.

I shrug modestly. 'It's not all down to me. I couldn't do it without you. And Ophelia, of course,' I add, hurriedly. Frankly, the whole operation would be quite a lot easier without Ophelia hanging around, as she contributes absolutely nothing to the organization of these events as far as I can tell, but I can't say that to Henry. He worships his twin sister.

Henry adjusts his bow tie – a real one, of course, none of those premade ones on elastic for him – and looks out over the heaving dance floor. We're in what is notionally the VIP suite for this evening, on the

23

balcony overlooking the ballroom of a grand old stately home, Tentingdon Hall, whose owner no doubt fell on hard times and resorted to having to rent it out for weddings, events and even teenage parties like ours. Or Smash Balls, as we call them. We've been running these events for less than a year, and this is the biggest one yet. We sold more than 1,000 tickets. It's not hard, especially since we were in the papers a few months back. Now everyone wants to come.

To start with, it was Henry, Ophelia and me simply ringing our mates at other schools, telling them about the party we were organizing, offering them a free ticket or two, access to the VIP area and complimentary drinks and fags all night as long as they sold at least thirty tickets. We rented a venue using some money advanced by Henry and Ophelia's dad, and more than covered our costs from the tickets and drinks sold, even from the first event. Since then, we make a tidy sum on each one, though fifty per cent of the profit goes directly back to Mr Cadwallader each time to cover his original investment. There's a proper contract and everything.

I don't have the connections the Cadwalladers do on account of being 'nouveau' as Henry would put it, meaning my dad actually made his money instead of inheriting it. This is somehow considered inferior by 'old money' in a way I don't fully understand.

I managed to blag my way through the first couple of balls and find people to invite by looking at the party pages in the back issues of *Tatler* and pretty much cold calling people at other boarding schools to invite them along. You'd think they'd be weirded out by it but they weren't – I got my spiel off pat and made them feel like we had chosen them because they were an important kingpin of the social world rather than simply because it was clear they had money, went to a lot of parties, and I'd managed to work out which school they went to, and therefore had a way of getting hold of them.

The balls themselves are great fun, and helping to organize them gives me a kind of kudos, I think, both at school and at the events, plus Dad's impressed that I'm earning money for myself, like he did at my age. But all of those things are added extras – the main reason I got involved in this enterprise was to spend more time with Henry.

After the first couple of parties, I no longer had to scrabble around to find people to invite, they started coming to me, asking when the next party was happening and how they could get tickets. The housemaster started complaining about the amount of mail and the number of phone calls I was getting on the communal house phone, grumbling that a school like Hamlington Abbey couldn't condone parties like ours and that they certainly couldn't be organized from school property. So I rented a mailbox in town, and I managed to persuade Dad I needed a pager – I agreed that I would pay from my earnings. The mailbox address and pager number were passed around and now everyone has them. We barely need to advertise the balls at all anymore – it's almost all done via word of mouth – and while school doesn't exactly encourage it, they pretty much turn a blind eye because Mr Cadwallader is an important benefactor for Hamlington – the school library is called the Cadwallader Library, for example.

In fact, our main problem now is finding venues big enough. We always have more people wanting to come than we can cater for, so we've ended up being more and more selective about who we invite. And as we get choosier, people are even more desperate to get an invitation, as we call the tickets, conveniently ignoring the fact that people are paying good money for them, so they're not actually invitations in the traditional sense at all. We've put the ticket entry up, added a larger commission for ourselves on all the drinks sold so that the prices are now, quite frankly, ridiculous, and still it doesn't put people off. Sometimes I wonder what it would take.

And there's even been a bit of press coverage. While the articles have largely had a 'shock, horror, won't someone please think of the children?' tone, apparently the editor of the paper who ran these stories is a Hamlington old boy who is quite fond of his *alma mater*. So the same articles, with their references to underage drinking, vomiting teens and sexual shenanigans also included quite a lot of information about the school's impressive cast of alumni and fabulous facilities, and apparently applications to be enrolled have actually increased since the first article was published. And even though the powers that be at school either largely pretend they don't know what we're doing or that we're doing it against their will, there is a part of them that quite likes the free publicity, I'm sure.

'The bucking bronco was a brilliant call, Xander,' Henry says, taking out another cigarette from his monogrammed case and lighting it with his trademark brass Zippo. 'Great fun. Look at them all. They're loving it.'

The mechanical bull swings round, tips and bucks the girl off, legs flying in the air, flashing her suspenders and stockings as her voluminous skirt flies over her head before she crashes into the huge crash mat and scampers off back to her friends, laughing. 'Plus a free eyeful for the boys. Win-win.'

I feel a stab of jealousy but laugh along with Henry. He doesn't know how I feel about him. He can't know, obviously. I am pretty sure I will never tell him, because he wouldn't want to know, and I would never live it down. But that doesn't mean it doesn't hurt.

One of the VIP area waitresses who Henry has dressed as Playboy bunnies (ironically, apparently) comes by with a tray of champagne and we each take a flute. Henry knocks his back in one. I sip mine slowly – I don't much like champagne but Henry has this thing about it being the only drink served in this area.

'I should go and find Ashley,' I say. 'Unless there's anything you need me to do?' Part of me hopes that there is, that he wants me here, with him, but he shakes his head.

'No, I think we're all good,' he says. 'You've done a great job, as usual. You go and have fun, find your girlfriend. Give her one from me if you like,' he adds.

DAY TWO – Sunday, 10 a.m.

Malia

The rest of the group is already gathered on the jetty when I arrive at 10 a.m. as instructed, plus Henry, who is in board shorts and a polo shirt, looking totally different to yesterday in his linen suit.

'Ah, Malia, there you are. Good. I think we're all ready to go? Is everyone diving today, or does anyone want to snorkel instead? The diving is excellent, but for safety reasons, only experienced divers can take the tanks. But you wouldn't miss out on much – the sea is so clear you can see almost as much with just a snorkel.'

'I think we're all diving,' Araminta says, 'At least that's what everyone ticked on the questionnaire I sent before the trip. But if anyone's changed their mind, that's fine too, of course. Anyone?'

There's a general murmur and shaking of heads.

'Great! So all of us then,' Henry says. 'Excellent. Let's get on the boat and get kitted up.'

The places I've dived before have all been run from surf-shack type places in cheap resorts by men with long hair in flip-flops and tie-dyed T-shirts where you're generally expected to sort out and check most of your equipment yourself, as well as lug it out to the water. The set-up is very different here.

Our equipment has already been loaded onto a gin palace-style dive boat, along with wetsuits. I assume they used the measurements which we supplied before the trip and try desperately to remember if I was honest when I filled in the form. Chances are I wasn't. The wetsuits are on top of each pile of kit and I can see that each has one of our names embroidered on it alongside the turtle logo of the resort, which seem to be then affixed to the suit using something like Velcro. There's also a second, smaller name tag on each BCD, the combined weight belt and flotation device which you use to control how you ascend and descend in the water. Cute.

'The name badges have been designed to be temporarily affixed so you can keep them if you'd like to,' Henry says, spotting me eyeing mine up, 'we thought they'd make a nice souvenir for guests. If you've got something with you such as a soft case or backpack that you'd like them transferred to while you are here, we can arrange that too. They're hand-sewn from recycled cotton by a local woman.'

Of course they are.

Claire offers her hand to one of the men, who are all dressed in the hotel uniform of black shorts and the logoed polo shirt, and steps gingerly onto the boat. River leaps on in one enthusiastic bound followed by Rob, who does similar but with a little less grace. Henry steps on to the boat, and then turns and puts his hand out to help Lucy, and then Araminta and me. Always the perfect gentleman.

Like everything else so far on this trip, the boat is nothing like anything I've been on before. Dive boats are usually small and functional – if you're going to be out all day there might be a manky Portaloo in something akin to a cupboard if you're lucky and maybe a cool box with some local beers and a couple of packets of crisps if you've paid a bit extra, but that's about it.

River and I settle ourselves on cushioned seats at the back of what is basically a mini-yacht, sipping freshly made tropical fruit smoothies which have been handed to us. The rest of the group is at the front of the boat, reclining on soft mattresses and soaking up the sun. The waitress from last night appears from the mahogany-wood interior of the boat with a silver salver of both sweet and savoury canapés of the kind you'd be more likely to see at a flash evening function. I take a toasted blini with what might be fish eggs but knowing how things are here, is probably the real deal, caviar again, like last night. Yum.

'Um, I don't mean to be weird, but you look really

familiar,' I say. 'I wondered if I'd seen you on *Below Deck*?' I peer at the name on her badge, Julia, and almost straight away I'm sure that I've got it wrong.

She gives a tight smile. 'No. I have worked on yachts before, but not been on TV. Just got one of those faces I guess!' she adds, airily.

'Have you been doing this kind of work long?' I ask. I'm convinced I've seen her before but can't think where.

'Yes, in various guises. I've worked in resorts around the world for a few years now.' She pauses briefly. 'If you have everything you need here, I should attend to a few things inside?'

'Of course,' I say. 'Thank you.'

'That was a bit rude,' River says quietly as she retreats back inside. 'Like she couldn't get away from us fast enough.'

I shrug. 'She's probably busy.'

'Yeah. Maybe.' There is a slight shudder as the boat starts up and we begin to move across the water. 'You dived much before?' River asks as we head towards wherever we are going. With olive skin and dark eyes, he is so perfect looking he almost doesn't look real. He started off doing male makeup tutorials on YouTube and Insta but ditched that pretty quickly and now does fashion, travel and restaurant reviews. And you can see why almost any brand would want him. He's secretive about whether he's straight, gay, or something else – says it's not relevant, though I suspect it's because he knows it makes him more interesting and enigmatic. Everyone laps it up, his followers, the brands, and I'm not ashamed to say, also me. I was thrilled when I found out that he'd be coming on this trip – I couldn't wait to meet him. And even though I know that he'd never be interested in someone like me in a million years, he's so exquisite I can barely speak to him without stuttering. Even though he appears to be absolutely lovely, so friendly and unpretentious, he still makes me nervous because he is so gorgeous.

'I've dived quite a lot,' I say. The breeze caused by the movement of the boat is welcome in the heat as I hold my sunhat in place. 'I learnt when I was fourteen – my parents were both massively into diving – and never looked back. Since then, most times I go on holiday I try to go somewhere I can dive. I love it. I've never been anywhere as flash as this though, obviously. Well, not obviously. But I haven't.'

I am gabbling. I blush and hope River doesn't notice or that if he does, he thinks it's just the heat of the sun that is making me act like an imbecile. Not that he will care. He is probably used to it. I'm sure everyone must turn to jelly around him. 'And what about you? Did you learn with your family?' I ask.

He smiles. 'No. it's not the kind of holiday my parents could have ever hoped to have afforded back when I was a child. They fostered children when I was small, there were always so many of us at home. And some of my foster brothers and sisters had additional needs which would have made travelling too far very difficult.'

I blush. I should have remembered. River's very proud of his upbringing and the work his parents did with children who had no one. He's now ambassador to a charity which protects the rights of looked-after children and heads up regular fundraisers for them.

'I went on a cheap holiday to Egypt with a mate when I was at uni,' he continues, 'and learnt to dive there. So, I have dived, yes, but not much. It was a few years ago now but,' his voice drops to a whisper and he taps the side of his nose, 'don't tell Araminta. I told her I was going to do a refresher before this trip but in the end, I didn't get round to it.'

I laugh, but it sounds hollow. 'OK. Your secret's safe with me,' I say. 'But aren't you worried that . . .' I'm a natural catastrophizer and would be terrified of forgetting something important if I hadn't dived for a while. Diving can be dangerous and you need to know what you're doing. Even a small mistake can potentially be fatal.

He shrugs. 'Worried that what? It'll be fine. If it was that dangerous they wouldn't let any old random person do it. It's like riding a bike, I'm sure. They'll brief us before we go, there'll be a divemaster and, tell you what, maybe you can be my dive buddy, if you'd be happy to?' He nudges my arm gently and I feel like I might die. 'Make sure I'm doing what I'm meant to be doing.'

I blush deeper and manage to stutter out, 'I'd love that, I mean, yeah, why not?' as Henry comes out from the boat's interior, now in a shortie wetsuit, hopefully distracting River from the fact that I've gone bright red.

'All good?' Henry asks. 'How were the smoothies?'

'They were delicious, thank you,' I reply, grateful for the change of subject.

He nods. 'Good, good. Well, we're nearly at the dive site now so if you want to head inside and get changed, now would be the time. Your wetsuits have been moved into the changing rooms, and there are both male and female attendants in the common area outside in case anyone needs a hand with zipping up or anything. The others are at the front, are they? I'll go and tell them it's time to get ready.'

Once the rest of the group has come back, we go through the sliding doors at the back of the boat into a lounge. There are two large sofas with a coffee table between, set with a plate of sliced melon and another fruit I don't recognize, a big crystal jug of iced water, several immaculate and delicate-looking tumblers on a silver tray and some small bowls of dried fruit and nuts. Julia and a man in the hotel uniform stand at the back of the room, hands behind their backs.

'Ladies? Your changing room is here,' Julia says. She opens a mahogany door to her left, where the shortie wetsuits with our name tags are now arranged on gold-coloured hangers. 'If you need anything, push this button here, and I will come and assist. Gentlemen, your room is here,' she says to Rob and River, 'and my colleague Caleb is here to help should you need it.'

'Not you?' Rob says with a leer. She smiles politely and I cringe. Everyone looks at the floor. 'As I said, my colleague will be here to assist you,' she reiterates without missing a beat, before continuing to direct everyone to their respective rooms. Good for her.

The changing room itself is compact but luxe, with a small dressing table with disposable hairbrush, a Dyson hairdryer, some mini high-end perfume bottles and shampoo, conditioners, shower gel, moisturizer and body lotion which are all Kalyana, the eco-brand used in the spa and locally produced, of course. There's also a small shower with a glass door, and a cupboard. I open the cupboard which houses several fluffy white towels and dressing gowns, all with the turtle logo.

'God that guy Rob is a knob,' Claire says, pulling off her dress, bra and pants as if she was alone in the room, stepping into her swimming costume and snapping the large, supportive-looking straps into place. 'There's always one on any press trip, isn't there?'

'Isn't there!' Lucy agrees as she gets changed slightly more discreetly than Claire, leaving her dress on till she's got her bikini bottoms on but swapping her T-shirt for a bikini top as she chats, seemingly not caring if she exposes her boobs which look like they are silicone to me. Then again, if I had a body like hers, I probably wouldn't care who saw it either. These women are both significantly older than me but much more toned. I make a mental note to join a gym when I get home. Perhaps I could see if I could get one to collaborate, even.

'Yes, always,' Claire continues. 'I always say if no one in your group seems obviously strange, then this time, it's probably you. Clearly though Rob the Knob, as he shall now be known, is the odd ball this time, so we don't need to worry it's one of us.'

'Come on ladies, let's all try to get on!' Araminta chimes in. 'He's not that bad!'

Claire snorts. 'Hmmm. But he kind of is . . .'

I tune out their chatter. I whip my sundress off over my head – I had no idea what the set up would be and certainly wasn't expecting anything like this, so I already have my fifties-style swimming costume on. I put my dress in the cupboard and take the wetsuit down from the hanger. It looks brand new, but as we are the first guests here, I suppose it would be.

I slip my flip-flops off and start easing the suit on as the others chat away between themselves, paying me no attention, heading out as I finish getting ready. Thankfully, although the suit is a little tighter than is ideal, it fits (kind of) and I can even do up the zips myself because they are at the front. It would have been simply too humiliating to have had to ask Julia or one of the others to help me. I consider putting the robe on before heading out but then decide that would be weird so I simply grab a towel, put my shoulders back and go outside. Body positive, I remind myself.

Outside, everyone is being handed their tanks, BCDs, dive computers and flippers, and being helped into them by the divemaster Ahmed, Julia and Caleb.

'Right, let's get everyone buddied up,' says Ahmed.

'I'm going to go with Malia,' River says, making me blush again. 'We've already decided.'

Ahmed nods. 'OK. Anyone else already made plans?' he continues.

'I'll go with Lucy,' Rob leers, openly eyeing up her neoprene-clad cleavage. 'Unless she's got other ideas?'

Fuck's sake. This really isn't OK.

'Actually, sorry, I'm going with Henry,' she says dismissively. 'There's some coral he was telling me about last night that he's going to show me.'

She shoots Claire a look and Claire smirks. I hide a smile. Rob the Knob indeed.

Rob shrugs but I see the tips of his ears go red. 'Fine. Araminta? How about you?'

'Of course!' she says. 'I don't mind. I'm happy to go with anyone.'

'OK, so that leaves me the lucky man who is buddied with Claire,' Ahmed says diplomatically.

'Pleasure's all mine, I'm sure,' Claire says.

'So, with your buddy, I'd like you to do your pre-dive checks,' he continues. 'I understand that you are all experienced divers and know what you're doing, but we will go through them together now to make sure that everything is completely covered.

'First, the BCD.' The BCD is arguably the most important scuba item after the tank itself as it's what regulates your buoyancy. I test the inflate and release mechanism on River's and he does the same to mine, though I notice he watches me very carefully while I do it and I assume it's so that he can check what he needs to do. Wasn't it some time ago he said he'd last dived? I was so flustered when speaking to him I've already forgotten.

'Next, weights,' Ahmed says. 'In this case, the weights are integrated into the BCD and they release like this,' he says, demonstrating on Claire who gives a lascivious wiggle as he fiddles with her belt. He smiles indulgently but looks faintly embarrassed. 'OK, good,' he says. 'Now the rest of you.'

I haven't used a belt like this before but it looks simple enough to remove the weights. I check it the way he showed and watch River as he does the same.

'Good. Now, releases.' He talks us through how these work and we duly test our own and each other's. But it is hot in the sun in our wetsuits and along with everyone else, I am desperate to get in the water. 'Air,' he continues, and demonstrates how to check our tanks. He remains serious and methodical but by now I can see that everyone is losing interest. Henry and Lucy are chatting as they half-heartedly carry out their checks. Rob is fiddling with his phone, God knows why because there's no signal out here, and Claire is twiddling her hair and batting her eyelids while Ahmed tries not to catch her eye. Araminta is trying to look interested and attentive but I can see that even she is struggling to keep her focus.

We are the very first guests in this high-end resort and the equipment is both brand new and no doubt top of the range like everything else here – I guess we are all taking it on trust that it's going to be OK. In theory you are supposed to do these buddy checks each and every time but the more you dive, the less worried you get about it. Or that's what I've always found, anyway.

'And a final overall check,' Ahmed says, carrying out an almost pantomime-like appraisal of Claire's dive equipment.

We all look each other up and down, sweltering in the heat.

'OK, I think you are all good to go,' he says. 'I will lead the way with Claire for anyone who wants to come with me, but as you are all experienced divers, if you wish to explore away from the group, that is fine too, as long as you don't go too far. Though you must stay with your buddy at all times, and keep a close eye on your air levels and the time, both of which are on your dive computers as you know. We meet back at the boat in maximum forty-five minutes. Any questions?'

Henry answers by flipping himself backwards into the water, quickly followed by Lucy. Rob theatrically pretends to hold his nose and jump in, while Araminta gently eases herself into the sparkling sea.

'Ready?' River asks.

'Ready,' I confirm. To my surprise he takes my hand and we jump in together, immediately followed by Ahmed and Claire.

The water is warmer and clearer than anything I've ever dived in before. I do the 'OK?' sign at River, making my thumb and first finger into a circle, and he does the same back to me. OK. Everything is OK. Really, how could it not be?

The flippers make moving through the water easy as we follow Ahmed and Claire. They sink a little deeper so I adjust my BCD so I can do the same. There are a few beats during which River floats further above me than I would like in the water and I wonder if he's forgotten how to change his buoyancy. That's the only problem with diving, beyond a few hand signals, it is difficult to communicate very much. But a few seconds later he sinks down so that he is alongside me.

OK? I ask with my hand again.

OK, he replies.

I wish talking to him on the surface felt so easy and natural.

By now almost everyone has drifted off in their pairs, though the water is so clear I can still see them even though they are some distance away. Colourful fish that don't even look real swim about between us and I'm briefly alarmed to see something which looks like a shark before I realize that it's actually a dolphin. Rays float past, their giant wings flapping. And the colours of the fish! Sergeant fish with their yellow and black stripes, Asian Sweet Lips which look like they are pouting, orange fish which hide among the tentacles of huge anemones, lobsters and lionfish (highly poisonous, apparently) crouching under rocks. And before I know it, the forty-five minutes are up and we head back to the boat. Ahmed helps haul me out and I see that Claire is already there, champagne in hand.

'That was amazing!' I gush excitedly as I pop up out of the water and pull myself up on to the boat, immediately followed by River. 'Incredible! Thank you so much, Ahmed!'

'It was my pleasure, Miss,' he says as he helps me take off my tank. 'I'm delighted to be able to share some of my beautiful country with you, and am very pleased that you liked it. I have the best office in the world.'

'You do!' I agree. Julia appears from the interior of the boat with both chilled water and glasses of champagne for us. I chug down a glass of ice-cold water and then follow River's lead by taking a flute of fizz too – it feels like a day which should be celebrated. We clink glasses and he and I smile at each other. What an amazing morning.

I'm nibbling on a slice of watermelon when Rob and Araminta arrive back, equally as thrilled with the whole experience as I was. 'Those fish!' Araminta exclaims as she's helped off with her tank. 'The colours! So amazing!'

'And we saw a shark,' Rob adds. 'That was pretty cool, once I got over the shock, and remembered that most sharks here aren't dangerous.'

'Indeed,' Ahmed says. 'There are more than twenty different species of shark in the Maldives, and there has never, ever been a serious attack recorded on a human here. Isn't that something? Even the sharks are laid back in the islands.' He smiles, and then his expression changes as he glances at his watch. 'Hmm. Fifty minutes. The other two should be back by now. Did anyone see them?'

Rob takes a long drink of his water. 'Not for a while. Lucy said Henry wanted to show her some coral, didn't she?' He takes another swig. 'Probably some kind of euphemism,' he adds.

Everyone ignores him. Ahmed looks at his watch again and starts putting on his flippers and hauling on his tank.

'I'm going to go and look for them. They should be here by now. Henry wouldn't take any unnecessary risks, especially not when buddied up with a guest.'

The mood on the boat instantly changes. 'Is there anything I can do?' Araminta asks.

He shakes his head. 'No. Stay here for now. Hopefully it's nothing and they simply lost track of time but to be on the safe side, one of my colleagues will radio the hotel and send another boat out to help look.' He glances at Julia and she scurries inside, presumably to get the radio.

But then I spot something in the distance. 'Is that them?' I ask. Whatever, or whoever it is is some distance away, but it looks like someone waving.

'Do we have binoculars?' Araminta asks.

Caleb hurries into the cabin and returns with binoculars, which Ahmed holds up to his eyes before saying: 'Start the boat. It's Lucy. And it looks like there's a problem.'

May, 1990

Ashley

Getting to this party was far from an easy task.

Jen and I have never been to a Smash Ball before. We're not exactly in with the Ophelia and Henry set, except for me with Xander, but he's different. Jen wasn't keen on coming at all, but I didn't want to go on my own. Or just with Xander, as I knew he'd be tied up with Henry much of the evening. Henry and Ophelia are the names and the money behind Smash Balls, but as far as I can see, it's Xander who does the vast majority of the work. And he's obsessed with Henry – thinks the sun shines out of his arse. Henry is not quite as awful as his sister Ophelia, I guess, but both of them are pretty up themselves.

'Why are you so desperate to go anyway?' Jen had asked. 'The balls are all a load of pretentious wank at the end of the day, aren't they? All that getting dressed up in black tie to go and get pissed. I don't really see the point.'

'I'm not *desperate* to go, but Xander's going and . . .'

'Oh *Xander*,' she'd sneered, dismissively. 'Of course.' Jen is my best friend, my only real friend at this school, but she's never made any secret of the fact that she doesn't approve of my going out with Xander. I've never entirely understood why.

Jen and I aren't like most of the others at our school – I guess that's why we gravitated towards each other from the time we both arrived, aged eleven. Neither of our families could afford the fees at Hamlington in a million years, and neither of them pay them. Jen's parents are in the army, stationed abroad and her fees are covered by some kind of military scholarship, as far as I understand. I did well in the entrance exam which Mum put me in for at the suggestion of a teacher at primary school who apparently thought I had great potential after noticing how quickly I got my lessons done compared to the other kids.

I was granted a scholarship and Mum was over the moon – way more excited about it than I ever was. Or am. I wanted to go to the comprehensive school that all my friends and my older sister Jade went to, but Mum said I'd be throwing away an incredible opportunity if I did that, and that I had to come here.

It's not a deliberate thing, but since I've joined the school, the words I use, the clothes I wear and even the timbre of my voice have changed in an effort to fit in.

But it's never enough for many of them, especially the likes of Henry and Ophelia who live in some stately pile – I have never been there, but everyone around here has heard of their home which is an actual castle, Cadwallader Castle.

Mum is easily impressed by that kind of thing. She does her best to make our council flat nice, but the longer I've been at Hamlington with all the panelled wood, portraits of masters (never mistresses) dating back to the fourteenth century on the walls, relics of some saint or other in the chapel and heavy velvet drapes on the windows, every time I go home, it seems pokier and pokier. Even the uniform here costs a fortune and Mum works two jobs plus extra temping shifts here and there to make ends meet, so every time I wish I wasn't at this school at all and was at the local comp with all my old mates from primary, I feel guilty. All Mum wants is for me to make the most of the fantastic opportunity I have in coming here (as she sees it at least) and she doesn't seem to care what she gives up to make it happen. In turn, all I want to do is make her proud.

Similarly, she's delighted about me going out with Xander. She hasn't met him yet, but I've told her a lot about him. His family are big in business, something to do with computers, I think. Mum spotted his dad in some kind of list of rich people in the paper. I don't care about that kind of stuff at all, but Mum really does.

And while Xander isn't snobby like most of the others here, and my background or the fact that I'm clearly not made of money doesn't seem to matter to him, there's still no way I could take him home. Mum wouldn't want him there either, I'm sure – she'd be embarrassed by the surroundings.

'I *could* go to the ball with Xander,' I'd told Jen, 'but I'd love it if you'd come too. It would be much more fun. Please, Jen.' I adore Xander, but I can't expect him to devote himself to me the entire evening, he'll probably have organizational things to do, and I know he'll want to spend time sucking up to Henry as usual. And as well as that, it's easier to stand up for myself against Ophelia and her coterie if Jen is there. She's better at that kind of stuff than me.

That's the other thing. Ophelia has made it quite clear that she fancies Xander, and is extra mean to me because of it since I've been going out with him. I trust Xander, I do, but Ophelia is so beautiful, has all the best clothes, and after a few drinks, especially if I'm not at the party, well, who knows what might happen? I try to believe Xander when he says he's only interested in me, but it's tricky when I find it hard to see myself as anything special. Plus, it's tricky to fully trust him when everyone knows about those stupid bets that he and Henry used to make about who they could get off with and stuff like that before he started going out with me.

The first time I got together with Xander, I worried that it was because I was the target of one of those challenges, but we've been together nearly four months now so I'm pretty sure that wasn't the case.

And there was another reason I wanted to go to the

party – I wanted Xander to know that I'm fun to be with, the kind of girlfriend he wants, not just the brainy girl that studies all the time. I've never been to a Smash Ball before – until this one, they'd always been held in the holidays, Jen was abroad with her parents and I didn't want to ask Mum for the money to go. Not that I'd have dared to go on my own anyway. But I've heard what they're like and while part of me hates myself for it, I was intrigued. They sound so debauched and glamorous, so unlike anything I'd ever been to.

Eventually, Jen agreed. But then there was another unexpected hurdle to overcome.

Mum said no. She said she'd seen the pictures in the papers of kids drunk, vomiting, boys' hands up girls' skirts, and worse.

But I ignored her. I had some money left over from the waitressing I'd done last Christmas so this time, I could pay myself. I faked her signature on the permission slip like Jade suggested, 'How's she ever going to know?' she'd rightly pointed out, and I handed it in.

I didn't really like lying to Mum. But as she'd never know, what would be the harm?

DAY TWO – Sunday, 6 p.m.

Malia

'I'm fine!' Henry exclaims, taking a drag on his e-cigarette and putting it down on the table. 'Honestly, it was all a lot of fuss about nothing and probably my own stupid fault.' We are drinking bright orange Aperol spritzes in enormous, bulbous glasses on one of the hotel's many terraces as the sun goes down. 'It was my first dive this season and I'm not used to those new whizzy combined belts. I probably did something wrong with the BCD, panicked, went all over the shop and used up too much air in the process. It was lucky I had Lucy on hand here to help me sort things out.'

She smiles modestly. 'I didn't do anything special, I did what anyone would do,' she protests.

Lucy, apparently an experienced diver, jettisoned Henry's weights for him as she also dropped hers and dragged Henry to the surface once she realized that his BCD wasn't inflating correctly and he was unable to ascend. The extra time and effort it took meant they only just had enough air between them to get to the surface rather than back to the boat too, which is why they didn't return on time.

They both seem very calm about it though. If it was me in a near-death situation like that, I'd be totally freaked out, I'm sure I would. I'm not sure I'd manage to stay calm. I'd probably panic and we'd both end up sinking to the bottom of the sea and dying.

But who knows? I never have enough confidence in myself, Mum was always saying so. Maybe I'd surprise myself, rise to the occasion and save the day.

'It's odd though because when I checked your inflate and deflate mechanisms before the dive, they looked like they were working fine,' Lucy adds.

Henry waves his hand. 'Honestly, don't give it a second thought. Any equipment is only ever as good as its operator, isn't it? I'm sure it was my own fault, I probably wasn't concentrating properly.'

'It was a brilliant day out, anyway,' Araminta interjects, clearly wanting to steer the conversation away from potential diving accidents in this idyllic resort which it is her job to promote. 'Now that everyone's a little less tired than we all were last night, why don't we all introduce ourselves properly to Henry so he knows who you're all writing for and can help you better with any particular angles you might want for your articles?'

'That sounds perfect,' Henry says. 'Though I think as you've all made the effort to come all the way out to visit us here, it's only fair that I start. My name is Henry Cadwallader and I am CEO and co-owner of Henphelia Hotels. This is the fifth in our small chain, with the other four being in ski resorts. All our hotels are small and aim to provide top quality service, while also employing local people and encouraging their career development, and using ingredients which have travelled less than fifty miles as much as possible in our restaurants. All our meat is organic, all our fish line-caught and sustainable breeds only. We encourage career progression and have won several awards for our training opportunities and HR policies – not easy when all except for this one in our small group of hotels are only open seasonally. We like to make our staff feel valued. Just as one small example, every staff member in every hotel has their own, admittedly small, private room – no stuffy dormitories for them. In this one they also have air conditioning and a small terrace with water access. We believe everyone is entitled to their privacy and we want them to be able to fully relax and enjoy their beautiful surroundings during their well-deserved time off.'

'We also dedicate one week each year to stays for families of children with terminal illnesses in each property, free of charge to them, of course. We're absolutely thrilled that you've come to visit us here and hope you are enjoying your stay so far.'

'Of course we are!' Araminta gushes. 'And we are all thrilled to be here too. Claire, why don't you tell Henry about yourself?'

'Yup, will do,' she says, smoothing down her emerald green maxidress, which I have to admire her for having the nerve to wear given her not inconsiderable bingo wings. 'I'm here for *Living the High Life*. I'm freelance these days, but for many years I worked in glossy magazines around the world, mainly in Dubai, but also Australia.'

'Rob?' Araminta prompts.

'I'm Rob, been freelance for years now, here for *Travel for Kings*, a membership website, and hopefully *Wherever You Go*, a glossy magazine. Also import wine these days.'

Henry nods. 'Perfect. I'll look forward to reading your pieces. River?'

'I'm not writing for a publication, I'm an influencer, like Malia. I have around one million followers and will be posting several pictures, stories and reels on Instagram every day, as well as TikToks.'

I blush at River referring to me as being an influencer like him, and hope that no one notices.

'Ah yes, I remember now! I was advised that . . .' Henry casts a look at the journalists and decides against whatever he was going to say. But I imagine it will have been something along the lines that his marketing or PR team told him that influencers do exactly that these days – influence – while the reach of traditional print magazines can sometimes now be fairly limited, especially now that so many publications are behind paywalls online.

'Have to say,' Henry continues, 'I'm glad social media wasn't around when I was your age though! Every moment captured for everyone to see and on the internet for eternity . . . anyway, I know that's not your kind of thing, River. I've seen your pictures, and they're beautiful. And you, Malia, you're an influencer too?'

'Yes. I don't have quite as many followers as River, but I'm working hard to develop all my social media channels and I hope that my posts will be useful to you. I'm grateful to you for inviting me and hope to do the best I can for you and for the resort.'

I don't state the number of followers I've got because it's not even vaguely in the same ballpark as River's numbers, it would be embarrassing. It fluctuates according to how much I post, and I'm still trying to get the measure of what works well. I also have a day job in a local library. There's no way I'd earn enough to live off from social media like River. Eventually, I hope to, but doesn't everyone? So far, I have occasionally been paid a small amount for campaigns and partnerships, but mainly I see my Insta life as a way of benefiting from a few perks which sometimes come my way such as spa days, meals out and the occasional nice piece of clothing in return for some posts, reels and stories.

'We're grateful to you for coming!' Henry says. 'Isn't that right, Araminta?'

She nods. 'Yes of course. All of you here were carefully chosen to provide the very best balance of coverage.'

'And I already know Lucy by reputation of course,' Henry continues. 'Not only is she one of the most well-respected national newspaper travel editors in the business, but she probably saved my life this morning!'

Lucy smiles graciously and says nothing. She and Claire are perhaps of around a similar age, though it's difficult to tell. They're both pretty attractive, but Lucy is natural and poised, while Claire is brash and, dare I say it, a bit embarrassing. I hope I am more like Lucy when I am older.

'Ah, here's Mohammed,' Henry continues, as a man in a smart suit and a subtle gold turtle lapel badge approaches. 'Mohammed is our hotel manager and keeps everything running smoothly for us. He will also be on hand during your stay to answer any questions you might have about the running of the hotel, or indeed anything else.'

'It's a pleasure to meet you all – thank you for coming,' Mohammed says, with a polite nod. 'I'm afraid I have a staff meeting this evening I must attend, but I hope to join you for dinner tomorrow. In the meantime, Henry, the boat is ready when you are.'

Henry claps his hands together. 'Right! Is everyone ready for dinner? We've got some very special experiences for you this evening.'

We are led along the jetty which is lit by flambeaux to a wooden boat with a cloth canopy – much simpler than the 'dive boat' we were on earlier, but very pretty and absolutely pristine. Julia is already on board, holding a tray of champagne flutes (it seems that champagne is on hand at pretty much every moment when staying on Ketenangan) and there is also man in the hotel uniform holding large fishing rods.

We step down into the boat and Claire wrinkles her nose as she sees the rods. 'Fishing? *Really?*' she says contemptuously. 'What's so special about that?'

Henry takes a glass of champagne from the tray and hands it to her, seemingly unfazed by her rudeness. If I was him, I would want to slap her. 'You will see, Claire. I hope you will find it special. But if you don't want to join in the fishing, that's fine too, of course. You can simply relax on board, enjoy your champagne and watch the sunset.'

She has the good grace to look faintly embarrassed at least. She mumbles something about fishing not being her thing and sits down on one of the upholstered seats which run along both sides of the vessel, sipping at her flute.

The staff cast off the ropes, one of them flips a switch and the boat moves almost silently away from the jetty. 'It's powered by solar energy which is captured during the day,' Henry says.

'Course it is,' Claire mutters.

'Zero pollution and less likely to scare the fish away,' he continues, ignoring her.

'How far can it travel?' Lucy asks, notebook in hand.

'I'm not sure exactly – I think it depends on the hours of sunlight, the speed we go, other factors that I don't understand too, quite possibly. I leave that to the experts like Yoonus here, who is driving us this evening.'

'It goes about twenty kilometres between charges,' Yoonus interjects.

'Thank you. There's your answer, Lucy, I knew Yoonus would know more about it than me. I'm still amazed by solar power. It both feels like magic, harnessing the power of the sun, and yet at the same time, makes perfect sense.'

Claire rolls her eyes and clicks her fingers at Julia, who immediately takes a bottle from the bucket of ice where there is, surely, far more champagne than we can possibly get through this evening, and refills her glass.

'But what if there's not enough sun during the day?' River asks.

'Then we swim back!' Henry says.

I feel a stab of alarm and swallow it down.

'Or, even better, we switch on the back up battery,' he adds. 'We don't want to leave any of our guests stranded, obviously.'

He was joking. No one is going to be stranded. I take a deep breath and tell myself to stop catastrophizing.

Yoonus flicks a switch, the boat slows down and he chucks an anchor overboard. Julia has been lighting candles in dozens of glass lanterns which are glistening in their various positions hung around the boat and, as the final glow of red dips beneath the horizon, they, the moon, and the distant glimmer of the lights of the resort we've just left, are all the light we can see.

It is magical.

'Pretty special, hey?' Henry says. 'Now, for those of you who want to catch your own dinner, I'll leave you in the capable hands of Yoonus who will provide you with rods and show you what to do. For those of you that don't,' he looks meaningfully at Claire, 'we have plenty of canapés and fizz.'

In the end, everyone takes a rod and has a go at the fishing, including Claire. We don't even have to put bait on the hooks – lights are lowered into the water apparently to attract the smaller fish (called bait fish) which, in turn, attract the bigger fish. I squeal as there's a tug on my line and I don't know what to do next, so Yoonus shows me how to reel the fish in, take it off the hook humanely and, once he's checked what type of fish and that it's 'not a protected species or one which is poisonous' he explains, makes me flinch by whacking it over the head. It immediately stills.

As someone who eats meat and fish, I know in my heart that it's almost inarguably better to catch and kill your own ethically sourced food than to buy it on a plastic-wrapped tray from the supermarket, giving the minimum-possible thought to how it got there and the animal it used to be. But even so, I still feel more than a little unsettled by the fact that I have killed a living creature and am now going to eat it.

'It was interesting, and I'm glad I caught the fish,' I tell Yoonus, 'but I think I'll sit back and watch now.'

'As you wish,' he says, looking at his watch. 'We only have another five minutes or so and then we have to leave for our barbecue.' He leans in closer. 'It's lucky that the chef will have come with spare fish as not everyone is an expert fisher-person like you.'

Our rods are gathered in and put away and the near silent boat rounds a headland. 'And there's Amaankan Beach,' says Henry. 'I believe it translates as Peace Beach.'

There is a collective gasp, even from Claire who has seemed to make a point of not being impressed by anything if she can help it so far. The beach looks like it is covered in tiny weeny lights.

'Amazing, huh?' Henry says. 'Nature's own fairy lights. They're little bioluminescent creatures which contain something called luciferin – and when it reacts with oxygen, it causes that glow.'

'A bit like fireflies?' Araminta asks.

Henry smiles 'Dunno. I only just learnt that from our turtle and conservation man who you'll meet tomorrow. You can ask him – I'm afraid what I've told you is as far as my knowledge goes when it comes to this. The best view of the lights is from the water rather than on the beach itself, so we're going to head over to that next cove,' he points to his left, 'where our guest chef Haruki is preparing your dinner and you can admire the view as you eat. Haruki will prepare and grill any fish you've caught if you would like him to, plus we have a few other surprises up our sleeve.'

DAY TWO – Sunday, 8.30 p.m.

Malia

A pagoda has been set up on the beach with candlelit lanterns like the ones on the boat. A large barbecue is flaming away, and a man in chef's whites is grilling jumbo prawns and langoustine. They are piled onto a platter by an assistant and placed in the centre of the round table in the pagoda.

The table is set for seven, plus there is one place where instead of a table setting, there's an ornate chopping board, a series of shiny and very sharp-looking knives, a large, shallow dish of water, a dish of salt and another, larger empty aluminium dish.

We are shown to our places at the table which I now see are set as if for sushi with what look like (but probably aren't given the resort's impressive eco-credentials) ivory chopsticks on granite rests and delicate little bowls of sauce, wasabi and pieces of ginger. There are also finger bowls with slices of lemon and small bowls of edamame.

I love sushi. Given the choice, I would eat it every day. And it would definitely be my death row meal, without a shadow of a doubt.

Julia circulates, serving us each a small goblet of sake. Rob knocks his back in one, as if it was a shot, causing himself to cough and splutter, but even so, he holds his cup up and indicates to Julia to refill it, which she does. I take a small sip. It's very strong, and also I happen to know that that's how you're meant to drink it rather than downing it like Rob did. I post sushi a lot on my grid and have been lucky enough to be invited to a smart new Japanese restaurant near where I live which I could never have afforded if I was paying. But while it was a step up from the usual high street sushi chains, it was nowhere near as upmarket as it is here, so I have very high hopes for tonight.

The chef walks over to the table and another man brings over a large, somewhat ugly fish on a salver and places it on top of the chopping board. They each give a little bow and the assistant takes a step back.

'I'm privileged to introduce you to Haruki, who we're delighted to have persuaded to come and join us from Japan for our opening with his sous-chef Itsuki,' Henry says. 'Haruki is one of the finest chefs licensed to prepare fugu, and the first to bring his art to the Maldives, we believe.'

Henry beams like a child at Christmas. 'Does everyone know what fugu is?' he asks.

'Isn't it that fish that's really poisonous?' Claire replies, with an undisguised look of disgust. 'As in, so poisonous it can kill you?'

'Yes, but also, no,' Henry says, tilting his head to the side. 'I'll leave Haruki to explain its history and how he prepares it safely. No one is obliged to try it, but I recommend that you do. It's an obsession of mine. I can personally vouch for the fact that it is utterly delicious, and that even if you don't want to try it tonight, watching Haruki prepare it is a spectacle in itself.'

'Thank you, Henry,' says the chef. 'First, a little about me. My restaurant Sakana in Japan has three Michelin stars. I trained for three years for my licence to prepare fugu, which is Sakana's speciality. I chose to specialize in fugu, which comes from the puffer fish, not because I wanted to exploit the danger and drama of preparing a fish which contains a poison 1,200 times more dangerous than cyanide, and which was banned entirely in Japan for 200 years, but because it is a genuinely exceptional fish which I think everyone should try at least once in their lifetime.'

'At least, those who can afford it,' Henry quips.

Haruki gives a small nod of acknowledgement. 'Indeed. It is illegal in many parts of the world, and can only be prepared by chefs like myself who are specifically trained and licensed. There are around 4,000 official fugu restaurants in Japan, but there are still a few dozen poisonings every year in my country, sadly. Most of those unfortunate deaths occur when people have tried to prepare the fish at home, which is an extremely foolish thing to do. I wouldn't go so far as to say that those people deserved what they got but . . . well.'

He rests his fingers gently on the skin of the fish.

'Scientists have now managed to breed a version of puffer fish which is not at all poisonous, which any chef can prepare. This has made it more accessible as no special training is required for that variety,' Haruki continues. 'It is also usually less expensive. If you are enjoying a meal of true fugu prepared by someone like myself, it can easily cost several thousand yen, or several hundred American dollars.'

Rob gives a long, low whistle. Everyone ignores him.

'I am a traditionalist,' Haruki continues, 'and I prefer to use a wild fish for many reasons, the most important being its taste. This one, a starry puffer, is native to the Maldives and caught today which is, of course, always the best way to eat fish. Straight from the sea, or at least as quickly as possible after it was caught.'

'So you're saying that if the fish isn't prepared correctly, by an expert such as yourself, it could kill us? Literally kill us?' Rob asks, frowning.

'That is exactly what I'm saying. If I did not correctly remove the poisonous organs, and you were to eat the fish, you would need medical help within one hour to have any chance of survival. If you didn't receive it, you would be dead within twenty-four hours.'

A hush falls over the table. 'There have been some very famous poisonings by fugu, but they almost all involve extremely reckless behaviour,' Haruki adds. 'In the 1980s, a very well-known Japanese actor died after eating four fugu livers. In 2012, two children sadly lost their lives after being given fugu for lunch – it's hard to imagine why any adult would think it a suitable dish for a child – and around the same time, two fishermen, who you think would know better, died, and seven were hospitalized after eating the skin of the fish.'

There is a shocked silence.

'But let me assure you that Haruki is an expert and no one is going to die,' Henry interjects quickly. 'I've enjoyed fugu prepared by Haruki several times, as well as by other chefs in his native Japan. I have been fascinated by it for many years, and eaten it at every opportunity I'm given, often making trips especially for the pleasure of consuming the dish, and am greatly looking forward to enjoying it again this evening. But, to reiterate, we have plenty of other delicious fish and seafood available this evening, and there is absolutely no obligation to try the fugu for anyone who is afraid.'

'I'm not afraid,' Rob says quickly. 'I simply don't like sushi.'

'Fugu is often eaten raw as sushi, but it is possible to grill the fish for those who prefer it cooked,' Haruki says, obviously quickly getting the measure of Rob, who quite clearly seems uneasy with the idea of a potentially fatal dish. 'I will prepare it both ways tonight. But I would never want anyone to taste anything of mine against their will. No chef worth their salt would, potential poison or not.'

A nervous laugh goes around the table, though Haruki himself remains entirely straight-faced. 'But today we are not here to talk about poison,' Haruki continues. 'This evening should be about good food shared among friends, yes?'

Henry holds up his goblet. 'Hear, hear. To good food, shared among friends.'

Haruki picks up one of the impressive-looking knives. 'Now, the most important thing to know is that only certain parts of the fish are poisonous. Not the white flesh that you will eat, but the innards – especially the ovaries and liver, and also the skin. Those are the places where the poison is. First, I will remove the skin. As you will see, it is not scaly like on some fish. I cut around the mouth, and pull it away, like so. Almost like a snake shedding its skin.'

I watch carefully as he drops the skin into a yellow box marked 'hazardous waste' at his side, a little like the sharps boxes you sometimes see in hospitals or doctors' surgeries.

'Then, using a smaller, very sharp knife, I remove the eyes.' Everyone winces, which is bizarre, as the fish is dead and if you think about it, all of this is pretty gross.

'Now, the most dangerous part. I remove the ovaries and liver which, as you may remember, are the organs which contain most of the poison. It's very important that I don't accidentally pierce these. If I do, the fish must be disposed of, as even a tiny amount of poison is usually fatal. If you were to swallow any poison at all, your mouth would go numb, and very shortly after that you would be paralysed. Within a few hours, you would be dead. Even the quantity you could fit onto the head of a pin would be enough to kill you. This is what the training is for – to ensure that I cut the poisonous parts of the fish away without any of the poison escaping.'

Everyone leans in as he removes the organs and places them carefully in the box.

'Now, assuming I have done my job correctly of course, the fish is safe.'

He smiles wryly at his own semi-joke, but no one laughs.

'It is then washed with salt, like so . . . .' he rubs the salt all over the large fish and then places it in a silver bowl to gently wash it away as we all look on, trans-fixed. The water is also poured into a second hazardous waste container. 'In my opinion,' he continues, 'the best way to eat fugu is as sashimi. Which I'm going to show you now.' He eases the knife into the flesh of the fish over and over again creating almost paper-thin, trans-lucent strips which he gently lays onto a large plate decorated with a brightly coloured pattern which can be seen through the thin layer of white fish. Within a few minutes, the plate is entirely covered. It is mesmer-izing to watch. Haruki holds it up at an angle for us all to admire.

'And there you have it. Fugu sashimi. Fugu is a fatty fish with a non-fishy taste, umami, if you will.' He hands the plate to his sous-chef. 'Itsuki will serve those of you who would like to try, and for our friend here,' he indicates Rob, 'who says he does not like to eat raw fish, I will grill some pieces. They will be delicious dipped in the sauces which you have in front of you.'

Itsuki circles the table, placing three pieces of sashimi in a precise fan onto each of our plates with chop sticks, except when he reaches Rob who says, 'I'll wait for the grilled version.'

My health anxiety wouldn't usually allow me to eat something like this, but it seems rude not to try and I did promise myself that I would start pushing myself out of my comfort zone more often, plus I absolutely love sushi.

'*Bon appetit*,' Henry says, before expertly picking up his chopsticks and pushing the first piece into his mouth. 'Mmm. As delicious as I remember,' he says.

I take a deep breath, grasp a piece of the beautifully presented fish with the chopsticks and hesitantly place it into my mouth. I chew gingerly and swallow, saying a silent prayer to a God I'm not sure I believe in. I feel a whoosh of relief and I mentally check myself over and realize there are no obvious ill-effects – at least nothing immediate. Didn't Haruki say you'd know almost straight away if you were poisoned? Are my lips tingling a little, or am I imagining that?

'Delicious,' I agree, though I am lying. Isn't this all a little bit Emperor's New Clothes? The fish is OK, but it's kind of like any other sashimi I've tried, only thinner and with less taste. Haruki comes over with the pieces of fish he has flash-grilled arranged on a small plate, which are slightly blackened and look much nicer. 'I'd love to try one of those too though, if there's one going spare?' I add.

'Of course,' he says, placing one on my plate along-side the two uneaten pieces of sashimi, before putting the other three pieces onto Rob's. 'I would suggest dipping a piece into the ponzu sauce, which is that one,' he indicates a small round dish in front of our plates, 'to best complement the delicate flavour and firm texture of the fish.'

'Bottoms up then,' says Rob, stabbing his fork into the fish, then dipping it into the sauce so that it splashes everywhere, before shoving the entire piece into his mouth.

He chews and gives an appreciative nod, before suddenly clutching at his throat with both hands, lurching to a standing position, seemingly unable to breathe. He staggers backwards and his eyes roll back in his head and he lets one of his hands fall to the table, bending at the knees as he appears to struggle to hold himself up before collapsing back onto his chair again and taking a laboured, rasping breath as he falls to the floor.

We all leap up from the table as everything seems to happen at once. Lucy and Araminta scream and grab at each other, Claire shouts, 'Oh my God, somebody do something!' and Henry rushes over to Rob, knocking a plate off the table as he goes. I burst into tears and for a horrifying second think I might wet myself. River is simply standing with his hand up to his mouth, staring, and Haruki is motionless, a look somewhere between horror and incomprehension on his face.

May, 1990

Ashley

When we're allowed out from school at the weekends, everyone knows which pubs will demand to check our ID and which don't care and are happy to simply take our money whether we're already eighteen or not, and obviously we choose to go to the right ones accordingly.

I thought they'd be stricter at a posh place like this country pile where the party is being held, and that was why so many people were already half-cut by the time they got on the bus.

But that shows how much I know – it's not like that at all. I'd say about ninety-nine per cent of the people at this party tonight are underage – quite a few don't look much older than fourteen or fifteen, but literally no one is being turned away from the bar. And they're not exactly ordering lemonade, except with their gin. There's some complicated ticketing system going on so you buy tickets at one stand and then pay at the bar with them, perhaps that makes it legal? Or maybe there's some loophole because it's private property rather than a pub? I don't know. Certainly there seems to be no limit on how many drinks you can buy, according to the shouts I hear going between some of the boys, boasting about how many tickets they're planning to get through this evening and how many they've already spent.

'ARE YOU GLAD YOU CAME?' I shout at Jen over the thumping music as we wait for our vodka and Cokes. We take the drinks and move away to stand near the bucking bronco where it's quieter apart from all the squealing as people, mainly girls it seems, get flung off.

'It's OK, I guess,' she says, noncommittally. 'Where's Xander?'

I shrug. 'Dunno,' I say, 'I'll find him later. He's probably in the VIP area with Henry. Xander could probably get us in if you like, but Ophelia will probably be there and I can do without her sneering at me. So unless you're particularly bothered . . .'

She shakes her head. 'Can't think of anything I'd like less.'

'You seen anyone you like yet?' I add, keen to make her admit something good about the evening, bring her out of herself. 'What about him?' I say, pointing at a guy with blond, floppy hair and a pink bow tie.

'Nah. More your type than mine,' she says, wrinkling her nose. 'All these posh boys look the same. They're of no interest to me.'

'Suit yourself,' I say, feeling a flash of annoyance and wondering for a second why I bothered to persuade her to come if she's going to be so grumpy about it all. 'Shall we go and give the casino a go?' I suggest. At least it will give us something to focus on.

They handed out ten pounds worth of gambling chips to each of us on the bus – the idea being that you use them up quickly and pay for more, I imagine. Any winnings can't be exchanged for real money anyway, only for rubbish merch like mugs, cheap and nasty T-shirts and key rings, not even for drinks tickets which realistically is what people actually want. Apparently if you buy more chips, a proportion of this money goes to charity, though which charity and the percentage is kept pretty vague.

But no one cares about that – it's all a bit of fun and after a few minutes of placing our bets on the roulette wheel, Jen finally seems to start cheering up.

'Yay! Black!' she calls, as the wheel spins and the ball bounces around, finally settling into number fifteen. 'I win again!' She takes her new chips and adds them to her pile, happily. 'If I can do that a few more times, I can win a shit T-shirt that I'd be embarrassed to wear,' she says, but with humour as she takes another pile of the plastic tokens and places them in the 'Even' section. 'I'm on a roll.'

'You are,' I say, finishing off my vodka and Coke. 'I'm going to get another drink. Want anything?'

She narrows her eyes and seems to be concentrating hard as the wheel spins, almost as if she thinks she can control where the ball lands. Bless. 'A vodka and Coke. Double. Please. Thank you.'

I head back to the bar, the queue for which is now a few people deep so I have to wait a while. My too-high stilettos are new and cheap and starting to hurt – I'm not used to heels. I stand up on tiptoes to slip my heels out of my shoes and then back in again, but they're still rubbing and I bet they'll give me blisters. I should have brought plasters.

I wonder again where Xander is. Looking around the circular bar, now and again I think I see him but then look again and realize it's not him after all. Chances are he's still with Henry. Jen is right, to a degree all these public school boys in their black DJs (with the occasional white one for those who think themselves a 'character') do look pretty much the same.

I push further in towards the bar. It's quite hot now – I wonder if there's anywhere we can get outside to get some air? Do we have access to the garden? Would I get back in if I went out? My tights are chafing around my waist and momentarily I wish I'd worn suspenders or hold ups, but Jen and I think the former are slutty and I'd be worried that the latter would fall down. Plus my dress is probably too short for either anyway.

I look down, rooting through my new Chelsea Girl evening bag for the drinks tickets. It's hard to hold anything properly in these elbow-length velveteen opera gloves which I thought looked classy and elegant when

I tried them on in Debenhams but are now making me itchy and hot.

'What can I get you, love?' the bar woman asks, interrupting my reverie.

I look up, and we look at each other in frozen horror and shock.

Oh my God.

'Mum?' I say hoarsely, when I can find my breath, looking around surreptitiously first to check that no one nearby can hear me. 'What are you doing here?'

Her face darkens and she hisses: 'I could ask you the same thing, missy' but then a man in a suit and slicked back hair passes behind her and asks, 'Everything all right here?' frowning, and she puts her fake smile back on and says: 'All fine, I'm just serving this young lady here. What can I get you?'

'Um . . . two Cokes please,' I say. I can't ask for vodka now, I'll have to tell Jen they wouldn't serve me if she notices, which hopefully she won't because I doubt she'd believe me anyway. Mum fills a couple of glasses from one of those nozzle things and shovels an ice cube tersely into each one.

'Four pounds, please,' she says, holding out her hand and glowering at me. £4! Daylight robbery. I hand her the relevant tickets and she leans in and says, 'Don't think we're finished here. You will regret disobeying me.'

'Mum!' I say, snatching my hand away, before a beat later, noticing who is standing next to me. Ophelia. Oh God. Could this get any worse?

'Your mum's here!' Ophelia cries, clapping her hands and jumping up and down like a little girl. I notice she is wearing similar gloves to me, but hers are much nicer, probably Dior or something. 'How cute! Don't you look alike? Well, it's absolutely *lovely* to meet you, Mrs Ashley's mum. I'd like two gin and tonics and four glasses of water please. On my VIP tab – Ophelia Cadwallader. Thank you.'

DAY TWO – Sunday, 9.30 p.m.

Malia

Henry leans over Rob on the ground, pulling him up by his shoulders and shouting 'Rob! Rob!' at his unresponsive body as his head lolls back. 'Shit!'

Julia has picked up a radio and is pressing buttons, gabbling something frantically in a low voice which I can't quite hear.

Suddenly Rob lifts his head, smiles, winks, gets up and dusts himself off. 'Ha ha, got you! April Fool! Brilliant! I never expected anyone to take that seriously.' We all stare at him in horror, dumbfounded. He looks around, grinning. 'Oh, come on! Can't anyone take a joke?'

Lucy and Araminta slowly let go of each other and Julia presses a button on the radio and speaks into it again, more slowly than before, I assume standing down whatever emergency procedure she had set in motion. Henry stands up and takes a careful step back from Rob. He looks furious. It's the first time I've seen him be anything except scrupulously polite since our arrival.

'It's not April,' Henry mutters, icily, 'and that wasn't even funny. Now, will you please kindly apologize to Haruki for your rudeness, and let us get on with our evening.'

The fish we caught earlier is prepared and served along with seafood and other local delicacies, and while the meal is delicious, the atmosphere has entirely soured. In spite of the magical setting and the little creatures still sparkling away on the next beach, it feels like no one can wait to get off the island and back to the privacy of our own rooms at the hotel.

Rob seems to try to make amends by being jovial and animated while Araminta, ever the professional, does her best to keep the conversation going. But it's all embarrassing and laboured and the evening is clearly ruined.

Henry remains stony-faced, barely saying a word or even looking at anyone as he eats his meal. He is entirely unlike I've seen him up until now. The rest of us, led by Araminta, continue to go through the motions and try to put on a face of jollity, but it's obvious that we are all relieved when Henry announces that the boat is ready to take us back to the resort. The journey passes in total and utter silence.

I'm glad to be back in my room and on my own. Being with other people the whole time can be so tiring, especially when the atmosphere turns the way it did after Rob's little stunt this evening. The turndown service has clearly been in – my bathroom has been tidied and towels rehung or replaced, scented candles have been lit, handmade chocolates and a fruit platter laid out on the bedside table, and the curtains drawn.

I'm not quite ready to go to bed yet though, so I open the curtains and step out on to the terrace. It's warm, still and clear and the moon is bright. Beautiful.

I take some pictures and sit down in one of the loungers and take some selfies. Candlelight is so flattering I barely even need a filter. But I fiddle with the image for a while even so before trying to post it to my story.

It doesn't work. There is no 4G here – no phone signal at all – but up until now the WiFi has been superfast. I go into settings, where I can no longer see any network at all.

How strange. Ah well. I guess my posts will have to wait.

May, 1990

Ashley

I take the Cokes and head back to the roulette table, where it seems that Jen has continued her winning streak and has clearly entirely shaken off her previous bad mood. She now has quite a sizeable pile of multi-coloured plastic betting chips, and is squealing and clapping her hands as she wins on yet another turn of the wheel and, most interestingly, seems to have acquired some bloke who she's pooled chips with. I don't recognize him – he's definitely not from our school.

I hand her a Coke and she takes a sip. 'Wow, that's weak,' she says. 'Can't taste the vodka at all.'

'Yeah, you know what these places are like,' I say vaguely, 'totally rip you off.' I'm not sure if I'm going to tell her about Mum being here or not, but even if I am, now is clearly not the time. 'Who's your friend?' I ask, changing the subject.

'This is Miles,' she says, staring at the wheel again as it spins. 'We were both doing best on the table so we thought we'd team up and now we're absolutely trouncing everyone!'

He gives me an apologetic smile. I guess he knows that that's a pretty lame way of chatting someone up but Jen seems happy and he looks OK, in that he's not so drunk he can't stand up and so far doesn't appear to be trying to grope her or anything.

'If you're alright here I think I'll go and see if I can find Xander then?' I suggest. 'I haven't seen him since we got off the bus.' I want to check Ophelia's not throwing herself at him or, oh God, I bet she's already telling everyone about Mum working here, shrieking with her bitchy mates about my mother, the poor woman who has to work for a living, serving spoilt cows like her.

Much as I absolutely don't want to and it's something I usually avoid at all costs, I need to see if I can get Ophelia by herself. See if there's anything I can do to stop her blabbing.

It doesn't take me too long to find Xander coming down the stairs from the VIP area. He spots me, his face breaks into a grin and I go over.

'Ashley!' he cries. 'There you are! I've been looking all over! Where have you been?'

Not looking that hard, I think to myself, *you knew I wasn't in the VIP area where you've probably been since we arrived.* But I'm not going to say that; the last thing I want to do is start a row or seem at all needy. No one wants a needy girlfriend, do they?

'I've been . . .' I start, but then I remember that Mum's behind the bar and I'm probably facing the biggest humiliation of my life and I can't work out whether it's better to tell him now and try and style it out or hope the problem will go away, that no one will notice and that Ophelia won't say anything. Neither seems like a good option. There's no way I'm going to get through this evening without something terrible happening – I'm sure of it.

'I've been with Jen,' I say, trying to push the problem out of my mind for now. I'll worry about the Mum situation later. 'At the casino. She's doing brilliantly. Can't drag her away.'

He takes my hand, pulls me towards him and kisses me, his tongue deep into my mouth. He presses against me, reaching round to cup my bum in his hand. I think he must be a bit drunk as he doesn't normally do stuff like that in public.

I've already had a few drinks so I kiss him back, but then I remember that Mum is here and might see me, oh shit, or what if there's a newspaper photographer who's sneaked in and I end up in the paper and make all Mum's fears come true, and I'm already in so much trouble for being here at all anyway.

I pull away abruptly. 'Not with people watching.'

I see Ophelia approaching with her gaggle of her awful friends and feel a lurch of panic. I take Xander's hand. 'Tell you what though, I'd quite like a go on the bronco,' I say. 'Will you come with me?' I don't want to go on the bull at all, hopefully there'll be a massive queue and I can get out of it, but I need to get Xander away from Ophelia as soon as possible in case she says something. But oh God, there's no way I can stay by his side all night and even if I did . . . she'll be bound to tell him eventually. I will probably introduce him to Mum at some point, but now is hardly the time or the place. The whole thing has the potential to be utterly mortifying.

What can I do? I need to stop Ophelia blabbing. Do something. I need time to think.

But for now, keeping him away from Ophelia is the best I can do. I take his hand. 'Come on. I want a go on the bull. It looks like great fun. Let's go.'

DAY THREE – Monday, 7 a.m.

Malia

The next morning we are up early for a full day of activities. I'm really excited about most of the things planned for today, though I wish there was more time to simply laze on my beautiful terrace gazing at the ocean. Plus not being able to update my Insta is making me angsty. I'm pretty sure I'll never get to River's level, but I'm hopeful that, given time, I can gain way more followers than I've got at the moment. A trip like this and the pictures which come out of it will go a long way to help with that, but it's frustrating not being able to do anything with them. They're not worth anything sitting on my phone.

The group has breakfast together today rather than in our rooms like yesterday. We're on the breakfast terrace, which is on the best side of the resort for the morning sun, apparently, and I can see colourful fish passing by off the edge. I get my phone out to film – it will make a lovely Insta story. When I can post it. Eventually.

I'm not sure if it's the early hour or whether we are all still feeling awkward after what happened last night, but everyone seems somewhat subdued. Without even being able to fiddle with our phones as most people probably would at breakfast time, checking out the news and updating their socials, the atmosphere is a little stilted.

Rob is certainly much quieter than he was yesterday – he barely says a word as he picks at his pancake decorated with fresh tropical fruit. His face is red – I guess he got sunburnt, and he looks tired.

'Any idea what's happened to the internet?' Claire asks the table in general, jabbing futilely at her phone before holding it up above her head and frowning at it as I guess she tries to see if she might catch some signal there. 'As a freelance, it's vital that I have access. God knows what kind of commissions I might be missing out on.'

Araminta tries to pull a sympathetic face but anyone can see it's not genuine. Fortunately, Claire is still pointlessly trying to scroll on her phone and not looking at her. 'I know. I have been asking,' Araminta replies. 'They think it's a problem with the satellite – they're not sure exactly what yet, but they're looking into it as a matter of priority.'

Claire squints up at the sky. 'It's not the clouds, is it?' she says. 'I don't know much about satellites but I guess that could mess with the signal?' It's hot and humid today and the sky is no longer as clear as it was yesterday.

'Maybe. I'm not sure. No doubt it'll be sorted soon. Shall I order you some more coffee?' Araminta adds, clearly trying to change the subject.

'No, thanks,' Claire says, testily. 'I want to be able to check my emails. Coffee won't help with that.'

'I understand,' Araminta says, turning away from Claire and rolling her eyes at me and River. We both smirk.

'I don't mean to be a pain,' I add, 'and I totally get that you can't do anything about the internet not working, but I'm worried that the resort is going to be annoyed that I'm not posting as much as was agreed. But obviously I can't because there's no network so . . .'

Araminta reaches over and squeezes my hand. 'Don't be silly. If there's no network, of course you can't post. Everyone will understand that. They don't expect you to work miracles! I'm sure they'll be absolutely delighted with whatever you share when it's back up and running, which will hopefully be soon.'

There is a sound of footsteps and Henry arrives. 'Good morning, everyone! I trust you all slept well?'

He is immaculately dressed in shorts and a crisp polo shirt and seems relaxed and cheerful. Either he's forgiven Rob for what went on last night, or he's simply excellent at hiding his emotions. As a hotelier no doubt skilled at pretending to get on with everyone, including difficult clients, I imagine it's the latter. I see Rob turn an even deeper shade of red but he doesn't say anything as he continues slowly forking his pancakes into his mouth and staring out over the sea.

There is a general 'Yes, thank you' murmur from the group as Henry continues. 'Good, good! I'd like to apologize for the lack of internet – I know you're all professionals and it will be a great inconvenience to you. Our technicians are looking at the problem and we hope to have it up and running as soon as possible.'

'Today, we thought we'd start with underwater scooters, followed by lunch, and then an island safari by quad bike and an introduction to the turtles, if everyone's happy with that?'

'Sounds wonderful!' Araminta gushes.

'I'll go and check the scooters on the beach are ready,' Henry continues. 'Rob?' He claps him on the back. 'Scooters sound good for you?'

'Yep,' he says. 'Listen, sorry about yesterday, Henry. I was out of order. I hope I, uh, didn't upset your chef. Or you.'

Henry pats his shoulder. 'I appreciate the apology. I won't lie to you, Haruki was quite annoyed, but I'll pass that on, and I'm sure he'll forgive you. As for me, I've forgotten about it already. No point dwelling on these things is there?'

Rob smiles weakly and mumbles, 'Cheers, mate.'

'Can we film on the scooters?' River asks. 'I'd like to make a reel.'

'They're all equipped with GoPros so I'm sure we can sort something out,' Henry says. 'I'll let you all finish your breakfast and see you on the beach in fifteen minutes? That work for you all? There's quite a lot to fit in today.'

The scooters – yellow, futuristic-looking things – are lined up on the beach. Julia is stationed behind a white-clothed table laden with fruit, tea, coffee, fruit juices and pastries in case we've suddenly got hungry or thirsty on the extremely short walk between breakfast and the beach, I guess, and Ahmed, the divemaster from yesterday is also there, talking to Henry.

'Hello again,' Ahmed says, looking up as we approach. 'We wanted to show you the dive scooters this morning. As I know from yesterday, you are all experienced divers, but these machines are ideal for those who are not confident using a regulator to breathe, or those who simply haven't dived before. They're also something different and a bit of fun, so we thought you'd enjoy trying them out.'

He walks over to the one at the end of the row and starts explaining how it works. 'They're a little like underwater motorbikes, or jet skis, except they only go very slowly – about two kilometres an hour. The slow speed makes them ideal for looking around you as you explore, taking in the coral, the fish and the turtles, just like when you are diving. Your head goes in here,' he indicates the bubble-like thing at the top, almost like an old-fashioned diving helmet 'and you can simply breathe as normal, from the air which is supplied by the scuba tank,' he indicates a tank on the front of the machine, 'here. You turn the handles left and right to steer, as if you were riding a bike, and this lever,' he indicates a bright red handle, 'allows you to go up and down. You can go to a depth of five metres and there is a gauge which checks you don't sink too far and won't allow you to go any deeper than that. There is no need for weights, or buoyancy aids, or any of those things that you need when you are diving traditionally. It is very, very easy.' He pauses. 'Any questions?'

Claire is frowning. 'Are these things safe?' she says. 'They look very heavy. What if you get trapped in them and sink?'

'They are very safe,' Ahmed continues, 'it is impossible to become trapped, and unless you are physically pressing the "down" lever, the natural inclination is for them to come up. So even if there is a malfunction, they would float.'

She wrinkles her nose. 'Hmm. A lever sounds like something which could get stuck to me. I'll take your word for it that they're fun, I think, and I'll give this one a miss. That Balinese bed and table of goodies that Julia has are calling me – I think I'll watch from there.'

'I'm going to sit this one out too,' Rob says. 'It looks interesting but I'm not feeling too clever.'

While Claire is clearly simply being lazy, to be fair to Rob, he does look pretty ropey.

He pats the top of his head. 'Also I think I left my cap at breakfast. I'm going to get that and then go back to my room for a nap out of the heat if that's OK. I didn't sleep at all well last night.'

'Not a problem,' Henry says, clapping his hands together. 'I appreciate you both taking the time to come and have a look at the scooters, and hope you have a restful morning. I have a few administrative tasks to get on with this morning and a meeting with Mohammed in five minutes, so I'm going to leave you in Ahmed's capable hands, while those who would like to can try out the scooters. I hope you enjoy them, and I'll look forward to seeing you later.'

The scooters are great fun. It feels odd being under-water and breathing without a regulator at first; I mean, can that helmet be totally airtight? But I quickly get used to it and it's kind of liberating not to have to keep checking a computer and doing all the things you have to do to keep yourself safe while you're diving. I watch the others through the glass of the bulbous helmets as we whizz about and, once we have settled into the weirdness of the breathing, we barely stop grinning.

'How was it?' Julia asks, handing us white, fluffy towels with the hotel's logo as we come back into shore and Ahmed arranges the weird-looking scooters in a neat line back on the beach. I notice Claire is already sipping a glass of champagne on her Balinese bed even though it can't even be 11 o'clock.

'It was fabulous! Thank you!' I say. She still looks familiar to me but I can't place her. Maybe she does just have one of those faces, like she says. We head over to the table where by now I'm grateful for a cold glass of peach juice with crushed ice and gulp it down, though this time I am strict with myself and hold back from the delicious-looking pastries, opting for a slice of water-melon instead.

'Such a shame the rest of your party didn't join you,' Julia says, though Claire at least looks far from bothered about missing out. 'I'm sure they'd have enjoyed it. I do hope Rob's feeling better soon.'

'What's up with him today anyway?' River asks. 'He seems in a right mood.'

Araminta shrugs. 'Dunno. I thought maybe he was embarrassed about the thing he did last night but . . . well, he doesn't seem the type to let something like that bother him too much.' She pauses. 'Maybe he simply didn't sleep well like he said. Hopefully he'll be feeling better after a rest,' she adds, snapping back into profes-sional mode. Julia is fussing around the table, collecting glasses and tidying, but I get the weirdest impression that she's deliberately trying to listen in and, even though nothing of any great consequence is being said, I feel uncomfortable. I take another sip of the delicious juice and try to dismiss my negative thoughts. I must be imagining things.

Araminta looks at her watch. 'Right. We've got about an hour now to relax and get changed before we head off to where we're having lunch. We'll meet in reception at 11.30. I'll let the others know. And meantime I'll go and see if I can find out what's going on with the internet so I can keep you all updated.'

Back in my room, the bed has already been made, the drapes opened, new glass bottles of water with the turtle logo placed on the bedside table and another platter of tropical fruit left on the occasional table, with a note which says 'With the compliments of the Ketenangan team.'

I go into the bathroom where the towels that I dropped carelessly on the ground after my quick morning shower have been replaced on the rails. The shower has been cleaned and even dried so it looks like no one has ever used it. My toiletries have been neatly arranged around the sink and the small soap I used yesterday taken away and replaced by a new one, with a note which says 'All hotel toiletries are sanitized and recycled into new products which are distributed to local women's centres and orphanages.' I put the note back. Impressive.

I head back out to the dressing room to find something to wear for the quad biking. I'm quite nervous about this particular activity, but I try to push my worries to the back of my mind. I'm overthinking it. I'm sure it will be fine.

May, 1990

Ashley

'My girlfriend would like a go on the bronco,' Xander tells the boy in charge of the queue, who is a minor acolyte of Henry's, I think. I feel a little thrill at Xander referring to me as his girlfriend, as I don't think I've ever heard him do that before, but this is quickly replaced by a feeling of dread. Why did I claim I wanted to go on the bull? It's absolutely the last thing I want to do. Why didn't I think of something else to get Xander away from Ophelia? 'And I can make it worth your while if you let us jump the queue,' he adds. 'We don't want to be waiting around all night.'

Xander glances around, takes a couple of pills from his pocket and presses them into the boy's hand, like a kindly grandma bestowing a 50p on a favourite grandchild when she doesn't want the parents to see what she's doing.

Fuck's sake. I was hoping he wouldn't be doing anything like that this evening. He looks pretty straight so far, bit pissed, though I don't think he's taken anything. But he's obviously brought a few pills along with him in case he or his mates feel like it later. Or maybe the dealer guy gives them to him and the other organizers as sweeteners; he must make an absolute fortune here. I know Ophelia's really into all that, not that I care about her, but I hate that Xander is.

The boy glances at him, drops the pills in his pocket and nods curtly. 'Nice one. No problem mate, she's up next.'

He presses a large red button, the bull suddenly speeds up, the girl on it (why is it almost always girls who go on this thing?) squeals and comes flying off in a cloud of shiny gossamer skirts. I feel a lurch of alarm as she hurtles through the air – should she be up that high? – before landing in the big crash mat. But she comes up laughing and scampers off to her friends.

'OK Alison, shoes off, then off we go,' says the boy. 'Follow me.'

'It's Ashley,' I say. 'And actually I'm not sure now if I want to . . .'

But he strides off towards the bull, clearly not listening. I'm suddenly really, really scared. What if I hurt myself falling? Or, I've already had a few drinks, what if the movement makes me throw up? That would be absolutely mortifying in front of all those people.

I'm still hanging back. I don't think I can do it.

'Come on!' Xander says, good naturedly, interrupting my fretting. 'I'll hold your shoes. You'll love it, I promise. I've done it before, it's great fun.'

I smile at him, trying not to show my nervousness, take off my black suede Top Shop stilettos and hand them to him. It's a relief to let my feet spread, I hate wearing heels, they're so uncomfortable.

It's too late to tell him I don't want to go on the bull now, especially since he bribed the boy, he'll think I'm a total wuss. 'OK. You'll wait here for me?' I ask. 'And make sure he doesn't make it go too fast?' I sound whiny and am embarrassed for myself.

He leans in and kisses me full on the lips. 'Sure. I'll be right here. You'll be great.'

I step up onto the thick mat and walk across, the plastic cool on my aching feet through my thin black tights.

I get over to the bull, where the boy is standing impatiently. 'Right. Up you hop then,' he says. It's impossible to do it elegantly but I grip the handle, throw my left leg up in the air over the brown leather of the bull and he gives me a gentle shove to get me into place.

'Good. That's it. I'll start it off slow, then speed up. It's kind of fun for people watching if you start off holding on with only one hand if you can, other one up in the air, like a cowboy.' I raise my left hand. 'Good. That's it. Ready?'

'As I'll ever be,' I say. He bounds back to the control panel and presses a button. Surely there should be two people doing this? No doubt it's just Henry cutting corners as usual – all he's bothered about is making money, according to Xander. Which is weird when his family are already so loaded. Maybe it's about Henry impressing his father? I don't know. Why am I even thinking about this now? Why do I even care? There is a lurch and the bull tips down to one side. I instinctively bring my left hand down to the handle to hold on better but once I've settled into the movement, forward back, forward back, I let go and hold it up in the air. I smile. It is actually quite fun, much less scary than I imagined it might be. I catch a glimpse of Xander and he gives me a thumbs up.

The speed goes up a notch and I try to grip with my feet too, but the sides of the bull are too smooth and trying to grip like that doesn't make any difference. A few seconds later it is going faster again and I have to hold on with both hands. The bull is also spinning now as well as jerking all the way forwards and all the way backwards. I try to see where Xander is but I'm spinning too fast now to see anything much. I start feeling something a little like car sickness so I look down at the handle but that makes me feel worse so I look up again at all the faces, brightly coloured dresses and the black and white of the boys in dinner jackets going past in a blur.

Up down. Forward back, spinning, spinning, I think I can hear whooping, the bull speeds up again, gives a sudden buck and I fly off with a lurch.

The thud as I land is harder than I expect and for a second I want to cry but I can't do that with all these people looking at me. I remember the girl before me, scampering away, laughing, I need to do that, be more like her. I wonder if anyone saw my knickers? I try to get up but the softness of the mat makes it difficult and I scrabble on my back like an upturned beetle.

A hand reaches down to me and pulls me up. At first I think it's Xander – he's seen that I'm upset and he's come to help me! But no, it turns out it's the boy operating the bull.

'OK, Aileen?' he says. 'Up you get. Next person needs to get on. People get bored if there's too long between riders.'

I nod and fight back tears. My neck hurts and pain shoots through my left leg as I limp back to Xander.

'Hey!' he says, taking my elbow as I gingerly step down from the large crash mat. 'You did brilliantly! Stayed on ages. Much longer than the girl before. How was it?'

I force a smile. 'It was fine. But I don't think I'd do it again.' He hands me my shoes and I slip them on, but as soon as I try to walk my ankle twists and I fall against him.

'Ow! I think I've hurt my leg. Can we go and sit down for a minute?' I bend down and take my shoes off. I can't balance in these heels when my ankle feels like this.

He takes my arm. 'Yeah, of course. Look, there's a free table there. Let's go.'

I hobble over, ease myself into a chair, and lift my left foot up on to my right knee. I can see that my ankle is already swollen and rub it.

'Better?' Xander asks, somewhat impatiently. He glances around, fidgeting, as if he wants to be somewhere else. Or maybe he has taken something after all. I'm not sure.

My ankle is throbbing. The music is suddenly too loud and I feel sick from all the spinning. When I go to the fair I never even go on the most basic of rides as they always make me feel nauseated so I don't know what I was thinking. I shouldn't have suggested going on the bull. I should have been stronger and said something when I changed my mind. Xander wouldn't have been annoyed, I'm sure.

Suddenly I don't want to be here. I can't remember now why I was so desperate to come. Part of me knew it was going to be a disaster one way or another. I should have listened to Jen. And Mum.

I just want to be at home, in my own bed in Mum's tiny and shabby but cosy fifteenth-floor flat. I can tell Xander has other things he wants to do rather than look after me right now, having a drink with Henry probably, or maybe he has things to organize this evening though it doesn't seem like it. I don't want to be needy, but equally, I don't want him to leave me here on my own.

An image of Mum serving at the bar flashes through my mind and for a second I want nothing more than to go and find her, ask for a cuddle and for her to take me home, but obviously I can't do that, that would be mad and probably make what is already setting out to be a terrible evening about 1,000 times worse.

I try to rotate my foot and a bolt of pain shoots up my leg. Shit. It's not broken, is it?

'It hurts quite a lot, to be honest,' I admit.

Xander frowns. 'Do you, uh, I dunno, do you want me to take you to first aid or something? I don't even know if there is anything like that here?'

I feel tears threatening. Is there a first aid centre? I've no idea. But even if there is, I don't want well-meaning people in a St John's Ambulance uniform fussing over me. They might even get wind of the fact that Mum's here and call her in to see me.

Or what if they think it might be broken and call an ambulance? How mortifying would that be? Being wrapped up in a blanket and taken out in a stretcher? Then Mum would almost definitely get involved and make a fuss and, oh God, no, I can't have that. I would never, ever live it down at school and Mum would never let me out of the house again.

'No,' I insist. 'Thank you. I'm sure I'll be OK if I sit here for a minute. Maybe you could get me a drink, and perhaps ask at the bar if they could give you a bag of ice? I could put that on my ankle. It's probably all it needs. Easier than going to find any first aid people, if there even are any.'

He touches my cheek lightly and looks at me thoughtfully.

'Tell you what,' he says, 'I've got some ibuprofen? That might help?'

'Ibuprofen?' I ask, sceptically. 'Or do you mean . . . your special pills.'

I blush. What did I call them special pills for, like I'm five years old? I've never made any secret of not being interested in drugs, but equally I've never made a big thing of it. And neither have I explained my reasons for it. Mum's drummed the evils of drugs in to me over and over again for as long as I can remember, the amount of damage they did to her when she was young, how she was lucky to come out alive, how my father didn't. How I mustn't go down that path, how you can never tell who is going to get sucked in. How even trying anything once is too much. Too dangerous.

Xander raises an eyebrow. 'I have *those* pills too. But I didn't think you'd want . . .'

'I don't,' I clarify. And I don't. Do I? I mean, for the first time ever, it's slightly tempting. After all, how much worse can this evening get? 'Not tonight, at least,' I add, to try to make myself sound less boring.

He shrugs. 'You're missing out. But it's your call.' He reaches into his pocket, opens an old-fashioned pill box and pops a capsule into my hand. 'Ibuprofen,' he says.

I look at it doubtfully. 'You promise?' I ask. It's too dark to see properly – it could be anything.

For a second he looks hurt. 'Ashley! Of course.' He pauses. 'I get migraines, you know that, so I always have painkillers with me. Especially in a place like this, the music and lights can set one off and that's no fun at all.' He pauses. 'Don't you trust me?'

I squeeze his hand, put the pill in my mouth and dry swallow it. Ugh.

'I trust you,' I say. And it's true, I do.

I think.

'Hopefully that will help. I'll go and get you a drink and some ice for your ankle now. What would you like?'

My head is swimming – I'm not sure if it's the after-effects of getting off the bull, like when you get off a boat and feel like you are still moving, if I had too much to drink earlier, or if it's adrenalin caused by my ankle hurting so fucking much which I am downplaying because I don't want to make a fuss.

'Just a Coke I think, thank you. I'll have a proper drink again later maybe.'

He kisses my forehead somewhat more paternally than I would like and walks off towards the bar.

'Be right back,' he says.

I wipe a couple of tears away surreptitiously as I watch his retreating back.

Right now I'd rather be anywhere else but here.

DAY THREE – Monday, 11.30 a.m.

Malia

As instructed, I head to the jetty to be taken to our lunch location. The rest of the group except Rob is already there, plus Henry, with a very beautiful woman who we haven't yet met.

'Ah! There you are,' Henry says. 'Brilliant. I'd like to introduce you to Ophelia – my twin sister and co-owner of the Henphelia hotel group. She will be your host this afternoon.'

Ophelia is like a willowy, feminine version of Henry and, now that he has said it, you can totally see that they are twins. She's in a pale blue, flowing dress which ripples in the slight breeze and wears a huge, white, floppy sunhat. For some reason she brings to mind an ancient Agatha Christie film Mum had me watch with her, *Evil Under the Sun*.

As is often the case when I see someone like Ophelia, I feel a stab of envy. I will never look like that. I push it away. I am my own perfect and authentic self though, I remind myself. Body positive, always. I try to ignore the sweat pooling under my boobs, pull out my phone and take a picture of the sea. Hopefully the internet will be back up later and I can start posting.

'It is beautiful today, isn't it?' Ophelia says. 'How did you enjoy the scooters?' Like Henry she is immaculate, polite and has not a hair out of place. Though on first impressions, she is somehow colder and more aloof. Henry is friendlier. Or that's how it seems to me, anyway.

'They were great fun, thank you,' I say. 'I don't mean to be weird, but would you mind if I take a photo of you? The way your dress is kind of floating in the breeze – it looks gorgeous against the blue of the sea.'

I feel myself redden as she is looking at me intently with a look of puzzlement on her face, but then her somewhat hard expression softens into a smile and I realize that, for once, I appear to have said the right thing.

'Of course!' she says. 'How sweet of you. I'm only sorry you won't be able to post your pictures straight-away as I'm afraid we haven't yet been able to sort the internet out. Though they are still working on it. It seems that the satellite has been damaged, they're not quite sure how, and we will need to get some replacement parts. Hopefully they can come from Male but it's possible they'll need to be sourced from further afield.'

'It is very tiresome,' Claire says. 'Though, I have to admit, not being at the beck and call of my editors for a change is quite nice. I could get used to it. But sadly, most of us need to work for a living.'

'Indeed,' Henry agrees. 'We appreciate your patience while it is fixed.'

I imagine he is being slyly sarcastic as Claire isn't being patient about it at all but, if he is, she doesn't seem to notice.

'Right,' he continues. 'I'm going to leave you in Ophelia's capable hands while I crack on . . . is everyone here?' He appears to do a mental head count. 'That's . . . almost all of you now I think? Who is missing?'

'Rob's not coming for lunch,' Araminta says. 'I'm afraid he's still feeling unwell and thinks, well, without putting too fine a point on it, that it's better he stays in his room for now.'

Ophelia frowns. 'Oh dear. I do hope it's nothing serious.'

'I hope so too,' says Araminta. 'It does sound like he's not in a good way though.'

'Probably drank too much,' Claire says. 'I wouldn't worry.'

A short speedboat ride away we land on yet another beautiful and tiny island. This one is clearly entirely uninhabited – as we disembark we can see pretty much the entire island. All that is here are a row of padded sunbeds with attendant umbrellas by the shore close to where we land, and a small cabin stacked with towels, a member of the hotel staff waiting patiently behind the counter. There's also a larger pagoda in the middle of the island with a straw roof and someone wearing chefs' whites standing in the middle, with a couple of assistants.

'This island is called Kalyana,' Ophelia says, 'which means wellness, I'm told. We also named our spa brand after it. We expect it to be very popular with honeymooners, or guests who simply want an extra private experience. We offer several options – one for couples where we can set up a table on the island with a meal in advance, a high-end picnic if they like, so they can simply arrive, help themselves and then . . . do whatever they want to do in complete privacy before radioing the boat to come and pick them up when they are ready. But today we are demonstrating the show-kitchen option for you – aimed more at people out here on holiday with friends, family or business clients looking for an out-of-the-ordinary experience.'

Julia comes over with cocktails on a silver tray and we all take one. I'm not sure I've been entirely sober since I arrived, the stream of drinks has been so steady. 'As you can see,' Ophelia says, indicating a kind of semi-circular bar with silver leather-topped bar stools in front of the chef, 'you can sit at the bar and watch as Bilal prepares your dishes in front of your eyes. Can I please invite you to take a seat for your starters? And then afterwards we'll move on to another dining location option for the main course. I think you'll like it.'

From a pile of glistening fish, meat, molluscs and vegetables laid out around him, chef Bilal's hands are almost a blur as he picks up items with tongs to throw them on the huge hot plate in front of him. They sizzle and steam invitingly as he flips them about before a couple of sous-chefs lay them delicately on small dishes ready-dressed with what looks like some kind of seaweed. They then drizzle them with oils and sauces poured dramatically from ornate silver ladles, before sprinkling them with seeds and passing the dishes to us. Even though they do it in a matter of minutes, each one is different and each one is beautiful. Mine is a delicate morsel of white fish wrapped in what I think is a banana leaf, subtly flavoured with something spicy. It is delicious, if tiny, and I am looking forward to the main course.

'Amazing!' Araminta gushes. 'It's so lovely to be able to watch while your food is cooked, isn't it?'

'Amazing,' Claire echoes, sarcastically. 'Though not exactly high-concept or particularly original.'

Ophelia smiles tightly as she finishes chewing the no doubt exquisitely tender beef tataki with sesame seeds she was served and swallows. 'It's not a new idea, no,' she agrees. 'But it's one our guests seem to appreciate in all our resorts and given that Bilal here has been awarded many Michelin stars for his restaurants around the world, we like to think that our show-kitchen experience is a cut above the rest.'

River, who is sitting next to me, smirks and subtly digs me in the ribs. I smile at him and roll my eyes.

'Now, let's leave Bilal to get on with preparing your main course, while we get changed for lunch.'

We are directed to changing rooms around the back of the 'pagoda' which is actually a fully plumbed-in building with toilets, showers and changing cubicles.

Each cubicle comes with a towel and a robe already in place, as well as black Ketenangan flip-flops with the ubiquitous gold turtle logo. Once I've got into my swimming costume, I wrap myself in the robe and head out to the loungers, which have now been sprinkled with flowers and the parasols opened. A fresh drink is placed on each table though no orders have been taken. I take a sip – mine is sharp, home-made lemonade with bright green sprigs of mint and I remember that a while back I posted something about fresh lemonade being my favourite drink on my grid. They clearly do their research here – it's quite impressive.

I sip my drink as I look out to sea, and I have to admit, it is pretty special. The wind is coming up a little and there are a few more clouds on the horizon, but the water is sparkling and for now the air remains warm.

My stomach rumbles and I hope they are going to bring the next course soon. As I drain my glass I notice a chain of immaculately uniformed but barefoot sous-chefs and waiters heading down the beach with trays. I'm expecting them to bring them to the tables by our loungers but weirdly, they appear to walk into the ocean, almost as if they're walking on water, before placing them down to float in the water and walking back into the shore. It's almost like some kind of live art installation, a performance.

Everyone has sat up a little in their lounger and is paying more attention – even Claire. Ophelia smiles, revealing just a hint of smugness. 'Several resorts in the Maldives now offer floating breakfasts, but it is usually in a pool or a hot tub. We believe we are the only resort in the islands to offer an entire floating meal in the sea. If you will follow me, lunch is served.'

Ophelia, also now in a swimming costume which I believe is probably Missoni, walks elegantly into the water and we all follow. As the warm water reaches her waist, Ophelia stops in front of one of the trays, which I now see is on a kind of float attached to a solid podium beneath the waterline which the staff must have used like stepping-stones. They're the same blue as the sea so that you can't see them from the shore – clever.

'There are two options,' Ophelia says, 'if you like, you can simply sit on one of the stools cum stepping stones, leave your tray where it is currently floating and eat from there. Or, you can take your tray and wade out to wherever you like. A little further into the ocean we have underwater recliners too. The food is designed to be eaten with your fingers and will bear a little extra moisture from wet hands; you'll see plenty of sushi and other small dishes, nothing that requires cutlery or that will fall apart too easily. So, take your trays and enjoy!'

I take my tray and push it out to next to one of the shaped recliners which I can now make out under the water. There's a wristband on a springy cord attached to the tray – they really do seem to think of everything, and I slip that over my hand to stop it floating away.

I hop onto the recliner and try to lie back in it but I'm too floaty and it's hard to relax. The food on my tray is beautifully presented and I try to savour the moment as I eat it but it kind of feels like a pointless novelty. It's awkward trying to manoeuvre myself into the right angle for eating – sitting up normally would have been much easier than reclining. I see that the others have all stayed where the trays were left, sitting on the underwater stools, and I think I should have done that too. I have made myself look stupid in my attempt to please, plus I left my phone in the cubicle too in spite of remembering to bring the waterproof pouch for it. So I can't even take a picture of the food on the floating tray, which admittedly does look beautiful, or at least did before I started eating it so clumsily.

The jet lag must be starting to catch up on me. I know none of this is a big deal, but I feel tears prick at my eyes. I push my unfinished tray to one side and dive under the water so no one will notice how embarrassed I am.

'I trust you all enjoyed your lunch?' Ophelia asks as we whizz back over to the main resort on the speedboat. She looks at her watch, and then casts her eye around the boat. 'Has anyone seen my sunglasses?' she asks, patting the top of her head as if to check they're not there. 'Damn. I must have left them in the changing room in the rush to leave. Caleb?' she calls to the boat driver. 'Can you get on the radio and ask someone on the island to bring them back when they come? Thank you.'

I wonder at the world she lives in when if you forget something, you can just order someone else to sort it out. Amazing.

'We're running a little behind, so can I ask that once we're back in resort you make it a quick change into something suitable for quad-biking, before we head off to see the turtles, please?' she adds. 'We've got quite a lot to pack in to today.'

It's all coming together. Everyone is here. I have waited a long time for this. People will be made to pay. Finally.

DAY THREE – Monday, 3 p.m.

Malia

After a quick change, as decreed by Ophelia, we meet back at the hotel's main entrance, outside which quad bikes are lined up waiting for us. Julia greets us with a tray of logoed insulated water bottles for the ride. 'And then there were six,' Ophelia says, with a sigh. 'I do think it's a shame the other one won't see the turtles,' she adds. 'We invited you all here hoping that—'

'We'll take lots of pictures,' Araminta interrupts, 'and all the group already has a lot of the information, as I wrote about it quite extensively in the press pack. It can't be helped if Rob's not feeling well.'

'Indeed,' Ophelia says, but her annoyance is clear. 'Anyway, never mind. I guess it can't be helped.'

Five of the quad bikes are red, and one is pink and a little bigger than the others.

'I love this pink one!' Lucy says, taking the helmet from the seat and straddling it. 'Can I ride it today?'

An awkward look passes between Julia and Araminta. Claire rolls her eyes. 'I think that one's Ophelia's?' Araminta says.

'Oh, is it?' Lucy says. She moves as if to get off. 'Never mind then. I mean, I wouldn't want to take it if . . .'

Ophelia waves her hand dismissively. 'Don't be silly. They're all the same, pretty much. And I can ride my bike any time. If you want to have a go on the pink one, Lucy, you must do that. I'd like you to. She is rather lovely – I call her Beatrice – and apart from anything else, she matches your T-shirt,' Ophelia adds with a smile. 'Shall we go?'

I have never ridden a quad bike before and had been feeling a little nervous about it ever since the trip itinerary arrived. I've read about several celebrities being injured or even sadly killed while riding them. I almost made an excuse and pulled out but then I reminded myself that if I want to be invited back on these kind of trips I need to make myself easy and amenable. So I gave myself a talking to, and told myself that I should just get on and enjoy the experience like the rest of the group was clearly planning to do.

'These quad bikes are very simple to drive,' says Ophelia, though it's easy for her to say as she obviously does it all the time. I've never been on anything like this in my life. 'On and off here, gears here, accelerator here,' she continues as she gestures to the various points on the handlebars, far too quickly for my liking.

'And braking?' I ask nervously.

'Like on a bike,' she says. 'All you need to do is pull the levers. But bring the speed down via the gears first ideally, and don't brake too hard. It's all common sense,' she adds, somewhat dismissively. 'If you can ride a bike, you can drive one of these.'

In theory I guess I can still ride a bike, but I haven't done so for years. I've never learnt to drive a car and I don't know what 'bringing the speed down via the gears' means. But now is not the time to bring any of this up. If I take it slowly, I'm sure I can manage. Can't I?

'I'll lead,' Ophelia says, putting the helmet on the seat of her quad to one side and mounting the bike, 'Just go where I go.'

I put my helmet on and close the visor. We start the bikes up – they're noisier than I expect, probably as loud as a motorbike. Ophelia moves off quickly and the others follow one by one in turn, so we form a kind of train.

I am at the back of the line and the gap between me and the others gets steadily larger for the first 100 metres or so as I get used to the machine. I feel like it might tip over at any time and if it did, what would happen then? Would the machine land on me and break my leg? Crush the air out of my lungs? The kind of juddering sound it makes is disconcerting. But as I settle into it I start to feel a little more confident, change up a gear and slowly gain pace and eventually catch up with Claire who is at the back of the rest of the group, but still going way faster than me. I'm pretty sure Ophelia and the others have slowed down deliberately to allow me to catch up but that's OK – I can live with that. There's certainly no danger of me overtaking anyone any time soon.

We pick up speed and I feel my shoulders start to relax. It is incredibly beautiful here. I soften my grip on the handlebars, which I realize I am holding so tightly that my palms are starting to hurt, and make the effort to look around myself rather than concentrating solely on the ground right in front of me.

The wide swathe of white sand we were driving along becomes narrower until it is no more than a strip a few metres wide with bright blue sea on either side. It's so beautiful. We drive along the spur for a few hundred metres until we go under a wooden arch labelled 'Turtle Island'.

Ophelia pulls up underneath some trees and switches her bike off. We all follow suit and take off our helmets. A man comes down the path.

'Welcome to you all,' he says. 'I'm Alex.'

The turtles are adorable. Alex is a marine biologist. He works here with a small team of rotating volunteers who rehabilitate turtles who have been injured. Many are apparently accidentally caught in fishing nets and other sea debris.

'More than a hundred turtles are found injured in the Maldives every year, probably an average of one every three or four days,' Alex explains, 'and around the world, the figure is hundreds of thousands annually.

'Six of the seven turtle species that live in the Maldives are threatened due to pollution but also due to hunting,' he continues. 'In some places, turtle meat is still considered a delicacy, sadly. Though thankfully its consumption in the Maldives has been banned since 2016, and it seems to be becoming more and more rare elsewhere too.

'Turtles which are brought to us are rehabilitated and released back into the wild where possible,' Alex continues. 'If they are too injured to be able to survive in the wild, which is sometimes the case, they will either be humanely put down or, if they can still have a decent quality of life in our large and protected tank, we will feed and look after them, which will allow them to live a comfortable and happy life, to breed and, usually, their offspring can be reintroduced to the sea when they are ready. As yet it is early days, but this way, we hope to be able to actually see the turtle population begin to rise again, rather than to fall.'

'Thank you, Alex,' Ophelia says. 'Now,' she turns back to us, 'if you can bear to get changed yet again, we can take you through to the rehabilitation tank where you can have a swim with the turtles if you'd like to? Our tank isn't so much an actual tank in the usual sense of the word as a section of the ocean which has been entirely walled off to protect the turtles from predators while they recover. They live in five-star luxury like our hotel guests.'

As Ophelia said, the tank certainly isn't a tank at all. A gently shelving beach with a few loungers and umbrellas slopes down into a bright blue sea in which literally dozens of turtles of all different sizes are swimming about.

'Oh, look at them!' Lucy exclaims. 'Can we go in?'

'Of course,' Alex says. 'We ask that you don't touch them, or otherwise bother them, but I'm sure that goes without saying. Afterwards you can help with feeding, and then it's Dodo's day to be released back into the wild, if you'd like to see that too. It's always quite an emotional day for us when that can happen, as it is our ultimate aim here.'

We wade into the water and start to swim. It's clear that the turtles have their own personalities – some seem curious and will swim close, even occasionally nuzzling against us, while others are nervous and dart away to the edges of the pen as soon as we go into the water.

It is magical. I take my phone with the waterproof cover which I managed to remember this afternoon, thankfully, and film myself swimming with the turtles using my selfie-stick. I'll no doubt need to bodytune and filter the images of myself later, but I don't want to think about that now. After around twenty minutes, Alex appears with a bucket of small fish and pellets and we get out to sit on the wall which separates the tank from the sea and throw pieces in as he tells us about some of the 'residents'.

'That's Giggy,' he says, indicating a green turtle about the size of a dinner plate. 'She's our newest, quite young, found exhausted and unable to move on a beach. We've been hand-feeding her since she arrived, and she's only been able to join the others here in the main tank in the last few days. But as you can see, she's loving having some playmates again. And there are Pickle and Pebble,' he indicates two almost identical-looking turtles dashing for a piece of fish thrown by River, 'rescued as babies from an illegal dealer. Their tank was tiny and they were very weak, but they've come on in leaps and bounds and should be able to be released soon. Speaking of which . . .' He indicates a large turtle not far from his feet, 'That's Dodo. He's back off to the sea today. He's been with us several months, brought in by some young guys who accidentally clipped him with a jet ski. It wasn't really their fault and they were utterly distraught. They made a large donation to the sanctuary and rather sweetly, one of them emails me regularly for updates. He's delighted that Dodo's made a full recovery, has made another donation, and is coming out to spend a few weeks with us as a volunteer next year. Isn't that great? Turns out not all people are cu— I mean, not all people are idiots.'

Dodo comes closer and Alex strokes his shell gently. 'I'll miss this guy. He's incredibly tame now, as you can see. But when things go well, this is no more than a temporary home for them. The whole aim here is to put these beautiful creatures back where they belong.'

As well as the wall which separates us and the sea, there is a short metal barrier between Alex and me which runs perpendicularly under the water. He pulls a lever just above it and I hear a faint grinding sound. 'Where I'm sitting here is a kind of airlock, or waterlock

121

I guess, more accurately. I've closed the door, separating Dodo from the others. Now I'll open the sea gate like this,' he pulls another lever, 'and Dodo can now go when he feels ready.' Dodo continues to paddle around Alex's feet and I may imagine it, but I think I see tears come to his eyes.

'Dodo has a comfortable life here though, and doesn't know he's better off in the wild, so he'll probably need some persuading.' Alex turns around, takes a large handful of pellets and throws them far off into the sea. Quick as a flash, Dodo heads after them. 'Off you go little guy,' Alex says. 'We'll miss you.'

'Oh!' I exclaim, welling up too. 'Will he be OK on his own?'

'He's fit and ready so we expect so,' Alex says. 'Hopefully he'll re-establish himself with a bale – a group. All the turtles that leave are chipped, and while we leave them to their own devices as nature intended, we also keep a discreet eye, and if it becomes clear they're not coping, we'll bring them back in. Hardly ever happens though – we don't let them go until we're pretty confident they're ready.'

'So how long have you been here looking after the turtles?' Lucy asks. 'Given that the hotel is so new?'

'I've been here three years. Including the set-up. So longer than the hotel. Henry was keen that—'

'Right, thank you Alex, that was a fabulous experience,' Ophelia interrupts, uncharacteristically abruptly. 'But I'm afraid we need to get changed and get back if we want to stay on schedule.' A look passes between the two of them which I can't quite make out.

'Understood,' Alex says. 'Thank you for coming to see our work here. If you are able to mention the turtles in your pieces, it would be much appreciated as it can really help with funding when—'

'Thank you, Alex,' Ophelia says, 'I'm sure everyone will do what they can. But we have to get a move on now.'

DAY THREE – Monday, 4.45 p.m.

Malia

Alex gives us each a little turtle pin and a USB stick as we leave and remount our quad bikes. I'm already thinking about the stories and reels I'm going to post – I want to make sure the turtle sanctuary gets some good coverage, at least from me. While realistically most of my followers could never afford to come and stay at this hotel in a million years, some might be interested in volunteering and others might make a donation. I imagine every little helps. I hope the internet is working by the time we get back to the hotel so I can start posting straight away.

I'm quicker on my bike this time, though I'm still at the back. I look up at the sky – the wind is picking up and there are more and more clouds appearing. I can feel the sand rubbing against my legs as it is whipped up by the growing breeze. Didn't someone say there was due to be a storm tonight?

As we come off the sandy spur which joins the two islands there is a downward slope. I think I hear someone shouting. At first I think I am imagining it because I am a little way behind but, yes, someone is definitely shouting something, a woman I think, not sure who, and then someone else starts shouting too and in the distance I see someone appear to throw themselves off their quad bike as the huge machine rolls away from them in the other direction.

I feel sick. I slow down to pretty much walking pace and as I get closer to where the others have stopped their bikes, I can see that someone is lying on the ground.

May, 1990

Ashley

I sit and stare into space as I wait for Xander to come back, rubbing my ankle absentmindedly. In spite of all the noise around me, it's actually quite nice to be sitting on my own. Not having to talk to anyone for a while, not having to smile, not having to think about what persona I'm presenting, whether I'm coming across the right way, whether Ophelia or one of her mates is going to say something bitchy to me, whether Xander still fancies me.

I see Jen a little way away, still with that same boy she was with at the casino. They're snogging at the edge of the dance floor and I can see his hand is creeping up under her skirt. I wouldn't let anyone do anything like that to me so publicly, but I'm glad she's having a good time. I wonder if she'll see him again after this?

I'd like it if she had a boyfriend. Sometimes I get the impression she's a bit jealous of me going out with Xander.

A boy who is clearly very drunk crashes into them, breaking them apart. Jen turns in my direction and I wave at her, still rubbing my ankle. She spots me, grins and rushes over. 'Ashley!' she cries. 'You OK? What happened?' She leans down and throws her arms around me, which is kind of weird because usually she hates that kind of thing – she's not very tactile. She squeezes me hard and for too long, it starts to make me feel uncomfortable. Her arms are bare and clammy against my skin and underneath the waft of Body Shop White Musk and pink Soft and Gentle deodorant I can smell a hint of BO. I try to wriggle away but it's tricky in my seated position, though she finally gets the message and stands up, looking at me intently as she strokes my cheek.

'I fell off the bull and hurt my ankle,' I say. She is still staring at me somehow both intently and vacantly at the same time, eyes glassy, jiggling up and down on the balls of her feet.

Oh. I see. She's taken something. The boy she was with earlier – Monty, was it? – turns up behind her, puts his arms around her and starts kissing her neck. Jen closes her eyes and giggles as they sway together in time to the music.

I can totally do without this right now. I don't want to watch this kind of thing. And she's absolutely no use to me in this state. 'Jen!' I say, loudly. Her eyes snap open but the pair continue to sway and the boy is still slobbering around her neck. It's pretty gross. 'Xander's getting me a drink. He'll be back in a minute. You don't have to look after me. You should . . . go and dance or whatever.'

She leans down to me again, smiling beatifically, puts her arms around me and kisses me wetly on the cheek. 'You're the best friend ever,' she says. 'I'll come and check on you in a few minutes.'

Believe that when I see it. There's a whoop of appreciation from the dance floor as Madonna's new song 'Vogue' comes on. Jen grabs whatever his name is by the hand and they rush off to join the throng.

I love this song. I love Madonna. I wish I could be at home, lying on my bed, listening to it on my Walkman. Maybe my cat Blue would jump up and lie next to me, purring, nuzzling me with his head the way he does. We could snuggle up together and then perhaps Mum might bring me a cup of tea. Or me and Mum could be sitting together on the sofa, watching something fun like Jeeves and Wooster, or maybe my sister Jade might have come to visit and we could have a pretend spa day, painting each other's nails and doing face packs. I miss her. I hope she comes home soon.

If only this ball wasn't in the middle of nowhere. If only we hadn't arrived on a bus, with no escape realistically possible before the set finish time of 1 a.m. If only I hadn't ignored Mum and decided I was coming to the party whatever her thoughts about it. If only.

May, 1990

Xander

Fucking hell. This is the last thing I need, Ashley and her stupid twisted ankle. I like her and everything, I do, but . . . I can't be bothered with this this evening.

People like Henry, born into money, they don't get it. My Dad's done alright for himself, and that's why I'm here, attending a posh school, mates with someone like Henry, the kind of person I'd never have met if I went to the local comp. Dad wants me to have all the advantages people like he and Ophelia have. The confidence which comes with centuries of living in draughty old piles, of having obscure titles attached to your name which don't really mean anything anymore but also somehow do, and of doors opening for you because you went to the right school or are a member of the right club.

Dad worked his arse off in his business from a very young age, even younger than I am now, and he built it all up from nothing. I think he got where he is today because he's sharp as a tack and works like a dog, but he's much more modest about it. He says that while those things might be true, he adds that he also got lucky, made some good investments at the right time, and he's always aware it could all come crashing down at any time. He's been bankrupt before, it could happen again, he warns. I don't see how – he's worth a fortune, but he still seems to feel like he's living on a knife edge. That his lifestyle, our lifestyle, remains precarious.

'I want something better for you and your sisters, son,' he says, repeatedly. 'Get your exams. Make the right connections. That'll stand you in better stead than hard graft and relying on luck of the draw.'

I'm not sure I agree. I'll never truly fit in at school. My accent's not quite right, nor my clothes. I have to hide the designer clothes Dad buys me – wearing too many labels is considered naff, having the wrong ones is considered lame. It's like there's a whole rulebook I'm not privy to. Most of the time I get it right, but when I get it wrong, they all take the piss. Even Henry. I pretend I don't mind, but I do. It hurts. Every time.

And I think that's why Ashley and I get on. She's the same. Doesn't come from money. Doesn't have the 'breeding'. But it's more obvious with her, because, not that we've ever talked about it, her mum clearly can't afford to splash the cash on pointless stuff like my family does. Ashley doesn't have the right trainers, or the latest music system, and some of her school uniform is quite obviously second-hand. She doesn't talk about her family much, and I don't prod. She lives locally, but I've never been to hers. She talks about her mum a little and her sister quite a lot, but I've never met her family. I don't know why she doesn't want to take me home, but I can guess. She's ashamed. She thinks I might judge. And although I would try not to, I know that realistically, I might.

She's been round to mine loads. And while she doesn't make a big deal of it, I can tell she's impressed by the plush carpets, the double garage with two BMWs in it, the home computer, the VHS players, the dishwasher, TVs in all the bedrooms and the huge kitchen island with the built-in waste disposal in the sink. Things that, conversely, Henry with his country pile stuffed with dusty old antique furniture, oil paintings of long-dead ancestors, creaking four-poster beds and a suit of armour which was worn at the Battle of Waterloo (or something like that, I forget) in the entrance hall, would consider the height of gaucheness, and Ophelia would actively sneer at. Ophelia has never been to my house, and I hope she never will.

Standing at the bar, the queue for which is about five people deep, I feel someone snake their arms around my waist and lean their head against my back.

I turn around. 'Ophelia,' I say. Her eyes are too large, shiny and staring, and there's a sheen of sweat on her forehead. I haven't taken anything yet today as she clearly has, but I've got a few in reserve for later, in case I feel like it. Although Ashley never actually says anything, I know she doesn't approve, so when I'm with her I usually stick to alcohol, maybe some weed now and again, but I tend to stay away from the powder and especially, the pills. Usually.

Ophelia and her mates take everything they can get their hands on at these balls, she makes no secret of it at all. Eventually, with a name like hers, she'll end up in the papers if she's not careful, I'm amazed she hasn't so far, but then again, that's probably a lot to do with who her dad might be friends with in the media, I imagine.

'Are you having a fun evening?' I ask, pleasantly. No point in riling her unnecessarily.

She touches my bottom lip with her finger and tilts her head. Her hair, which was pulled into a tight French plait at the beginning of the evening, has become a little dishevelled and her cheeks are pink. Her large boobs are encased in fitted velvet above her tiny waist and I think she has dusted her cleavage with something glittery. The skirt of her dress appears to be made of gossamer and glistening silver feathers which match her sparkly makeup and I have to admit, she does look pretty fabulous tonight. In spite of myself, I feel a stab of desire.

It was only once. That time at Henry's, a few months ago. Henry had invited me for the weekend, and I'd allowed myself to get my hopes up about admitting to him how I felt about him, but when it came to it, of course I couldn't. Henry would never be interested in me in that way anyway, he's only into girls, I'm ninety-nine per cent sure, so it's too much of a risk to say anything. I'd never live it down at school. Plus I'm pretty sure Dad would never accept that side of me, and I want him to be proud.

While Henry was out riding with his father, Ophelia and I had shared a spliff or two at her suggestion in what they call their 'snug' in spite of it being absolutely enormous – what anyone normal would call a TV room. As we sat on the old, saggy sofa with light streaming in through the huge, leaded windows, she put her hand down my trousers and before I knew it we were rolling around on the no doubt ancient rug. She'd lifted her tartan mini-skirt and guided me into her – it was my first, first and only time. It was only afterwards that it had occurred to me, as we sat on the sofa smoking another spliff and watching the rest of *The Rachel Papers* (we rewound a bit to catch what we'd missed, it wasn't much), that she hadn't been wearing any knickers and I wondered if she'd planned the whole thing. Had she engineered it so that she and I would be left alone?

'You, um, you won't tell Ashley, will you?' I'd said, shyly. My head was swimming from the spliffs and from the shock of what had happened. I couldn't believe what I'd done.

She looked at me and laughed. 'Of course not. Why would I do that?'

'Or, um, Henry? You won't tell Henry?'

An evil glint came into her eyes and she leaned towards me, her face so close to mine I could feel her breath. 'Are you worried he might beat you up for defiling his sister?' she said quietly.

I blushed. 'Um, no. If anything, you defiled me,' I said, trying to make light of what had just happened.

She leaned back and took another long drag on the spliff before passing it to me. I did the same and then stubbed it out.

'Ophelia? So you won't say anything?' I persisted.

She pulled a 'hmmm' expression and then smiled, touching the tip of my nose in the way you might to a cute child who was being cheeky. 'Don't you worry about a thing,' she'd said.

But she didn't answer the question. And I still don't know if Henry knows. I'm not going to ask, but he's never said anything. I'm certain Ashley doesn't have any idea about it, because she would never put up with such an awful betrayal I'm sure, especially not when it was with Ophelia. I need to do whatever I can to keep it that way, even if it means pandering to Ophelia more than I might want to. I like Ashley a lot, and Dad likes me having a girlfriend. It makes me more of a man in his eyes. Neither of them deserves to be let down by a combination of my failings and Ophelia's love of shit-stirring.

I drag my mind back to the present. 'Are you? Having a fun evening?' I repeat, because she is still staring at me in that 'out of it' way and hasn't said anything.

'I am!' she says, pushing past me to get closer to the bar, brushing her ample tits against me. It is pretty crowded here, but I'm sure she's doing it deliberately.

I feel hot and undo the button under my bow tie. 'So thirsty though. And you?' she asks. 'You having a good time?'

'Yeah. It's OK,' I say. 'I'm getting a drink for Ashley. She hurt herself falling off the bull.'

She pulls an exaggerated clown-like sad face and says, 'Poor little Ashley,' sarcastically. She leans in towards me and I get a whiff of her perfume – I don't know what it is, that one that comes in a purple bottle which a lot of the girls like, I think, and it takes me right back to that afternoon on the sofa. 'Do you want to hear a secret?' she half-shouts into my ear, to ensure that I hear her over the music.

I turn towards her. 'What secret?'

'It's about Ashley,' she shouts back, putting her finger to her lips.

I feel a lurch of alarm. Does she mean she's going to tell her what happened with us? Or even that she already has?

'No,' I reply. 'I'm not interested in stupid gossip,' because it seems like the right thing to say. There's nothing she can tell me about Ashley that I need to know. Surely.

Her face darkens. 'I'm going to tell you anyway. You'll like it, I'm sure. It's funny.'

'I don't want to know,' I say, waving my hand, and turning back towards the bar, brandishing a wodge of tickets to try to get the barmaid's attention. Does that ever work? Probably not.

'Ashley's mum,' Ophelia continues, ignoring me. 'She's here. Isn't that hilarious?'

I turn to look at her again. She's grinning so widely it's more like a gurn.

'What do you mean, here?'

She points at the barmaid whose attention I'm trying to get.

'That woman. That's her mum. Ashley's mum.'

I shake my head. 'No it isn't. Ashley would have said. I don't believe you.'

She shrugs. 'Whatever. It's true. I heard them talking earlier.'

'What can I get you?' the same barmaid asks, finally coming over to me.

'A large Coke and a vodka and Coke please,' I say. I look the woman in the eye and I guess there is something about her face which looks a bit like Ashley's. At a push. But it's dark, difficult to tell and Ophelia is probably talking bollocks, trying to stir things up, I imagine. I don't understand her aim with this particular piece of info and neither do I want to. 'Could you also put some ice in this bag for my friend?' I say, handing over a small plastic bag which had my little stash of pills in before I emptied them into my pocket. 'She's hurt her ankle.'

'And a large glass of water for me too,' Ophelia pipes up. The woman looks at me, raising an eyebrow.

'Yeah. Some water for my . . . friend too,' I agree, reluctantly, regretting my idea of charging for tap water at these events to up our profits. I don't want to buy Ophelia a drink but then again, saying 'no' to her doesn't feel like an option right now.

138

I take the extortionately priced drinks and the bag of ice and we push back out of the crowd. I'm suddenly desperate for a piss. 'Can I leave these with you a sec?' I ask Ophelia. 'Need a wazz.'

We put them down on a table. 'Sure. I'll be here waiting,' she says, leaning in closer, 'my luvveerrrr.'

Fuck's sake. 'Thanks. Won't be long.'

DAY THREE – Monday, 5 p.m.

Malia

Someone jumps off their quad bike and whips off their helmet – River – and runs down the small slope. The next two people pull up and take off their helmets – Araminta and Ophelia – and follow him. As I get closer I can see Claire, who has taken off her helmet but is still sitting on her bike, gawping at what is going on a few metres away from her. With a sick lurch I realize that it must have been Lucy who fell. River has already reached her and is on his knees next to her – I can't see exactly what he's doing – but I can see she's still lying on the ground and it doesn't look like she's moving.

I feel wobbly and sick as I park my quad up and head down the slope – I'm not as fast as the others but I don't want to risk twisting my ankle or anything when it looks like someone is already hurt. That would be

141

the last thing any of us needs. The pink quad bike is on its side a few metres away from Lucy.

Ophelia is barking instructions into her radio – I can't hear what she's saying but I assume she's trying to summon help from the hotel, and Araminta is simply standing and staring, wide-eyed, hand to her mouth.

Meanwhile River is touching Lucy's arm gently, and it looks like he's talking to her, but she's not moving. Oh God. I hope she's not injured. She might even be dead for all I know.

Ophelia gets off the radio and moves closer to River and Lucy, as do I. To my relief, I see Lucy open her eyes, though her expression is pained and she is wincing. She moves her right hand across her chest and gingerly touches her left shoulder.

'Help is on the way, Lucy,' Ophelia says briskly. 'They're sending our first aiders down from the hotel right now and we'll . . . work out what to do from there.' Ophelia looks pale and rattled, it's the first time I've seen her customary cool demeanour slip. 'Do you think you can sit up?' she asks.

'I think it's best she stays where she is for now,' River replies, tersely. 'We don't want to make things worse than they already are. Let's wait until someone professional can have a look at her.'

'Who put you in charge?' Ophelia snaps. 'I think we should see what the first aiders say when they get here.'

'That's exactly what I suggested, basically,' River replies, evenly.

'Lucy? How does it feel?' Ophelia asks, somewhat unsympathetically.

'It . . . hurts,' she says. 'But I think maybe I could move if . . . ow!' she cries, as she tries to sit up. 'Maybe it's better if I wait a minute after all,' she adds, easing herself back on to the ground.

Araminta is still standing a little apart from the rest of us and, I notice, crying. 'Will Lucy be OK?' she asks, her voice almost a whisper.

'I'm sure she'll be fine,' River says. 'She just needs to get her shoulder looked at.'

I feel a fat drop of rain land on my arm, followed by another and then another. The wind has picked up further and the sky is now entirely covered in thick black clouds. Claire arrives at my side. 'What's going on?' she asks. 'Is Lucy alright? It's lucky she wasn't killed. Death traps, those quad bikes are. Not sure who thought it was a good idea to send us out on those. I was half-minded to refuse to go but I thought it would be impolite.'

'Don't you think we should move her?' Ophelia says, ignoring Claire, as a golf buggy comes into sight. 'It's about to start raining and the weather can get quite full on here sometimes. She'll get soaked.'

'I think we should wait and see what the professionals say,' River repeats.

I'm not sure quite what I was expecting from the first aiders Ophelia mentioned, but it was something more than a golf buggy and, as it gets closer, judging by the uniforms, two members of hotel staff.

River clearly has the same thought. 'I thought you said a medic was coming?' he says.

Ophelia clears her throat. 'I said first aider. Fadi and Julia are our first aiders in the resort.'

He frowns. 'But, with all due respect, Lucy might have broken her shoulder or arm. Surely you can call the mainland and get them to send some, erm, I don't know, paramedics? Or an air ambulance, even?'

The rain is already falling harder now and the wind is much stronger. Fadi opens two large golf umbrellas with the hotel's turtle logo and tries to hold them over Lucy, but it is too windy. They don't keep the water off her at all and within a few seconds one of them has broken. Lucy is still wincing as Julia kneels beside her.

Ophelia takes her hat off which is already almost soaked through – this rain is wetter and denser than anything I've ever experienced before. My hair is drenched and I can feel the water running in thick rivulets down my back. Claire wraps her arms around herself and tuts.

Ophelia takes a deep breath and exhales slowly before replying. 'I don't think there's any need to panic yet. We don't even know if Lucy's broken anything. Let's get her back to her room and get her comfortable first. Then we can consider what to do.'

'There's no one properly medically qualified on the island then?' River persists.

'Our resident doctor is due to arrive before our first paying guests,' Ophelia says, tersely. 'She was sadly unable to be here this week, having to work notice in her previous post. But in the meantime, Fadi and Julia have undergone full and comprehensive first aid training,' Ophelia continues, clearly trying to keep her voice steady and polite but unable to keep a slight wobble of something I can't quite put my finger on – anger? impatience? fear? – out of it.

'It's OK,' Lucy says, 'It's not that bad.' But it's clear that she is extremely uncomfortable and it looks like she's struggling not to cry.

'Someone could take her to a hospital by boat?' River persists. 'Look at her. You can see she's in pain. I think she should be seen to as soon as possible.'

Ophelia looks up at the sky again. 'Perhaps. We can look into that, though we wouldn't normally do transfers by boat – it's a long journey. Plus it very much looks like a storm is coming in, it certainly wouldn't be comfortable to leave the island in choppy water, and I'm not sure it would even be safe. I will ask the boatmen, but we need to consider the safety of our staff, as well as Lucy.'

'What about a helicopter?' Araminta asks.

Ophelia flashes her an undisguised look of irritation. 'Again there are likely to be difficulties because of the distance and the weather . . .' she says before her voice is drowned out by a large crack of thunder. 'Look, let's get everyone back into the dry, get Lucy comfortable in her room and see what the best way is to proceed then.'

'But she needs to be seen!' River persists. A look of horrified realization crosses his face. 'Are we stuck here?

Is that what you're saying? No one can get here or leave?' he demands.

'Don't be such a drama queen,' Ophelia snaps, her cool demeanour slipping further. 'That isn't what I'm saying at all.'

An uneasy silence falls over us. Because we all know that what River said is true. If the weather makes it too dangerous to leave, we are stuck here. Like it or not.

It seems that Julia and Fadi are actually a little better equipped than they first appeared, and with the help of what Julia tells Lucy is like the gas and air some women use for pain relief when they have a baby, Fadi straps Lucy's arm across her body to immobilize her shoulder before helping her into the golf buggy and driving her away.

By now we are all thoroughly soaked through and miserable. There is another clap of thunder and a flash of lightning forks across the sky. I feel tears threatening. I've never liked storms and I'm desperate to get back to the safety of the hotel.

Another golf buggy arrives. 'Hop onboard,' Ophelia commands, 'we should all get inside as soon as possible, given how quickly the storm seems to be coming in. We'll send people to retrieve the quads later.'

The short journey is completed in total silence bar occasional snivelling from Araminta, who still seems quite tearful. I'm not sure why she's so upset. I guess she's one of those ultra-empathetic people. Or perhaps it's because

146

one of the journalists has been injured on the trip she organized – that can't be a good look for a PR, I suppose. Perhaps she's worried that someone will blame her? Or even that Lucy might sue? No. Surely not. She's probably simply feeling sad that Lucy was injured.

As we arrive in the (thankfully covered) area outside the hotel entrance, Claire gets out of the buggy and immediately storms off, muttering something about not coming all this way to get soaked to the bone. Once we are all out of the buggy, we look towards Araminta as usual for instructions as to what to do next. By now she seems to have pulled herself together and moved back in her PR role of pretending that everything is brilliant at all times.

'Right. I think we could all do with some time to . . . dry out and generally regroup and relax, so how about we meet in the bar at seven for pre-dinner drinks?' she suggests.

She smiles tightly, wipes her eyes and walks off towards her room. Ophelia is talking animatedly to Mohammed in a low voice. River catches my eye and I smile weakly.

He touches my arm. 'You OK?' he asks. 'That was all quite shocking, wasn't it?'

I nod and to my horror, feel tears rising. 'Yep,' I agree. 'It was. Will Lucy be alright? You were amazing out there,' I add, and immediately feel myself go red. Mustn't act like a little girl with a crush.

River smiles. 'That's sweet of you. But I didn't do anything special. I started training to be a paramedic at one point and then . . . life kind of got in the way. But to answer your question, while Lucy's clearly in pain, and I hope she can be seen by a doctor sooner rather than later, I'm hopeful there'll be no lasting damage, and she'll certainly live. Which . . .' he trails off.

'What?' I press.

He leans in closer. 'I don't mean to scare you, but from what Lucy said to me, and what I saw of the underside of her quad, her *living* may not be what someone intended. She lost control on that slope because her brakes failed, and it looked very much to me like someone may have deliberately stabbed a hole in the brake fluid reservoir.'

May, 1990

Xander

As I get back from the loo, I see Ophelia popping a pill. She's not even subtle about it. Bloody hell, she's already totally off her face as it is. I hope she knows what she's doing. It's easy to overdo it if you're not careful.

But she is not my problem. Fuck her. 'I should go and find Ashley,' I say, picking up the drinks. 'She'll be wondering where I am.'

Ophelia stands up and moves close to me. Too close. 'If you must,' she whispers. 'You know . . .' she adds, tracing her finger gently down my arm, from my shoulder to my hand, her eyes following her finger as she does so, and then letting her gaze flick to my groin before she looks back up at me, 'I think about that time . . . at home often. I think about it and I touch myself.'

She leans in closer to me and I can feel her breath, hot on my ear. 'We should do it again sometime,' she says.

She licks my ear and then moves away, looking directly and intensely at me again. I lurch back in alarm. Fuck's sake! I look around to see if there's anyone who knows us nearby. What if someone saw that? What if they tell Ashley? Ophelia's pupils are huge. I wonder how much she has already taken. More than one pill, I'm almost sure of it. I open my mouth to say something, but realize I don't know what to say so I simply turn away and leave.

Fucking hell. I should never, ever have gone with her. However exciting it was at the time, Ophelia is now basically a ticking time bomb. I bet Henry knows, and while I imagine he will probably keep it to himself, it's only a matter of time until Ophelia tells Ashley, I'm sure.

I've messed up badly on so many levels here.

Thankfully Ashley is still sitting in the same place when I get back with the drinks, staring into space and vaguely rubbing her ankle. Her face breaks into a smile as she sees me. I feel a pang of regret. She is so sweet. I should never have done what I did. But it's too late to change things now.

I pass her the Coke and she takes a large gulp. She pulls a face. 'Ugh. It tastes so weird when they make it with that awful syrup stuff from the nozzle, doesn't it?'

'Yeah, guess so,' I agree, though really, who cares? It's just Coke. 'Sorry I was so long. How's your ankle?'

'Bit better. Think that ibuprofen is helping already.

And it doesn't matter at all that you took a while – I saw Jen while I was waiting for you.'

'Jen?'

'You know. Jen. My friend. I told you about her before – she didn't want to come tonight. But she's hooked up with some boy now and looked like she was totally off her face. Seems to be having fun, anyway.'

'Oh, yes Jen,' I agree, not really listening. I've no idea who she means. I don't know any of Ashley's friends and I'm still distracted by worrying about whether Ophelia's going to say anything about what we did.

'Great,' I continue. 'You, um, ready to rejoin the party?'

She smiles. 'Just give me a few minutes. And then I'll probably be OK.'

DAY THREE – Monday, 5.45 p.m.

Malia

Before I could ask River anything about what he meant about the quad bike being sabotaged or whether I'd misheard as surely I had – why would anyone want to tamper with Lucy's brakes? – Henry comes over and starts spouting his usual pleasantries, reassuring us that everything is being done to find out what is possible as regards helping Lucy. It must be exhausting being so relentlessly positive and nice to everyone all the time. I don't know how people like him do it.

'So unfortunate what happened,' he says. 'All our guests in our resorts seem to enjoy the quad bikes but, well, I guess they're not without their dangers.'

I look at River, thinking he'll say something about his theory that the bike was deliberately damaged, but he doesn't. He doesn't say anything at all.

Henry is still speaking. Maybe River simply doesn't want to interrupt? It seems odd though. 'We're going to see how the weather goes for the next half an hour,' Henry continues, 'and if conditions improve, we'll consider taking Lucy to the mainland by boat. But it's a long and bumpy journey, and if we're not 100 per cent sure it's safe, obviously we won't do that as we can't risk putting her or our staff in any danger. And she may feel that a long and potentially uncomfortable boat trip would make her feel worse. A sea plane can't fly in the dark, and nor in this weather. If it feels necessary, we can see whether a helicopter might be possible, though given the incoming storm, I'm not sure they'd come unless it's life or death. Mohammed is assessing what the options are as we speak. But in the meantime, we'll do everything in our power to keep her as comfortable as possible here, of course.'

'How is she?' I ask.

'Julia's taken her to her room in case she needs any help getting out of her wet clothes, and I'm going to pop along in a minute to see what else we can do for her.

'Ophelia tells me you took charge of looking after her, River,' Henry adds, turning towards him and clasping his hand between both of his. 'And I understand you have some paramedic training? I wanted to make sure I personally said thank you. You are our guest, you shouldn't have to take on that role. Once we are fully open we will have a doctor on site to help us deal with something like this, but even so, it's thrown up some things for us to think about, how we might do better next time. Again, thank you.'

'It wasn't a problem,' River says. 'Anyone would do the same. And to be honest, I'm not fully trained, and I didn't really do anything. But I do think that shoulder needs to be seen to as soon as possible. By a doctor,' he adds, pointedly.

Henry nods. 'Absolutely, without a doubt. But I think you'd also agree that we can't be sending Lucy or our staff into a potentially dangerous situation, surely?'

'Of course,' River says stiffly. 'You're in charge, you must do what you feel is right.' He plucks at his wet clothes. 'If you'll excuse me now though, Henry, I'm starting to get cold and I'd like to go and dry off.'

Henry claps him on the shoulder. 'Sorry, yes, please don't let me hold you up any further. I'm going to go and check on Lucy personally now, see if she needs anything. If there's anything else we can do to make her more comfortable. Thanks again, River.'

We watch Henry's retreating back until he is out of sight. I turn to River. 'Why didn't you say anything about your theory about the quad being sabotaged?' I ask.

River leans in closer towards me. 'Sssshhhh! Not so loud. I didn't say anything because I'm pretty sure he'd deny it. No one wants that kind of thing happening at their hotel, do they? Especially not in a luxury outfit like this, and definitely not while a whole load of journalists are visiting.'

'But don't you think . . . if someone's doing something like damaging bikes, Henry should know about it?

155

Especially as someone got hurt?' I want to add 'And could have been killed,' but I don't because I know I'm prone to overreacting and catastrophizing and River will probably think I'm being ridiculous. Instead I take a deep breath and try to push the thought away.

River shrugs. 'Maybe I should have said something. But then again, who's to say it wasn't Henry who did it? Could have been anyone here. And if it *was* Henry, I wouldn't want him to know I was on to him. Would you?' He pauses. 'Imagine for a minute he deliberately damaged the bike. Who knows what he might do next?'

I feel a lurch of alarm and for a second I think I might be sick. My legs feel shaky. I take a deep breath. 'I don't understand though. Why would anyone want to hurt Lucy? Least of all Henry?'

He throws his hands up in the air. 'Who knows why anyone does anything? None of us on this trip know each other at all, do we? There might be many reasons he might want to hurt her. Maybe she's written negative reviews about their other places in the past? Perhaps he fancies her and she knocked him back? Perhaps he's a psychopath and likes hurting people?'

I stare at him aghast, somewhat shocked by his outburst. Does he really think that Henry, or anyone here, wants to hurt Lucy?

'Equally, there might be no reason at all,' he continues. 'Then again, everyone has secrets, don't they? Can you honestly say you don't?'

I realize I am still staring at him. I don't know what to say. Why does he think I have secrets?

He touches my arm. 'Don't look at me like that. I'm not having a go, I promise. Hopefully I'm wrong, it might have simply been an accident. Perhaps a rock or something damaged the brakes. But look, either way, these wet clothes are annoying me now and I'm freezing. I'm going to dry off and warm up. I'll see you at dinner.'

May, 1990

Xander

'Come on, I'm feeling better now,' Ashley says, slipping her foot back into her shoe. 'Let's go and dance.'

'You sure?' I ask, though in all honesty, it's a relief. I'm pretty bored of sitting here now and am about ready to go and do something else. 'I thought you said it was hurting too much?'

She shakes her head. 'It's fine. That pill you gave me has made a huge difference.' She leaps up. 'See? Good as new! Come on!'

She takes my hand and pulls me towards the dance floor. I catch Ophelia's eye as we cross the room and she makes a lascivious face at me, running her tongue around her lips and groping her own breasts before collapsing into a heap of giggles with her up-themselves mates.

They are coming towards us. I need to keep Ashley away from her.

'Excellent,' I say, pulling Ashley towards the heaving floor as she stumbles slightly and then rights herself. 'Let's go and dance.'

DAY THREE – Monday, 6 p.m.

Malia

Back in my room, I'm surprised to find Adhara already running a bath for me, the hot bath I'd been fantasizing about pretty much since the rain started while we were still out in the sand. All that seems ages ago now, though it was probably only an hour, if that.

'Wow, how did you know I wanted a bath?' I ask. I realize I am shivering – I'm not sure if it's simply from the cold or from the stress of what's happened, and what River said about it. Poor Lucy. I hope she's not in too much pain.

Adhara smiles, as she adds oil which smells like jasmine to the water and throws in a handful of pretty rose petals which float on the surface. Scented candles have already been lit and placed around the edge of the freestanding bath. It looks lovely, extremely

161

inviting, and above all, warming. Exactly what I want right now.

'I didn't know,' she says. 'But you've had a long and busy day and I heard that you all got caught in the downpour.' Right on cue, there is a loud clap of thunder and a flash of lightning. 'I thought you would appreciate the chance to relax and warm up. I've also taken the liberty of making you a fresh herbal infusion – it's one of our own we prepare from dried local flowers. It's warming, but it has calming properties too.'

She indicates a small table by the side of the bath where there is a large mug of steaming, dark liquid with petals sprinkled on top, with what look like a couple of homemade truffles next to it in one dish, and a small bowl of nuts and dried fruit in another.

'This all looks absolutely perfect, thank you,' I say.

Adhara turns off the taps. 'At Ketenangan, we like to not only provide everything our guests ask for, but also things which they haven't yet asked for, or sometimes which they don't even know themselves that they want.'

'You've certainly done that here,' I say, suddenly wondering if I should be leaving a tip, and if I can afford to do so. Have I even got any cash with me?

'I'm glad,' she says. 'I will leave you to enjoy your bath.' She hands me a cotton tote bag emblazoned with the hotel's turtle logo. 'If you'd like to leave your wet clothes in here, I'll come and collect them when you're at dinner and ensure they are attended to.'

She gives a little bow and then closes the door with a soft click. I throw off my clothes which are starting

162

to chafe now and ease myself into the water. I'll put them in the little bag later.

The water is exactly the right temperature, and the tub is huge. I press a button and the water jets start, gently massaging my legs and back. I press it again and the pressure increases. Nice.

There is a skylight above me, I guess the idea being that you can lie in the bath and look at the stars or a nice blue sky. But it's now raining so hard that all I can see is water and hear the 'bam bam bam' of the massive rain drops which are now falling so hard they almost sound like hail. It can't be hail though. Can it?

There is another crash of thunder and a bolt of lightning shoots across the sky, with jagged forks going off in countless directions. It's like nothing I've ever seen before. I breathe in deeply, inhaling the scent of the oils in the water, and reach over to get the mug and take a sip of the tea. Normally I'm not that bothered about herbal tea; while they might smell nice, they all taste the same to me, of nothing much. But this one has an unexpected sweetness, and is delicious.

There is another crash of thunder. Poor Lucy. I don't think they'll be able to get her back to the mainland tonight.

I feel much better after my bath. It's a relief to be warm again and the towels I use to dry myself are the largest, thickest and softest I have ever used. My skin feels and smells amazing – I guess it must be the oil Adhara poured in, and the candles are casting a beautiful light. I feel like I could stay here forever.

I go to post a picture I took of the bath before I got in it and then remember that I can't. I wish the internet was working. I feel like my followers are missing out on so much, and I'm worried I won't get invited on another trip like this if I don't get enough engagement. The longer you go between posts, the more followers you're likely to lose, and it's extremely unlikely that you'll gain any if you're not creating regular new content. Everyone knows that.

I put my phone away and pad over to the huge sliding doors. I go to open one to see if I can maybe take some video from the covered terrace to post later, because I've never seen a storm like this in my life, but as soon as I open it even a few inches the wind howls in and my feet get wet. I close it again. It's not the kind of storm you can watch from out in the open.

Dinner tonight is in the underwater restaurant Aqua, which is accessed by a little glass tunnel. Given the weather, it is probably the best option for tonight as most of the other eating areas in the resort are all very much geared to outdoor dining.

'I'm afraid you're not seeing this place quite at its best,' Henry says, frowning. We are seated at a round table surrounded by a glass dome with water all around. 'Normally, if the moon was full as it is tonight, there'd be moonbeams cutting through the water and you'd be able to watch fish and other sea creatures, maybe even seahorses, starfish and sharks. And you can even see part of the coral reef through that wall,' he indicates to the left, 'when it's particularly clear. We light it with solar floodlights while people are dining, and the light from the restaurant carries a little way too.'

But this evening the water is choppy and churning and it's stirred up the sandy sea floor so you can't see very far at all. It's actually making me feel kind of seasick if I look at it too long, so I try to keep my gaze on the others' faces and the table as much as possible.

To my surprise, Lucy is here to eat with us. Her arm is strapped up in what looks like quite a professional way and she seems quite cheerful, if a little pale. 'I'm fine,' she reassures. 'I've had loads of painkillers and my shoulder's not as sore as it was earlier. I'm not sure it's broken at all – it's probably just a sprain or something. It's kind of you all to worry about me so much, but I think it was more the shock of falling off the bike that upset me than anything. I'm quite sure it can wait a few days before being looked at. I'm not keen to try to venture off the island with this storm going on, even if it were possible. Too scary.'

Her words sound a little slurred and I wonder if they've given her more than painkillers – maybe some diazepam or something? Something to make her feel a bit more compliant about staying, given that it sounds like it's going to be impossible to get her off the island any time soon? Then again, it's probably better she has some meds to dull the trauma of it all, as well as the pain, so whatever the reason, perhaps it's not a bad thing.

'It was so strange the way the bike seemed to go out of control so suddenly,' she muses. 'It was almost like the brakes failed or something.' Her eyes are glazed – she's definitely taken something.

'They're very heavy, those machines,' says Mohammed, who is joining us for dinner tonight. 'It can feel like they have a life of their own if you're not used to them. We very much intend to learn from this unfortunate incident and will be looking at how we can make them safer – perhaps put in speed limiters or something. Anyway – has everyone looked at the menus yet?'

He clearly wants to move the conversation on. 'Have you decided what you would like to eat this evening? Our chef is one of the best in the islands and will be happy to answer any questions if you're not sure – you're in for a treat I promise.'

I tune out as Mohammed starts talking about the provenance of some of the dishes on the menu, how they aim for zero miles where possible and what is grown in the resort's kitchen garden. I try to catch River's eye to see if he's going to say anything about his suspicions of deliberate sabotage of the bike, but even if he was, the moment has now passed and he's staring at his menu as if his life depended on it. I'm surprised at him being seemingly afraid to say anything and, I have to admit, a little disappointed. But it's not my place to voice his suspicions as I didn't see anything wrong with the bike myself.

'Where's Rob?' I ask, instead. 'Is he still unwell?'

Araminta pulls a face. 'I'm afraid so. I knocked on his door after we got back from the quad biking but there was no answer. I checked with his butler and he said Rob had assured him via the room service app that he didn't want anything – he felt it was best to sleep it off.'

Mohammed is now wanging on about the chef's background and credentials – Bilal is Maldivian, the youngest chef ever to be awarded a Michelin star, he was poached from one of the other five-star resorts, and the resort's flagship restaurant Aqua specializes in traditional dishes of the Maldives. I opt for boshi mashuni which is an intriguing sounding banana flower salad, followed by a Maldivian vegetable curry. The boshi mashuni is a beautifully presented single large leaf containing, as the waiter explains in careful detail, shredded banana flowers and coconut, delicately spiced with curry leaves, cumin, turmeric, plus chilli and limes grown in the hotel's garden. The vegetable curry (Maldivian name tharukaaree riha), is nothing like the homogenous and somewhat gloopy thing I might typically order from my local takeaway at home, but rather sweet potato, pumpkin, beans and other local vegetables, beautifully peeled and cut and arranged in a shallow bowl, along with a couple of other vegetables which are not generally native to the island, such as ackee and bok choy, which are grown here to use in the kitchen garden to add a twist. Once the waiter has introduced every vegetable and its provenance in detail while I hold my 'interested and listening' face, though I lose track after the first couple of ingredients like surely anyone must, he pours over a sauce from a white jug and delicately places two large pandan leaves on the top.

For dessert I choose gulab jamun, which are balls of sponge soaked in rose syrup which has been created from roses in the garden, and afterwards we are served tea and huni hakuru, a kind of sweet made of grated coconut, flour and sugar. Claire turns her nose up at the tea and instead insists on a 'proper drink' of Cointreau.

'So how did you all enjoy today?' Ophelia asks, as we are finishing our tea. It's about the first time she has spoken this evening and I notice she's been drinking quite a lot. 'Apart from Lucy's mishap, I think it all went rather well – don't you?'

'Yes it was fantastic!' Araminta enthuses. Claire rolls her eyes and take another large slug of her drink. 'It was so marvellous to see your work with the turtles!'

'Ah yes, Alex's pet project,' she says, and I may be imagining it, but I think I hear an edge of bitterness to her voice. 'Good old, lovely, kind, Alex,' she adds. 'He's an old school friend of ours. Well, of Henry's really. No love lost between me and him, I don't mind telling you.'

There is an awkward silence around the table. Ophelia's bald statement seems somewhat weird and inappropriate but Henry laughs uproariously, as if she's made some kind of hilarious joke.

'Ha ha yes indeed!' Henry exclaims. 'Xander, as he called himself then, and Ophelia at school – well, that's all in the past now; you wouldn't want to hear about all that teenage pettiness, who fancied whom and who was caught doing what with who and so forth. Wouldn't go back to being that age again for all the tea in China.'

He smiles and sighs, as if dismissing memories of silly childish rows. 'A few years back, I came across an article in one of the Sunday papers about the work Xander was already doing around turtle conservation; it sounded like such a worthy cause and such a good way of our new hotel being able to give back to the local ecology, I was keen to get involved. I got back in touch with Xander and the years simply fell away,' he continues, seemingly keen to move the conversation away from whatever Xander and Ophelia's teenage spat might have been about. 'We stayed up all night reminiscing and by morning, we'd come up with a plan for the turtle sanctuary, and Xander was on board. I even managed to persuade Ophelia, though that took a little longer.'

Ophelia drains her wine glass and motions for the waiter to refill it. 'Hmm. Recollections may vary on that I think – I seem to remember it took quite a lot longer than one night for you to bring him round to your way of thinking. And it was, and remains, very much against my better judgement,' she mutters.

'The most important thing is that it all worked out and that, with Alex's help, we are able to help conserve the turtles,' Mohammed interjects. 'And I'm very pleased that we were able to show you the great work he is doing there before the storm came in, and hope you are able to give his work a mention in your articles – I know he would appreciate it.'

'Of course! I'm sure everyone will!' Araminta gushes as there is a general non-committal murmuring and nodding around the table.

'Right then,' Henry says, standing up abruptly, 'I think it's already been quite a long day so, if everyone is happy to, perhaps it's about time we turn in, or at least head to the bar so that the good people of the restaurant can clear up?'

There is a cacophony of 'thank yous' and 'it was all delicious', as we stand up and push our chairs back. And then there is a scream.

Ophelia is staring at the glass-domed ceiling, wide-eyed and with her hand over her mouth.

'What is it?' Henry snaps, somewhat unsympathetically, in my opinion, even though Ophelia is a bit pissed and seems quite snarky tonight, she is clearly upset.

'I . . . saw something,' she says. 'It looked like . . .'

A look of annoyance flashes across his face. 'Like what?' he persists.

We all look up. Initially there is nothing but churning water. But then there is a loud clap of thunder, followed by a flash of lightning which illuminates a ghoulish face, eyes open but unseeing, their arms floating above them lifelessly in the water.

May, 1990

Xander

Ashley has taken something. I'm sure of it.

She's dancing like I've never seen her dance before, throwing herself around and grinding against me, which isn't normal behaviour for her at all, and might almost be OK if she wasn't doing the same to pretty much everyone else as well.

'What did you take?' I shout, over the music. I don't understand. I didn't give her anything. I didn't.

She mentioned she'd seen her friend. Did she give her something? Surely not. Wouldn't Ashley had mentioned if she had?

Eyes still closed, Ashley shakes her head. 'I haven't taken anything!' she shouts back, opening her eyes and grinning. 'It must have been you who gave me something. That painkiller. It wasn't a painkiller, was it?'

171

She leaps and twirls.

It *was* a painkiller. It was ibuprofen.

Wasn't it?

'But that's OK,' she says, leaning in again and kissing me harder and deeper than she ever has before, 'because this feels amazing! And you only did it because you love me! I know that! You wanted me to have fun this evening! You were right! I should have done this ages ago! I should have listened to you! All this time, I've been missing out, when I could have been doing this!'

'I didn't give you anything!' I repeat. I feel sick. Oh God. I didn't give her the wrong pill, did I? It was the ibuprofen, surely? I know it was dark, but I'm sure I gave her the right one.

Or, at least, I *think* I'm sure.

I would never give anyone something they didn't want to take. Never. Least of all Ashley. I wouldn't. I can't have done it by accident. Can I? Please, please, please, no.

I know she's loving it now, but once it wears off, and she has days of feeling depressed, tired, shaky and sick, not only will she blame me, but she'll also think that I gave her something against her will. She will never trust me again. She will hate me, even though I'm sure I've done nothing wrong.

In a flash, it hits me what happened. Ophelia. She must have put something in Ashley's drink when I went to the loo.

That's what must have happened. Shit.

DAY THREE – Monday, 10.30 p.m.

Malia

There seems to be nothing now in the room except noise in between the screams around the table and the wide-eyed waiters shouting at each other in their own language, Dhivehi.

'Now let's stay calm,' Mohammed says. 'Surely you are mistaken, maybe it was—'

'Who was it?' Ophelia interrupts. 'There was someone there! A body! Who was it?'

We are all staring at the roof in horror, but now that the lightning has gone it's impossible to see anything distinct. The waiters' usual professional and unrufflable veneer has entirely disappeared and they are shouting, gesticulating and pointing, running to and fro.

'I think the best thing . . . is if everyone goes to their rooms,' Henry says, 'and we organize . . . well, see if it's safe to send someone out to . . . either way, if everyone could leave the restaurant while we, uh, assess the situation.' His voice is strained and tight, his usual cheerful and 'anything goes' demeanour totally vanished.

We all look at each other. We can't all have imagined it, surely? Those blank, staring eyes and a strangely contorted face. Whoever we saw was quite clearly dead.

'I saw a flash of red,' Lucy says, pale and quite clearly shaken. 'Rob was wearing a red T-shirt this morning. He's not here. I think it must have been him.'

I stare at the glass dome but there is nothing to be seen except for the churning water now. No one moves.

'As I said, I think if everyone can go to their rooms while we . . .' Henry reiterates, looking severely rattled now. 'And I'll go to check on Rob to see if he's . . . before we jump to any conclusions.'

I feel weird about going to my room and being on my own but then again, I'm probably safer that way. After all, like River said earlier, how can I know who to trust? Unless we all stay together, or I'm on my own, how would I know who I'd be safe with?

Everyone else is clearly having similar thoughts as we eye each other suspiciously and no one says anything.

Except Claire, who appears totally unruffled. 'Must have managed to fall in the water somehow,' she says somewhat brusquely. 'Or maybe it was deliberate. Put himself there, I mean. I heard he was having some financial problems. And after all, here is a nice place to go if you're going to go, no? A good place to spend your final days?'

Everyone looks at her aghast. How can she be so insensitive? She rolls her eyes. 'Ah. I appear to have said the wrong thing again,' she says, entirely unapologetically. 'I seem to have a talent for that. When you've been around as long as me, you'll all no doubt have heard stories about random people getting themselves onto press trips as freebies by lying about their credentials, especially if they know they're going to be checking out, so to speak, before too long.'

What is she talking about? I looked Rob up online before I came out, like I did with all the others. He is – was – legit – I'm sure of it. What a horrible, disrespectful thing to say about anyone, least of all someone who is probably dead and can't defend themselves.

There is total silence in the room. I guess everyone else is as horrified by what she said as I am. But if they are, it seems to totally wash over Claire.

'Well,' she adds, looking at her watch, 'It's quite early yet. If we're going to be sent to our rooms like naughty children, can I at least get a bottle of wine?'

Bloody hell. I expect Henry, or at least Ophelia, to tell her that that is hardly the most pressing concern right now but Mohammed simply says smoothly: 'Of course. And once we have arranged that, I agree with Henry. I think the best way forward would be to clear the restaurant so we can talk to the staff and arrange a plan of action. But first, can we see if we can ascertain who last saw or spoke to Rob, and when?'

'He was at breakfast,' Araminta says, 'and said he wasn't feeling well. To be honest, he didn't look too good then. I knocked on his door when we got back from the, uh, quad biking as I said, but he didn't answer so I assumed he was asleep and I didn't want to bother him. His butler said he'd communicated that he didn't want to be disturbed.'

'Has anyone else seen him since breakfast?' Henry continues.

'I checked on him just before 11.30,' says Araminta, 'when he said he was still feeling very unwell and needed to stay in his room.'

Henry nods. 'OK. Mohammed, can you please check his movements with the staff? Find out exactly when his butler heard from him. And ask security if and when his door has been opened today, and if so, by whom. Thank you.'

Mohammed gives a nod and leaves the room.

'Meantime,' Henry continues, 'I'll go and check his room and . . . hopefully this whole thing is a huge mistake.'

I was already not exactly in the best of moods the day of the diving because I was exhausted – I got up even earlier than my various duties demanded of me that morning, with the excuse prepared of a dawn walk to watch the sunrise if anyone spotted me. My plan was to get to the dive equipment and put a small hole in the BCD, the flotation device, on Henry's gear. His was easy enough to spot, thanks to the lovely name badges on their rigs and wetsuits.

There was a risk that he might notice before he got in the water, though he was far too busy playing the part of the fake and genial host, and even if he didn't notice the damage to his equipment before the dive, I knew my tampering quite possibly wouldn't kill him. If all went to plan, he probably wouldn't notice the hole until it was time to ascend at the end of the dive, by which time it would be too late to do anything. But it was never going to be an exact science.

Henry was too busy showing off to bother to do his ABC checks properly. And I was pleased when, as I thought he might, he decided to head away from the group. More chance of things going wrong. Less chance of rescue. Maybe Henry would sink to the bottom of this beautiful, clear sea, never to be seen again.

Clearly, it didn't go to plan. Henry is still alive. Ah well. It was worth a go. I haven't yet entirely fine-tuned exactly how I am going to hurt those who deserve it.

Though I have a few ideas up my sleeve. I have to take every chance I can get.

People like Henry think they are invincible, they always do. Like nothing can touch them.

He's wrong.

DAY THREE – Monday, 11 p.m.

Henry

This was not how I expected this trip to go.

Once Mohammed and I have finally managed to sort Claire out with the wine she was totally inappropriately demanding and get everyone to fuck off to their rooms out of the way, Mohammed goes to speak to Rob's butler and the security guys to try to find out more about his movements today while I brief the restaurant boys about attempting to get the body out of the water, stressing that they must only do what they can do safely. Ophelia and I then head to the office to get a master key to access Rob's room, hoping and praying that somehow we've got this all wrong, that Rob is hungover or has a dodgy stomach and the thing we saw in the water was just something like a dead tuna or shark.

Ophelia has clearly drunk too much this evening. I wish she'd learn to rein it in when we're hosting guests. But I get that she's stressed out about what went on earlier on the bikes, while she was notionally in charge, so I'm not going to have a go at her about it right now. I will talk to her when she's sober though. Again.

Once we are in the office and alone, I sit down and take a moment to pause and take a few deep breaths. I know we need to get on with things, but this might be the only chance I get to speak to Ophelia by herself this evening.

'I think River might know about that bike potentially being sabotaged,' I tell her. 'Fadi told me about the hole he'd spotted in the reservoir when they were tending to Lucy, but obviously we kept it from the guests. I heard River talking to Malia about it earlier. But I don't understand why anyone would do anything like that to the quad.'

Ophelia leans against the windowsill and shrugs. 'They wouldn't. Fadi should know better than to be saying things like that. And River's being a ridiculous drama queen. Lucy probably hit a stone or a sharp stick or something, I don't know. Or maybe I did last time I was out – I go all over in that thing. I'm annoyed it's been damaged, actually. I probably shouldn't have let Lucy ride it. I love that bike. It's the best one yet – I ordered it especially. It's got wider wheels for the sand and . . .'

'Fuck's sake Ophelia!' I hiss. 'That hardly matters right now! There's something going on here. But I don't understand what. I don't understand why anyone would want to hurt Lucy. She seems so nice, like she wouldn't hurt a fly. Rob, OK, he's annoying and a bit of a twat, but that's not a reason to kill anyone, is it?'

Ophelia gives me a withering look. 'I don't know. Isn't it?' she says. 'Only yesterday you were ranting about all that business with Haruki and the fugu. Haruki's quite a coup for us, we wouldn't want him to cut his residency short over some joke played by a bellend like Rob, would we?'

I look at her in horror. 'You can't seriously think *I* killed him over a stupid practical joke, can you? Or that I tried to hurt Lucy? Why on Earth would I do that?'

'Don't be ridiculous,' she snaps. 'I'm not suggesting anything like that. Quite apart from anything else, you simply wouldn't have the balls. All I'm saying is that in general, in life, people have killed for much less than the way Rob behaved.'

I stare at her. 'You don't mean Haruki? I mean, I know he was upset but—'

'Henry!' she shouts. 'Pull yourself together! That's not what I'm saying at all. Haruki is a big boy and I'm sure he can handle a stupid, if insensitive prank like Rob's. I'm just saying it's not beyond the realms of possibility that staff members, he, you, or indeed, even I, might eventually end up under investigation for this.'

I feel bile rising. No one would ever think we would deliberately *kill* someone, would they? Surely not.

'That is, of course, if it turns out that Rob was actually killed by someone else at all,' Ophelia continues, 'which, as yet, we've no real reason to suspect is the case.'

181

Yes. She's right. I'm panicking. He probably died of natural causes. No one killed him. Surely there's no reason that anyone here would want to kill him. These people didn't even know each other before this trip. Did they?

'Like Claire said, it might have been an accident or suicide,' Ophelia continues. 'Or even something like a heart attack. But I still think we should be careful what we do and say around all this, especially in front of the journalists, in case it does turn out to be something sinister. That's all I mean. We need to put ourselves first, think of the business.'

How can she be so cool and calm about this? The thought flits through my mind that maybe *she* did this, maybe she killed Rob, but I discount it quickly. She wouldn't get her hands dirty. Then again, maybe it's not beyond the realms of possibility that she'd commission someone else to do it?

No. I'm being ridiculous. Why would she want to kill someone like Rob? He was irritating and crass, but if people were habitually bumped off for that kind of thing, there'd be almost no one left alive. And Lucy. Ophelia would have no reason to want to hurt Lucy.

Focus. Focus. Of course Ophelia didn't kill him. No one did. It was probably a simple accident. And the thing that happened with Lucy, just bad luck. Ran over a stone, like Ophelia said. The two things, a terrible coincidence. Coincidences happen all the time. Get a grip, Henry.

'And while we're on the subject of Lucy,' Ophelia adds, 'for all you know she might not be as sweet as she seems. Most people have their secrets. You just fancy her, is all. Get your mind out of your pants, for a change.'

'Don't be so ridiculous,' I counter. 'She's a guest. I always behave professionally with guests. And anyway, I don't fancy her. I just respect her as a journalist.'

She snorts. 'Yeah. That'll be it. You respect her mind and her way with words. Ahmed told me you were all over her when you went diving.'

Fuck's sake. I'll have to have a word with him about discretion. I don't want him gossiping with the other members of staff, and certainly not with Ophelia.

'I was not. I wanted to show her the coral,' I tell her.

'Pathetic,' she sneers. 'I heard about how you pretended to be struggling in the water so that she had to rescue you on the dive. Bet you loved sharing her regulator. Probably used it as an excuse to brush up against her arse.'

'I wasn't pretending!' I protest. 'I messed up. I've been so busy lately with the opening, I haven't been diving for ages. It wasn't deliberate. I must have done something wrong with the weights or the buoyancy thing or something.'

She stops and stares at me intently. 'Perhaps we're looking at this wrongly, Henry. Perhaps there *is* something going on. If you weren't pretending, then maybe someone sabotaged the dive equipment too. Let some air out. Cut a pipe. Fiddled with the O-ring. Slashed the BCD. I don't know. I'm not a dive expert. Ask Ahmed to have a good look at your rig – maybe he can check. Maybe he even saw the damage after the dive and didn't say anything in case he got in trouble for not checking it properly.'

What? No. Why is she saying this?

'And the bike. I'm not saying it *was* deliberately damaged, but *if* it was, maybe it was me they wanted to hurt and not Lucy at all. It was my bike, after all. There's a possibility that you and I are the targets here. Perhaps Rob was collateral damage of some sort.'

'What? Why would anyone want to hurt us?' I ask. Why is she being so paranoid? This isn't like her at all. Normally Ophelia considers herself invincible, like nothing can ever touch her. That anything bad will bounce off her, or that she can pay to make it go away. Which, to be fair, she usually can. Or, in the past, get our father to do so for her.

She throws her hands up in the air. 'I'm not sure who. Yet. But I have a few ideas. Think about it. Can you honestly say that there's nothing we've done that people might want to get revenge for? In fact, several people I can think of, right now, off the top of my head.' She pauses. 'One of whom *you* personally invited onto the island. Who we know very well is here, with access to us and the ability to cause bad things to happen if they wanted to, in order to damage our reputation.'

What is she on about? 'Alex?' I splutter. 'Don't be ridiculous. Xander is my oldest friend. He . . . wouldn't.'

She shrugs. 'Maybe. Maybe not. He can access all areas on the island, he could easily have damaged the

184

bike or the dive equipment. And we didn't exactly treat him very well over the fallout from Smash Balls, did we?'

I feel the wave of nausea I always feel when I think back to what happened back then. I take a deep breath. 'That was . . . all a long time ago. And Father pretty much forced us to do what we did. Xander understands that now. And I've done everything possible I can since to make it up to him. I basically gave him the turtle sanctuary to make amends. He knows that. All that stuff . . . was years ago. Water under the bridge. He's forgiven us. I'm sure of it.'

I pause. Is that really true? 'Or he's forgiven me at least,' I add. 'It's no great secret that he never liked you much anyway.'

Ophelia sighs. 'For what it's worth, I don't think it's him either. You and he are cut from the same cloth. All mouth and no trousers, or in his case, not even much mouth either. I can't see he'd have the guts to do anything to us, or the business, even if he wanted to. Plus, he's happy as a pig in shit here with his little turtles, so I don't see why he'd want to mess that up.' She pauses.

'However, let's say, for a minute, that something sinister is going on here. Xander is hardly the only person we've ever pissed off in our lives, is he? Not even the only person we upset while we were still at school.'

Upset. That's somewhat of an understatement.

'But the people here – they're nothing to do with anything that went on then, surely?' I counter. 'They're

185

random journalists and influencers. Why would they be at all bothered about anything which happened thirty odd years ago?'

'*Aren't* they bothered? Are you sure about that?' She moves her face up so close to me I can smell her favourite Chateau Margaux wine on her breath. 'And are they all just journalists and influencers, simply here on a nice free trip to write about our lovely resort? I don't think so. I have a nasty suspicion someone here is not actually who they say they are at all.'

May, 1990

Xander

'I'm going to go and get you some water,' I say, 'I don't think you're drinking enough.'

Ashley is holding her arms above her head, swaying with her eyes closed and with a blissed-out expression on her face which is covered in a thin sheen of sweat.

'Ashley! Did you hear me? I'll be right back. Don't go anywhere.'

She nods and continues swaying, her eyes still closed. Her annoying friend is now next to her, dancing in the same way, possibly even more out of it than Ashley, being periodically groped by some random. She doesn't seem to mind and anyway, she isn't my problem.

Thank God I hadn't taken anything before this happened. I need to make sure Ashley's OK, keep an eye on her.

Part of me doesn't want to leave her side but I need to get her some water. Again, it takes an absolute age at the bar but eventually I manage to get to the front. There is no bottled water because it's not meant to be that kind of party, but I get her a lukewarm glass of tap water.

I hold the extortionately priced glass above my head as I push back out through the bar throng to the centre of the dance floor, where I left Ashley.

She's not there. I feel a lurch of alarm. Where is she? I look around wildly to see if there's anyone I recognize that I can ask but there's no one.

'Did you see a girl in a red dress? Where she went?' I shout at the person nearest to me but they either don't hear me or choose to ignore me, turn their back and carry on dancing. It's a pointless question anyway, there are loads of girls in red dresses. I look around to see if I can see her mate or her handsy boyfriend but they're not there either.

Shit. I need to find Ashley. The dance floor suddenly surges and becomes even more crowded as Soul II Soul's 'Back to Life' starts up and it becomes harder and harder to push through the throng.

Someone knocks my elbow and most of the water spills. Fuck. I push through to the edge of the dance floor and look around wildly. I spot Thalia – one of Ophelia's lot. I grab her arm.

'I'm looking for Ashley, have you seen her?' I shout, trying to make myself heard over the music.

She wrinkles her nose. 'Who?' she shouts back.

Fuck's sake. This is pointless. Thalia probably doesn't even know Ashley's name – Ophelia's set are only interested in each other. Everyone else is considered unworthy of their attention.

I barge my way around the crowds of the party, desperately looking for Ashley but it's useless, I can't see her anywhere. Why is it so hot in here? Why are there so many people? Did some of them gatecrash? I need to find Ashley. I don't know where she is. I don't know what to do.

And then it occurs to me. Maybe she's gone to the loo. I rush over to the girls' toilet and dither outside – I can't go in. Perhaps I can ask someone?

It's a lot quieter here, round the corner away from the music and frankly, it's a relief. The door bursts open and two girls I don't recognize come out. 'Probably just wasted,' one says to the other. 'I wouldn't fancy lying on the scuzzy ground in there though.'

Shit. Who is wasted? Who is on the ground? Is it Ashley? I can't stand out here doing nothing. Panic rising, I shove the door open. I expect to be met with a chorus of 'What the fuck are you doing in here?' or similar but no one pays me any attention.

They are all staring at two girls on the floor, one hunched over the other, crying.

DAY THREE – Monday, 11.15 p.m.

Henry

I hold the key card to Rob's door and it clicks open almost silently. I feel a little thrill of pride. I love how well this hotel in particular of all of our group is designed. All the things that annoy me in high-end hotel rooms – too many confusing light switches, overcomplicated showers, too few plug sockets and none by the bed, have all been thought of and arranged to make guests' lives as easy as possible. There's even fresh milk in the fridge and scissors in the desk drawer, always so useful and not something anyone brings on a trip. But then I remind myself that there are more pressing matters at hand, this is not the time to be mentally patting myself on the back, and I rein myself in.

Rob had 'Do Not Disturb' marked on his room service app which guests use internally to communicate with their butlers, which isn't that surprising as he wasn't feeling well. The system is still working, thankfully, because it runs on an intranet independent of the external internet. So while the rooms are generally tidied up several times a day and little gifts left – a fruit platter here, a box of chocolates there, perhaps an item hand-made by a local craftsperson of some sort – Rob's butler will have stayed away and left him alone.

'Rob? Rob?' I call, knocking. 'Are you there? We're coming in.' I'm ninety-nine per cent sure it's pointless but part of me is still holding on to the vain hope that this is all a massive mistake.

I see immediately when I open the pleasingly heavy door that the room is a tip and, not to put too fine a point on it, absolutely stinks. I go straight through to the sliding doors which lead out on to the terrace to pull one open and get some air in but the rain and wind immediately hit me in the face so I close it again.

'What's that awful pong?' Ophelia says as she follows me in, holding her noise. 'It smells like someone died in here.' She smirks.

'For fuck's sake, Ophelia, have some respect!' I snap. I slide the bathroom door open and the stench instantly gets worse. I only need a quick glance to see what the issue is, and slam it shut. There's vomit and shit abso-lutely everywhere. Gross.

It's very quickly evident that Rob isn't here. My stomach lurches – a combination of the awful smell and the real-ization that it is looking increasingly more likely that we do indeed seem to have a dead body on our hands.

'Rob was clearly quite ill, given the state of the bathroom,' I tell Ophelia. 'But that doesn't explain how he ended up in the water.'

'We should probably have a look on the terrace,' Ophelia suggests. 'It seems unlikely he left his room today, so he probably entered the water from there. Security will confirm if his door was opened or not.'

'OK, good.' I open the terrace door again at Ophelia's suggestion but, again, the rain and wind drive me straight back in. 'I think we'll have to leave it till the storm dies down,' I tell her.

'Meanwhile we should get someone in to clean this place up,' Ophelia adds. 'We can't leave it like this, it's disgusting. We should give whoever does it a bonus though, I don't envy them.'

'Don't you think . . . given that a man is dead, we should wait until the police have been before clearing up?' I ask. 'They might want to . . .'

She gives me a withering look. 'In theory, we probably should. Then again . . . remember what I said. If we're not careful, we could be put in the frame for this. It's even possible that someone might actively *want* it to look like we did it.'

What is she talking about? 'To frame us, you mean? What for? Why would they want to do that?' I ask.

She rolls her eyes. 'For God's sake Henry, for the same reasons someone might hobble my quad bike or try to drown you on the dive trip. We're hardly whiter than white, are we?' She looks me up and down. 'Either of us.'

I pause. 'It seems somewhat—'

'Maybe it does sound far-fetched,' she interrupts, 'But stranger things have happened, and I think we need to seriously consider it as a possibility. So let's have a look round the room. See if we can find anything which might help us work out what happened. Before we get any outsiders involved.'

I frown. 'Is that . . . ethical?'

She snorts. 'Since when have you worried about if something is *ethical*?'

'I'm not the same person as I was back at school, Ophelia,' I say, quietly. I don't much like being reminded of what happened. 'You know very well I helped Xander – Alex – out with the turtle sanctuary to try to make amends for the way we treated him. At least in part. And the other thing . . . well, sadly there is no real way to make amends for that.'

She waves her hand dismissively. 'Yeah, yeah. Whatever. You and your little friend Xander and his pretty turtles,' she says sarcastically. 'Your inviting him here had nothing to do with those kind of eco-credentials – creating a brand new turtle sanctuary – helping ease the planning and permission process, of course, Saint Henry. No, no, it was all about saying sorry to Xander and helping the poor little shell-dwelling creatures. Of course it was.'

I feel a wave of shame. If I am entirely honest with myself, there was an element of that. 'But I wanted to make it up to Xander because—' I protest.

'Anyway, as things stand,' Ophelia interrupts, entirely uninterested in what I have to say, as ever, 'the police

194

can't do anything for now because they wouldn't be able to get here. I took the precaution of grabbing the satellite phone on the way down,' she waves it in my face, 'so that we can control who is called and when rather than Mohammed deciding. And as we all know, the internet is currently broken so there will be no leaking of information from the journalists.'

'But . . .' I protest.

'We can't go anywhere,' she continues. 'No one can get to us here. So for the moment, we are all stuck here on this beautiful island in a storm with everything we could ever wish for as far as luxury fittings go. The only snags are that we are now also sharing it with a corpse, and that there is also someone here who may have tried and failed to kill you, hurt Lucy, possibly while trying to get to me, and potentially offed Rob.

'All these things may end up being unfortunate co-incidences,' she continues, 'but I think for now, we should at least entertain the possibility that they are not. And so I think we're well within our rights to have a hunt around, don't you?'

'Rob might have just got drunk and fallen in the water? Or been disorientated given that he was clearly so ill?' I venture. I'm still desperately trying to cling to the idea that all these mishaps are indeed simple co-incidence. Ophelia rolls her eyes.

'Possibly. But also, quite possibly not. I think there's something strange going on here after all. I'm going to have a look through his things, you have a look at his computer and phone,' she says, pointing at the desk. 'I'll nip out and get us some gloves from the kitchen. It's probably better if the police don't know we've been snooping, when we do eventually get them here.'

DAY THREE – Monday, 11.30 p.m.

Henry

While Ophelia is gone I stare out of the glass doors, trying to see if there's anything obviously wrong out on the terrace which might give us a clue as to what happened. It's impossible to see much with the rain driving against the glass the way it is. But as I far as I can tell by straining hard to see each time there is a flash of lightning, the simple rope rails around the edge of the terrace look like they are intact.

But even if they are, that doesn't tell me anything. The terraces are just above sea level, aimed at honeymooning couples and high earners who want to get away from it all. They're not the Empire State Building or the Eiffel Tower – there are no proper security rails around their edges as we assume that no one is going to fall off the platforms. They are designed to offer easy access to guests who might want to go in the water to enjoy a paddle or a swim, depending on the time of day and the tide. We are an adults-only resort for many reasons, but one is that we don't have to worry about water-safety for children. The ropes are simply decorative barriers, not designed to prevent anyone falling in or being pushed off. Neither is a scenario which ever seemed very likely.

Mohammed comes in. I see his nose wrinkle but he doesn't say anything. So much more respectful than Ophelia. 'Henry? Just to let you know, security say Rob's door wasn't opened all day after he returned to his room after breakfast at 9.13 a.m.,' he says, 'except briefly at 11.25 when I understand he spoke with Araminta. His butler Tamir heard from Rob via the app at 6.18 p.m. replying to a message that Tamir had sent much earlier, in which the client confirmed that he had everything he needed and simply wanted to sleep. Tamir hasn't physically entered the room all day, and neither have housekeeping.' He pauses. 'I'm going to head up to the deck now to see how they're doing with getting the body out of the water.'

'Thank you,' I say. At least that adds credence to my hope that this was simply some kind of accident or unfortunate yet natural incident rather than anything more sinister.

In which case, surely Rob can't have already been dead when he went in the water? I shudder. For whatever reason, he must have fallen. Or put himself in the ocean deliberately. I'm not sure which is worse.

Drowning doesn't seem like a traditional suicide method. My best guess is that he stumbled and fell because he was ill and disorientated, and perhaps he was too weak to get himself out again. Poor guy.

I should get back to the rest of the staff with Mohammed. It might be still too stormy and dangerous for them to do anything, but the idea of him floating around the restaurant with his eyes open is simply too awful. We can't just leave him there unless there really is no other option.

I cast an eye over the fruit platter which is by the bedside and will have been brought in last night, ready for when Rob returned from dinner. Each butler informs housekeeping when the guest is away from the room so that they remain entirely undisturbed. Housekeeping leave chocolates when they do turn down, of course, but we find that in a hot climate like this, especially after a large, rich dinner like the type we serve here, guests often appreciate something fresh to nibble on too.

And Rob clearly did, because much of the platter has gone. There are remnants of melon, papaya, guava and mango, and . . .

Oh God. Surely not? I need something to take the edge off this. I dig in my pocket for my vape, but, shit, it's not there. I must have left it somewhere.

The door opens and Ophelia reappears clutching a handful of blue disposable gloves. 'Right, I've got the . . . what is it?' she says.

I point at the fruit platter where among the fruit there are some small, white fruit which look a little like lychees. But we don't have lychees on the island, and I know exactly what these are.

'The ackee,' I say. 'That shouldn't be there. The chef grows it in the kitchen garden to use in various dishes but it's highly poisonous if it's eaten raw and unripe. That's what will have caused the vomiting.'

Ophelia frowns. 'But could it have . . . killed him?'

My heart is beating too fast. The stench of this room isn't helping and I feel like I might throw up. 'I'm no expert, but I think that while it's unlikely, it's possible.'

She pulls a face. 'How would the ackee end up on the plate though?' she asks. 'Could it have been put there accidentally? A lot of these fruits look the same to me.'

Oh God. I've no idea. It must have been an accident, surely? Why would one of the staff want to hurt Rob? How carefully were they vetted? I have no direct input into employing staff. Could someone here have a vendetta against him? But even if they did, how would they know he was going to be a guest here?

This is all too much for me. 'I don't know,' I say. 'It must have been a mistake, I think. Maybe. No.' Oh God. I have no idea about anything anymore. 'But either way, the ackee didn't throw him in the water. So even if he did eat it, which it looks like he did, he either then fell, or someone pushed him.'

May, 1990

Xander

I breathe in sharply as I see that one of the girls on the bathroom floor is Ashley. Oh God. Her face grey, her eyes closed, motionless. She couldn't look more different from the last time I saw her. How long ago was that? Twenty minutes? Half an hour, maximum?

Her friend – I can't remember her name – is kneeling next to her, shaking her shoulders and screaming in her face.

'She's dead,' she wails, 'I think she's dead!'

I rush over and pull her back – she is banging Ashley's head against the floor and that can't be good. 'For fuck's sake!' I bark. 'Calm down! You'll hurt her. Let me see.'

She gives me a dirty look but sinks back to rest her bum on her heels to give me some room and starts crying even harder. I wish she'd stop. It's not helping.

I kneel down, put my hand under Ashley's head and try to sit her up but she flops backwards and her eyes roll back in her head. I always imagined girls' toilets to be way more civilized than our own but the floor is filthy, covered in discarded pieces of loo paper, many with lipstick marks, and I can feel water soaking in through the knees of my trousers. The already short skirt of Ashley's dress has ridden up and her tights have laddered.

'She's dead!' She's still shouting. 'She's dead!'

Ashley's skin is pale and her lips are blue but, thank God, I can see that she is breathing. 'For God's sake will you shut up!' I yell. 'She's not dead!'

I am trying to sound confident, but Ashley is so heavy and lifeless in my arms I feel like I might throw up. It might not be as bad as it looks, I tell myself. It's probably something like a whitey. She'll be back to normal in a few minutes, wake up and just be a bit embarrassed, I'm sure. She hates a fuss.

I lift her up onto my shoulder, fireman style, and stand up. Even though she's small, the movement makes me stagger. I've never carried anyone like this before but I've seen it in films. Ashley's shoes fall away but I leave them where they are, I can't bend down again and I don't want to involve anyone else by asking someone to pick them up. I can buy her some new ones. She is totally limp and still doesn't stir. A dead weight I think, with a pang of alarm, and push the thought away.

She's not dead, I tell myself. She'll be OK.

'I'll get her some help,' I say, trying to sound like I know what I'm doing and am in control, hoping no one notices the wobble in my voice. 'She'll be fine, I'm sure.'

'Oh God this is all my fault!' her annoying friend is wailing. 'I should have been looking after her! I shouldn't have left her with you!'

'I didn't do anything!' I snap back at her, but she is sobbing and keening, literally clawing at her own bare arms like some kind of animal.

'I'm coming with you!' she screams. 'I need to help her!'

Fucking hell. She's totally out of it. The last thing I want is her snivelling over Ashley and adding to my problems so I pretend not to hear her and stride off, taking care not to let Ashley's head bang on the door frame, but her friend scurries after me, crying and trying to stroke Ashley's hair which is not helping anyone, least of all Ashley.

Back in the main body of the party, everyone parts around me like the Red Sea around Moses, gawping as I push my way back through the throng and up the stairs until I get Ashley into the VIP area and drop her as gently as I can into an armchair. I'm not entirely sure why I brought her here but at least it's a little quieter and there's more space. As I didn't arrange a first aid area of any kind, it seems unlikely that there is one. I certainly haven't seen anything like that.

Ashley's head lolls back again and a thin line of drool rolls from her mouth. She doesn't look any more awake than she did in the loos.

'Christ,' Henry says, coming over and frowning. 'What's the matter with her?'

'I don't know,' I say. 'We need to try and wake her up.' I turn to one of the ludicrously dressed Playboy bunny waitresses, their costumes now seeming more ridiculous than ever. 'Can you, I don't know, get some cold water or something please? Ice?'

She nods and races off. I feel bile rising and swallow it down. I really thought Ashley would have come round by now and I'm starting to get worried.

'Ashley?' I call, tapping her cheek gently again. 'Ashley!' A little harder. 'Wake up!'

'Is she pissed? How much has she had?' Henry asks.

'No,' I say. 'She was fine before. I think . . . someone put something in her drink.'

By 'someone' I mean Ophelia. I'm pretty sure it was Ophelia. But I can't say that now. Henry wouldn't have anything like that said publicly about his sister.

'What a terrible thing to say,' Ophelia says, suddenly appearing seemingly out of nowhere. 'Who would do something like that to an innocent, pure of heart girl like Ashley? I hope you're not actually accusing anyone of such a thing. If you're not careful, someone might have you done for slander.' She pauses and a mischievous gleam comes into her eyes. 'And anyway, I saw you giving her a pill earlier – so who's to say it wasn't *you* that did this to her?'

'She'd hurt her ankle,' I say, through gritted teeth. 'It was a painkiller.'

'*You* might say that, but who's to say what anyone looking on might think?' she retorts, before shooting me a look of triumph and stalking off. Bitch.

The Playboy bunny reappears at my side with a Bollinger-branded champagne bucket full of water and ice. I take an ice cube and rub it over Ashley's forehead and across her cheeks.

'Ashley!' I call again, louder, tapping her face again, more firmly this time. 'Wake up! Please!' I feel tears pricking at my eyes as there is no response from her at all. Her lips are blue and her skin looks even more grey now. I touch the skin of her chest lightly above her now-filthy strapless dress; she is hot, but I can feel she is breathing at least, thank God.

The small group of us now gathering around her are staring at her uselessly, saying nothing as she lies slumped in a chair, floppy as a ragdoll.

'We need to call an ambulance,' Ashley's friend shrieks, still crying. Shit. I hadn't realized she'd followed me in. 'I'm going to find someone.'

DAY THREE – Monday, 11.45 p.m.

Henry

After a quick discussion with Ophelia, we agree that it's best we don't mention the ackee to anyone for now. Before I know it, she has picked up the plate, opened the terrace doors and hurled all the remaining fruit out, slamming the doors shut again as quickly as possible to keep out the howling wind and rain.

'What did you do that for?' I ask, horrified. 'I just meant we shouldn't mention it to the other guests so as not to freak them out. The police will need to know about it!'

Ophelia shrugs. 'I don't know. It seemed simpler. We already have a dead body on our hands; flagging up a potentially deliberate poisoning seems to complicate things. I think we should try to work out what has happened and then . . . decide what story we want to present to the police.'

I sink down into a chair and put my head in my hands. For a second I feel dizzy, almost like I might faint. This takes me right back to what happened at school, when Ophelia once again took charge, decided how best to control the narrative. And I just went along with it.

Ophelia is all of five minutes older than me. Anecdotally, though I don't imagine it has ever been studied scientifically, the first-born twin is usually the stronger. The leader. The one who takes charge.

In our case, that's definitely the case. When we were children, Ophelia was always first to the top of the slide, but would make me go down ahead of her to test the waters. As we got older, she'd often get me to do her bidding, to play a trick on someone or do something mean to them, simply to see what would happen. And then as we got into our late teens, when I would no longer do something simply because she told me to, she could still bend me to her whim by presenting her tasks or challenges to me as competitions or bets. Sometimes she would win and sometimes I would, but I only realized years later, after very many months of therapy, that this was her way of still controlling me as I became older and less biddable. That it was how she was continuing to get me to do what she wanted.

I've got better at saying 'no' to her and at spotting her manipulations, but sometimes it still feels easier to simply sit back and let her take charge. And one of those times is very much now. I can't think straight. I don't know what to do.

There is another clap of thunder and a flash of lightning. Ophelia hands me some gloves.

'You have a look at Rob's phone and computer while I check out the rest of the room. Let's get on with this.'

'I thought I should go and see if they've managed to get Rob out of the water?' I protest.

She shakes her head. 'The restaurant boys are doing that and Mohammed will be keeping an eye on them. They don't need you there. It's a manual task which, with no due respect, you'd be no use at helping with; in fact, you'll probably just get in their way. Let's do this first.'

May, 1990. The morning after the ball

Henry

'Well, this is all extremely disappointing, isn't it?'

Ophelia and I have been summoned to Father's study, along with the family solicitor, Mr Harwood, whose presence has also been demanded even though it is early on Sunday morning.

Father is sitting behind his walnut, leather-topped desk and is surrounded by books. No one is allowed in here unless expressly invited, and if you *are* invited, you know you're in deep trouble.

Up until now, when I've been in this room, it's been for fairly trivial transgressions. Back when we were tiny, it was usually because Ophelia had dobbed me in for doing something to annoy her, maybe messing up her room, pulling her hair or stealing her sweets. Then as we got older, if it wasn't down to her, which nine times out of ten it was, it would be something like disappointing exam results. Being caught smoking at school. Whatever I was being called in for though, coming in here and having father chastise me always inspired fear and dread. It's hard to say exactly why. I suppose it was the look of abject disappointment on his face. Something Ophelia never seems to get from him. She can do no wrong.

Except, perhaps, this time. But I imagine that one way or another, I will end up shouldering most of the blame. Like usual.

I didn't sleep at all last night. After the ambulance was called, the ball was shut down by the police. Someone pointed out the main guy who sells the drugs and he was arrested, I believe. I don't even know his name, he's not from our school. The whole thing caused complete havoc because the party was in the middle of nowhere and, being school kids, the vast majority of whom were both underage and totally wasted, almost no one had their own transport. So coaches and taxis had to be recalled earlier than planned, which is no easy task at pub chucking out time on a Saturday night, parents were summoned, teachers at boarding schools alerted.

There was no way we were going to be able to keep all this from Father, especially considering his close ties with school, so I figured it was best to make the first move. We didn't get back to school until nearing 3 a.m., but I called Father a few hours later at 7 a.m. – he is

212

an early riser and always up by then. I hadn't slept anyway, and by the look of Ophelia, neither had she, though probably for different reasons than me. She's never had much of a conscience and doesn't ever seem to consider anything her fault, but the pills will have kept her awake.

I drove us both home in my vintage Frogeye Sprite, which was foolish as I was probably still over the limit. By the time we arrived, Mr Harwood was already here, in his usual three-piece suit, for fuck's sake, with his pad of paper out and glasses perched on the end of his nose.

'I invested in your venture in good faith,' Father is saying. 'I advanced you the money to hire the venue for your first party and to help with publicity. And to your credit, you made a go of it, and I have already seen some return on my investment.'

That's mainly down to Xander, especially the effort he put in in the early days, but obviously I'm not going to tell Father that. Xander is the business brain behind this and does most of the donkey work. My role is little more than phoning up a few of my mates, pulling in some favours and sometimes sorting the venue as I have better contacts, and that's about it. Ophelia lends the operation some extra glamour. Xander does pretty much everything else.

'I, wrongly and somewhat naively, it seems, assumed that these parties would be no more than fun events where teenagers could meet other teenagers from similar backgrounds to their own,' he continues. 'Something akin to the balls of the past at which debutantes were presented to the Queen. Quite clearly, that is not the case.

'I allowed you the benefit of the doubt when those articles appeared about the goings-on at these parties, thinking it was simply a few bad apples, or press exaggeration,' Father continues. 'In retrospect, I should have acted sooner. And now I find that you were allowing people to sell drugs on the premises. Extremely disappointing.'

Ophelia is weeping softly. For fuck's sake. I'm not sure whether this is part of her act to get Father to not be too hard on her or whether she's coming down from her pills. Either way she's not saying anything. Leaving it to me.

'We didn't allow it. We didn't know,' I lie.

There is silence in the room, bar the tapping of Father's pen on the leather of his desk and Ophelia's stifled (possibly fake) crying. Mr Harwood makes a note.

'And you expect me to believe that?' Father sneers.

'Whether you believe it or not is beside the point,' I say evenly. 'It's the truth.'

Ophelia continues to sob and Mr Harwood makes another note. Father throws his pen down.

'Right. This is getting us exactly nowhere and I have things to be getting on with. I don't plan to waste my entire Sunday on your error of judgement. We need to decide what to do to protect the family's good name. Mr Harwood, what do you think is the best way forward?'

He takes off his glasses and rubs his eyes with his thumb and middle finger. 'Like you, Mr Cadwallader, I think that the school and the public at large are going to find it hard to believe that, as organizers, Henry and Ophelia were entirely unaware of the sale of drugs at their events.'

Mr Harwood glances at Ophelia here. Maybe he isn't quite as blinkered as Father, and realizes the reason behind the state of her this morning.

'Though, looking at it in a more positive light, it might be difficult for anyone to actually prove that they *did* know. We have that in our favour,' he adds.

Father nods sagely. Ophelia looks up at me in alarm and then back down at her hands. While I prefer alcohol to that chemical pill shit and pretty much never take it, it's not exactly a secret at school that Ophelia likes an E or two. So I imagine that, by extension, it would potentially be more difficult for her to claim that she had no idea the drugs were being sold. Though, as Mr Harwood says, possibly difficult to prove.

A thought strikes me. It would be difficult to prove, unless anyone has photos. Could there have been a press photographer there? They've sneaked in before. And many people will have brought their own cameras, no doubt about that. Might anyone have snapped anything incriminating? Perhaps we should ban cameras from future events.

'Though with a young girl so gravely ill,' Mr Harwood continues, interrupting my racing thoughts, 'there will be pressure on the police and the school to find someone

215

to blame. Especially, God forbid, were the situation to worsen.'

How could the situation be worse than it already is? And then I realize what he means.

He means if she dies.

Oh God. She won't die, will she?

The room is near silent again. Even Ophelia's sobs have stopped, though I can hear that her breath is still ragged. Perhaps she isn't faking after all.

Mr Harwood is tapping his pen against his thin, pale lips. 'What would be most desirable in this situation, is if the blame could be apportioned to someone else.'

'A scapegoat you mean?' Father barks.

'I would hesitate to use that word, but in essence, yes,' Mr Harwood agrees. 'I believe a young man has already been arrested on suspicion of selling drugs. So that is something. Though, at present, we have no way of knowing how things are likely to proceed, or if he will be prosecuted. And even if he is, the ideal would still be if we were able to link him, or indeed another person, directly to the unfortunate girl. It is extremely unlikely that anyone would be able to prove beyond doubt that he sold the substance which injured the young lady, in my opinion.'

Ophelia lifts her head and looks directly at Mr Harwood. 'But I think I know who actually gave her the pill,' she says. 'And I think I even have an idea how we might prove it.'

17-year-old girl from exclusive Hamlington Abbey on life support after controversial Smash Ball

A teenage girl is on life support at the Royal Berkshire Hospital after taking Ecstasy at a party attended by children from some of the country's top public schools.

The teenager, who has not yet been named, is described as being in a stable, yet critical condition.

A spokesperson for Hamlington Abbey said: 'We are all devastated about what has happened to our student and are praying for her speedy recovery. We have spoken to the ball organizers who have assured us there is a strict no-drugs policy at the events but sadly someone slipped through the net this time. Our thoughts and prayers remain with the girl and her family at this extremely difficult time.'

DAY THREE – Monday, 11.50 p.m.

Henry

Unsurprisingly, I can't get into Rob's phone because I need his face to unlock it and he is currently floating around dead in the sea. Ophelia finds his passport and at her insistence I try various permutations of his date of birth to try to work out his passcode for the phone but nothing works. I have to admit I'm not trying very hard because I don't see the point of this exercise and don't understand what Ophelia thinks we might find.

His computer, though, isn't password-protected, so I browse through it while Ophelia picks through the items in his cupboard. His desktop screen is a mess, a picture of two small children covered in icons all over the place, seemingly in no order at all, and there are literally thousands of unread emails in his inbox. How can

219

people live their tech lives like this? It's like an email version of a teenage boy's bedroom.

'What exactly am I meant to be looking for?' I ask Ophelia in exasperation. This feels wrong. A man is dead and we're nosing around his room and his devices for no good reason I can fathom.

'I don't know,' she snaps, picking a huge pair of boxer shorts gingerly out of the cupboard, peering into the space they vacated and putting them back. 'Perhaps have a look at the emails between Rob and the PR. See how he came to be here – maybe there'll be something there.'

I sigh. 'OK. And then after that, can we go? I don't feel comfortable doing this at all. We should check on the guests, and . . . what's the PR's name again?' I ask. 'Arabella?' Even though she and her team have been working on the account since we started the build several years ago, it's usually marketing that deal with her. I generally stay out of the organizational side of the PR, simply turning up when the journalists arrive to play genial owner, which is what I'm good at. I think it's better that way.

'Araminta,' Ophelia says. She shoves the papers back in and picks out his suitcase, unzips it and sticks her hand deep into all the various pockets. She pulls out a box of condoms and wrinkles her nose at it. 'Ewww. Looks like Rob was hoping to get lucky.' She shoves it back into the cupboard and moves on to start looking through the drawers.

I search 'Araminta' in the emails and am surprised to find there's more than one. After reading through the subject lines for a few, I work out which one is our PR and search again, 'Araminta Fernsby-Smythe'.

The first email from her to Rob is the standard invitation to the group press trip with dates, some details about the resort, the restaurants, facilities and the activities, plus an image of the island taken from above by the best drone photographer in the business, who we had come in especially from Singapore. I vaguely remember signing the invitation off but, as usual, didn't pay much attention to the details because I knew marketing and Mohammed would have it all in hand. A few days later, there is a second email which says:

Hi Rob – wanted to check you got the invitation to Ketenangan – hope you can make it! Feel free to get in touch if you have any questions!

There are two more along those lines, with no reply from him as far as I can see, until he finally sends back a short message.

Thanks Araminta, it sounds like a great trip but I'm a bit out of the game lately – mainly been focusing on my wine import business – and I'm not sure who I'd pitch this to. Thanks for thinking of me though – I'll give you a shout again in the future I'm sure.

That email arrived at 15.10. At 15.12, she emailed back: The client is really keen for you to come though!

They asked for you especially! Can I please give you a call to discuss – I'd love to be able to make this work! Let me know when would be a good time for you?

He doesn't reply, and there are a couple more emails from her asking if she can call. Eventually he sends his number and they arrange a time to speak.

Why was she so persistent? It can't be that hard to find people to come to a luxurious resort like ours completely free of charge, surely?

After that, there are no more emails between Rob and Araminta until she sends the itinerary and boarding passes to the entire group the day before they left the UK.

'Find anything?' Ophelia asks. 'I think I'm about done here.'

I frown. 'Nothing significant. Though Araminta seemed very keen for Rob to come. Who does he write for?'

'Dunno. I forget. I think he's freelance. Probably writes for a magazine marketing think we should target.'

'In her emails she says we asked for him especially. Did you ask for him?'

She snorts. 'No. Why would I do that? Never heard of him before and, even if I had, he's the last person I would want here out of choice. He's an oik. *Was* an oik, I mean, sorry.'

She chuckles to herself at her own tasteless and unfunny joke. Even though I've known her since birth and love her more than anyone else in the world, there are still times when she totally appals me. I should no longer be surprised by her, but sometimes, it seems, I still am.

'Well, I didn't ask for him to come either. So why would Araminta say that?'

Ophelia throws her hands up in the air. 'I don't know! She probably means the marketing people thought some publication he writes for would be a good fit rather than meaning us *personally*, I imagine. Marketing always seem to have a lot of opinions about where our press coverage should be. Maybe she was trying to appeal to his ego by saying we'd asked for him personally? I don't really care, to be honest. Shall we crack on? We don't need to waste time talking about this right now. I'll go and check on the guests, find out what they're talking about and nip any potential gossip in the bud. You go up now and see what's happening with the body.'

The storm is still raging so I swing past the storeroom and get some wet weather gear for myself – we bought a whole load during the set up though we hardly ever need it. We get bad weather, of course, but there's usually no reason to be outside then. And that's partly why we have facilities like our underwater restaurant and beautiful spa, so that tourists will still come during the rainy season when the weather isn't always likely to be good. Though even then, the storms tend to pass through pretty quickly, so you can still get out snorkelling and on the water or whatever, as long as you pick your

223

moment. I sincerely hope this one blows over quickly too, so we can get Rob out of the ocean, get Lucy the help she needs, and get our communications back up and running properly.

Bloody hell, this trip is turning into a disaster. It's probably a good thing the internet's down, or they'd no doubt be posting on Twitter, ruining our reputation before we'd even opened. Would River and Malia be posting reels and TikToks or whatever those little videos are called, detailing disaster after disaster? Or would they be doing what they were invited here to do and focusing on the positive? And there's always the chance that one of them would be straight on the phone to the tabloid news desks; they are all journalists, after all. My money would have been on Rob, had it been someone else in his position. Though I imagine Lucy as a staffer at a national news-paper would have been pretty quick off the mark too.

We're not going to be able to keep any of this secret for ever, obviously, but hopefully we can at least do some crisis comms and mitigate the disasters as much as we can. When you charge the eyewatering prices we are going to be charging, everything needs to be abso-lutely just so. A dead body floating past when you're trying to enjoy your Michelin-starred meal is very much not part of the deal.

I head up to the hotel's main terrace, which overlooks Aqua. I can hear people shouting to each other, so I assume this is where the action currently is.

Mohammed seems to have disappeared; perhaps he's in the office. Almost all of the waiters and kitchen staff are out here though, most of them simply in their uniforms, and I wonder about sending them off to get properly kitted out in wet weather gear – I wish they'd put it on first like I did. But it's probably too late now, they're already soaked and apart from anything else, it's hard to make myself heard over the howling wind. They are shouting to each other in Dhivehi and while I am making the effort to learn it when I have the time, in these conditions it's impossible to grasp more than the occasional word – I hear 'man', 'water' and 'dead', none of which help me at all, as all of these things are patently obvious.

'Please don't put yourself at any risk!' I holler as absolutely the last thing I want is someone else in the water but, if they hear me at all, they don't seem to take any notice. There are no proper barriers around the terrace – simply an ornamental white rope which is twisting like an angry snake – and none of them is wearing a lifejacket. I wonder about running to the water sports centre to get some but I'd have to get the key and get them to stop what they were doing to put them on, they're never as bothered about safety as I am, and it would all take time and . . . I'm not good in a crisis. This is probably why I have always let Ophelia tell me what to do. I should have sent her up here and seen to the guests myself. She would deal with this better than me. I'm not sure what I was thinking. She was right earlier when she said I'd be useless at helping with this.

Where is Mohammed? The scene in front of me is almost farcical, though the guys are clearly all mucking in and doing their absolute best. Between them they have huge torches, a large fishing net and a couple of boat hooks and are shouting to each other as, I realize, they try to move Rob's body into the net. Three of them are kneeling close to the edge as they try to manoeuvre the net – shouldn't they be tied on or something? 'Be careful!' I yell, ineffectually. God, this is embarrassing. This could barely be further from their job description and I make a mental note to ensure they are properly rewarded. I feel bile rising and swallow it down.

The shouting and pointing suddenly ramps up and I realize they've finally got Rob into the net. I brace myself as they haul him in from the water and manhandle his bulk onto the terrace edge. It is all so undignified. But then the staff step back for a moment and bow their heads, and Fadi moves his hands over Rob's face to close his ghastly staring eyes, thankfully.

'Thank you all,' I say, uselessly. Now that the urgency of getting Rob out of the water has passed, in Mohammed's absence they are all looking at me for instruction, and I am totally at a loss. 'We should, erm, we should . . . move him,' I say.

But where shall we put him? I haven't thought this through. We can't leave him in a guest room, surely? Does he need to be refrigerated or anything? I wonder momentarily about the restaurant freezer and quickly discount the idea simply because it's so awful. I've no idea what to do. I look at the sky to see if the storm is showing any sign of passing yet and am rewarded with more rain in the face, a clap of thunder and lightning for good measure.

Fadi is straightening Rob's limbs and lying him on his back so he is not simply in the heap he was when he was landed. His skin is a terrible grey colour and, horrifically, I think I can see marks on his face – perhaps they are shaving cuts but I've a feeling fish have already been trying to feed on him. For a wild moment I wonder if we can just throw him back in the water and pretend this never happened but obviously it is too late for that, plus that is not the kind of person I like to think I am. Ophelia would probably do it in a heartbeat if she could get away with it. I push the thought away, feeling guilty. My twin sister isn't that unfeeling. Is she?

Mohammed reappears. 'Sorry – I was looking for the satellite phone but I couldn't find it.' He looks at Rob, lying on the terrace. Poor guy. It's so undignified.

'There is an emergency stretcher in the water sports centre,' Mohammed continues. 'We should get that. And then perhaps we can take him back to his room until the storm has gone and we can get him moved to the . . . mainland.' It's possible Mohammed couldn't remember the English word for morgue, though more likely he was simply being tactful but, either way, for me the word hangs unsaid in the air.

I think about the state of Rob's room. Taking him there seems wrong. Disrespectful. 'No,' I say. 'His room is . . . no. He shouldn't go there. There are other rooms which aren't being used, we'll take him to one of those.

I'll speak to housekeeping and find out which would work best. Perhaps villa twenty – that's the, um, furthest away from the main part of the resort.'

DAY FOUR – Tuesday, 1 a.m.

Malia

After Rob being found dead like that, I think we all felt too shaken to simply go back to our rooms by ourselves and go to bed, and certainly way too freaked out to sleep. So when Claire suggested we join her in her villa for a nightcap before turning in, we all very hastily agreed. 'Better make that a couple of bottles of wine rather than just one in that case,' she told the waiter. 'Actually, all good things come in threes, don't they? Or is it all bad things? Either way, let's say three. Please. Maybe one of each, red, white and rosé?'

In spite of the dead body in the water of which we were by now all painfully aware, Claire was brought a wine list and the sommelier discussed the bouquet and notes of various bottles, as if it was a totally normal evening and it mattered at all which bottles of wine we might choose to drink. Claire took her time selecting the bottles she wanted before we all followed her back to her room.

My room is by far the most luxurious place I've ever stayed in my life, and I had assumed all the villas were the same here, but that clearly isn't the case. Claire's villa has two bedrooms, two bathrooms, a living/dining room with elaborate hanging spherical lights and a table which would seat at least eight, plus two terraces (each with a pool – who needs two pools?), and its own sauna. Part of the living/dining room has a glass floor which I imagine is designed for watching the fish swim by but today all you can see is the water churning.

I wonder how they decide who gets which room on a trip like this? Did Araminta allocate them? Or the Ketenangan people? I guess the powers that be here feel her readers are more likely to book to come here than mine which, to be fair, is probably the case. Most of my followers are young, single women in their twenties or early thirties who might be able to afford a cheap week on the Costa del Sol once a year if they are lucky or a short city break somewhere served by a budget airline.

We sink into chairs and sofas as Julia, who has followed us from the restaurant with the wine and glasses, fusses around the table, placing coasters and little snacks on tiny salvers in case we haven't already eaten enough, plus a small plate and white linen napkin in front of each one of us. She asks us in turn which wine we would like, pouring it and arranging the white and rosé in ice buckets and the red on its own little coaster, before checking we have everything we need and leaving. It's so weird the way everyone here is simply carrying on as normal.

'Well,' Araminta says, 'that was all a bit strange, wasn't it?'

Claire snorts. 'That's the understatement of the year.'

An expression of hurt flashes across Araminta's face momentarily before she swiftly rearranges it into something more neutral. I get the impression she, unsurprisingly, doesn't quite know how she should be acting now, keeping up the perky and professional PR woman act around her charges, or being serious and sombre as befits the fact that someone has died. She seems to have opted for something between the two, which somehow makes it seem more like she's commenting on a duff episode in a usually reliable Netflix series than expressing regret or surprise at someone's death.

'Shocking,' Lucy says, taking a sip of her drink. 'And very sad. What do you suppose happened to him?'

I notice she is still moving very carefully, wincing a little most times she does so.

'I think it's pretty obvious,' Claire says, as she drains her first glass of wine and pours herself another. Wow, that was quick. 'While I appreciate that you don't generally expect to have a dead body floating at you while you're having your dinner, I don't understand why everyone is acting like there's anything particularly sinister going on. I'd be willing to bet quite a lot of money it'll turn out to be nothing more than some afternoon drinking when he was bored, followed by falling off the terrace and drowning. Happens all the time.'

'Does it?' River says, frowning. 'I've never heard of that happening in a place like this. Aren't drowning accidents usually children, or when people get in trouble while they're out swimming, or on a boat or something? Not usually grown men somehow falling out of their room in a luxury hotel.' He whips out his phone, no doubt to look it up. 'Oh yeah. No internet.' He pauses. 'And don't you think that the lack of connectivity is a bit convenient too?'

'I'd say it's the absolute opposite of convenient,' Claire counters. 'Whatever that would be.'

'Inconvenient, that would be,' River retorts. 'No, I mean, with the internet down, we can't let people know what's happening easily. Or check anyone's credentials. So if anyone is . . . trying to hurt anyone, they've got more time and space to do it. The staff here don't seem to have found an answer yet as to why the internet isn't working. Perhaps they've even deliberately disconnected it so we can't let people know what is happening. It's not the kind of publicity they'd want, is it?'

Claire gives a contemptuous snort of laughter. 'Oh dear, River. I think you've been watching a few too many true crime documentaries. Let's hear this though – who do you think is trying to hurt whom?'

'Well . . . I'm not sure,' he admits. 'Lucy was lucky not to have been more badly hurt. And don't forget, when the brakes failed, she was riding what is normally

Ophelia's quad bike. Maybe whoever did whatever they did was actually trying to hurt Ophelia, and not Lucy at all.'

Lucy looks up. 'You think someone sabotaged the bike deliberately?'

River nods. 'Yeah. It looked like it to me. I didn't say anything before because I didn't want to . . . scare you.'

Lucy frowns. 'Hmmm. It takes more than something like that to scare me. And like you say, no one would have known in advance that I was going to ride that bike today. If it was deliberate, surely they must have been trying to hurt Ophelia.' She pauses before adding, 'And there was that thing with Henry's dive equipment on our first day. He shrugged it off as his own mistake, but I'm not so sure. It seemed to me like his BCD was damaged. When I suggested that he said he must have caught it on the coral but . . . maybe he didn't.'

'How else could it have happened?' Claire snaps. 'Listen to you all! You sound utterly ridiculous.'

Lucy ignores her. 'I guess it's possible, assuming it was damaged, it could have happened before he put it on, and he might not have noticed till it was time to ascend,' she concedes. 'It would only take a small hole to make it malfunction and it would be easy not to notice something like that. It was lucky I knew what I was doing because with someone else, it may not have turned out that way. I didn't make a big deal of it at the time because I didn't want to undermine or embarrass him but now . . .'

Claire slams down her glass and fills it up yet again. 'Right. I've had enough of listening to this nonsense. So according to DCI River and PC Lucy here, someone has so far tried to kill Henry while diving, off Ophelia on the quad bike, accidentally hurting Lucy in the process and, what, killed Rob as well? Why on earth would they want to do that?'

Lucy takes a slow sip of wine, looking at Claire darkly but saying nothing.

'DCI River?' she persists. 'Any ideas?'

I'm surprised to see him blush – he always seems so confident. 'I don't know,' he replies. 'Maybe none of it was deliberate. Perhaps I'm wrong. But you have to admit it's odd, isn't it? So much happening in such a small resort in such a short space of time?'

Araminta finishes off her wine and refills her glass. 'No. I don't think it's odd. I think it's just unfortunate. Unconnected incidents, coincidence, synchronicity, call it what you will.'

'Rob wasn't looking too good at breakfast,' she continues. 'Perhaps he was ill, I mean, more than a hangover like we assumed. It's not like, well, not to put too fine a point on it, he was the fittest looking of blokes. Overweight. Liked a drink. Perhaps he had an underlying condition no one knew about. You hear about things like that all the time. Maybe he had a heart attack or something and fell in the water. Anything could have happened. I think it's pretty disrespectful you all talking about him like this, to be honest, and very rude towards the Cadwalladers to be speculating that something so

234

terrible is going on at their resort when they're so generously hosting you here.'

Ah. Back into PR mode I see. 'So, if we can kindly change the subject, please,' she adds. 'Assuming the weather has calmed down, what would everyone like to do tomorrow?'

There is silence as everyone looks at her in horror. I can't quite get over that, when one of our number has died, Araminta seems to be expecting us to continue with the trip as if nothing has happened.

Then again, unless the storm abates, it's not like we can get away from the resort anyway.

But before we have a chance to answer, there is a sharp knock at the door. Claire frowns, but gets up to answer it.

It's Ophelia. 'Ah, here you all are!' she cries, following Claire back into the room. 'I was worried when I couldn't find anyone.'

'Yes, we're all here,' Claire says. 'Just having a little nightcap to steady our nerves after the unfortunate incidents of this evening. Would you like to join us?'

I see Ophelia's eyes flit towards the door which Claire has already closed. I imagine Ophelia was about to make an excuse not to stay, but Claire has picked up a spare glass from the hospitality tray and is heading for the bathroom, saying 'I'll give this a quick rinse, save bothering Julia again, plenty of wine to go around,' and Ophelia can now hardly say no.

She eases herself down into a chair. There is another clap of thunder and a flash of lightning. 'Wow, it's still really coming down out there,' she says conversationally.

A general murmur of agreement goes around the room. I'm not sure this evening can get any more surreal. Here we all are, fresh from having been confronted with a dead body, and we're Britishly talking about the weather.

Returning from the bathroom, Claire plonks the still-wet glass down on the table and says: 'Red, I think, if I remember rightly?' not waiting for an answer before she pours it in.

'Yes, red will be lovely, thank you,' Ophelia replies. She takes a large glug before asking, 'How are you all feeling? If that's not a silly question?'

Araminta says, 'We're shocked but OK,' at exactly the same time as I say 'All feeling a bit on edge, I think,' and we give each other an apologetic look.

Ophelia nods. 'Totally understandable,' she says. 'Hopefully we can get a better idea of . . . what happened to Rob soon. It's all terribly upsetting. The poor man.'

There is an awkward silence as we all sip our drinks. The atmosphere is even more stilted since Ophelia arrived. I suddenly feel incredibly tired and want nothing more than to be on my own, in my enormous, comfortable bed with pillows like clouds. It'll be alright, won't it? Nothing is going to happen. It's not like someone is going to come and attack me in my room.

Is it?

Maybe Araminta is right. Maybe everything that has happened has been no more than a series of unfortunate coincidences.

I stand up. 'I think I'm going to go to bed now,' I say, triggering a chorus of, 'Yes, me too', 'It's been a long day', etcetera and we all leave *en masse* to go off to our separate rooms.

'I hope you'll all sleep well,' Ophelia says, draining her glass and also getting up. 'Given the, uh, circumstances, I want to assure you all that we have extra staff on tonight, who will be monitoring the systems carefully to ensure that no room doors are opened unexpectedly in the night. While, as you know, there is no CCTV on the island for reasons of privacy, we do have a record of which doors are opened and when. We hope this will make you feel safer. It's probably best if you stay in your villas if possible, but if you do feel the need to leave your room for any reason, can I please request that you inform your butler first via the app, to avoid any unnecessary alarm?'

I am relieved to hear this. It makes me feel safer. Surely with the place locked down like that, nothing else can happen.

DAY FOUR – Tuesday, 8 a.m.

Henry

I feel like I have only just closed my eyes when there is a hammering on my door and someone is shouting 'Henry! Henry! Wake up!'

I'm surprised to see that it is already light – I thought I'd barely slept at all but I suppose I must have done. The memory of the horrors of last night wash over me and I feel a wave of nausea. Oh God. The poor, dead man. What happened to him? And what are we going to do about it?

The waiters, Mohammed and I took Rob's body to villa twenty where we put a tarpaulin over the bed to protect the bespoke handmade mattress. I wonder if we will ever be able to offer that bed to guests again – would that be creepy? It can't be the first time someone has died in a hotel bed, surely? Do they always throw them away? I doubt it.

Focus, focus, I tell myself. This is not the time to be thinking about this.

We laid him out as respectfully as we could. One of the waiters brought some pink roses, the Maldives' national flower, to surround Rob with before we covered him with a sheet. As we left, I discreetly turned the air conditioning up to full to make the room as cold as possible. I don't know much about dead bodies, but I do know that ideally they'd be stored in a fridge. I've no idea how long we have until . . . well. It doesn't bear thinking about.

'Henry!' the shouting continues. 'Wake up! Please! You must wake up!'

I stumble groggily out of bed and open the door, only then remembering I'm only in my boxer shorts. It's Julia, and she's white as a sheet.

Oh God. What now? Surely there can't be something else? I grab a robe and wrap it around me. 'Julia. What is it?'

'It's Ophelia,' she says. 'I went to take her breakfast and . . . I can't wake her. I think . . . something's wrong.'

Fuck's sake. Ophelia was really putting it away last night and she's probably still pissed. She's always hard to wake after a heavy night. I know yesterday was pretty full on, but she could have behaved more professionally. Given what's happened here, and the fact

240

that we have several journalists visiting, it's more important than ever that we are absolutely at the top of our game.

'Hang on, let me put some clothes on and I'll go and sort her out. Thank you for letting me know, Julia. I hope I can rely on your discretion? It's been a very difficult time. I imagine Ophelia's . . . exhausted.'

I'm quite sure Julia isn't stupid and no doubt knows exactly what I mean by 'exhausted', but even so she replies, 'Of course, goes without saying. Let me know if you . . . need any help with anything.'

I haul on some shorts and a T-shirt, grab my 'access all areas' key and head to the apartment where Ophelia is staying, just along from mine.

'Ophelia!' I shout as I enter. 'Get up you lazy mare!' As I go into the bedroom I see that Julia has dropped the tray on the ground and simply left it, which is extremely unlike her on both counts.

I feel a lurch of unease as I step around the tray. And then I see Ophelia lying on the bed. And it's immediately obvious that she's not simply wasted. Something is very, very wrong.

No one should look like that. She is dead. My breath catches in my throat and my knees go wobbly. I hold onto the door frame and try to take a deep breath, but it's almost impossible to get air into my lungs.

Should I call someone? I close my eyes and open them again, but nothing has changed.

Oh God. Oh God. Not my sister, please. I let go of the door frame and walk over to the bed, sinking down on to it next to her.

She is still in yesterday's clothes and lying in a strange, contorted position, her eyes open, bloodshot, and staring at the ceiling.

There is quite clearly nothing that can be done. I feel nausea rising and leap up to rush into the bathroom to throw up. Then the tears come. I sink down to the floor, racked with sobs as the rain continues to beat against the glass roof.

What the fuck happened to her?

The night before the quad biking, I went out to the shed where the bikes are kept and stuck a screwdriver in the brake fluid reservoir on Ophelia's flashy pink bike so that it would leak out slowly. I'd looked up how to do it in advance. I already knew I was going to disable the satellite – I'd researched how to do that too. I found the satellite and threw some large rocks at it, which I figured would be a good way of damaging it and messing up the signal. It wasn't a particularly scientific approach, but it seems to have worked. As it turned out, the storm might have done my work for me anyway.

But back to the quad bikes. It turned out you can't actually find (at least not easily) 'how to sabotage a quad bike' however much you google. Instead I watched a few mansplainers on YouTube boring on about how quad bikes work and how they maintain theirs (why are their videos always so long???) and so it was easy enough to work out what to do to scupper hers. I knew Ophelia loved quad-biking – she's always posting pictures of herself on her stupid girly pink bike on Insta. Apparently she has a signature pink one in each of the resorts, for fuck's sake.

All that was easy enough, though I was pretty exhausted after waiting up half the night until everyone was in bed to sneak out to do what I needed to do. It was a pleasant, warm night so it would have been easy enough to claim a nice walk to look at the stars had anyone spotted me. Which they didn't, anyway.

With everything else that's been going on, I don't know if anyone's actually got around to checking the quad bike over yet. If and when they do, it's possible they'll notice it's been deliberately damaged, though I guess it would be easy enough to write off as something that happened when Ophelia hit a rock or a sharp branch on a previous ride.

Then again, if someone does realize that the damage was deliberate, it doesn't really matter. I've got a plan for that too.

May, 1990. Two days after the ball

Henry

'Thank you for coming in today,' says Mr McKenzie, the headmaster.

It's my first time in this office since my entrance interview as a terrified eight-year-old. Mr McKenzie sits behind a huge leather-topped mahogany desk. Behind him is an enormous portrait of a monk who I believe was the school's first headmaster. The walls are wood panelled and light streams in through the large arched, mullioned window, casting cheery sunbeams on the walls, entirely at odds with the sombre mood in the room.

Ophelia, Father and I are sitting in overstuffed armchairs facing the desk.

'You will be well aware of why I've called you here today,' he begins. 'We need to talk about the, ah, unfortunate incident at your May Ball.'

245

Sunday was horrendous, spent being grilled by both Father and Mr Harwood about what we did and didn't know, followed by being aggressively coached about what we could and couldn't say to Mr McKenzie, and potentially to the police too. I'm almost surprised Father didn't bring Mr Harwood along to this meeting today as well, but I guess he would think that might suggest we were in any way to blame for this thing. Which of course we may be, but we are not allowed to concede that under any circumstances.

'How is the poor girl?' Father butts in. 'I understand she was – is – not a full fee payer at Hamlington. If there are any . . . financial implications to her accident I'd be very happy to help her family in that way if they would allow me to.'

Accident. What kind of euphemism is that?

Mr McKenzie clasps his hands together and looks at Father with a grave expression. 'Thank you,' he says. 'Miss Pennington is, sadly, still extremely unwell and remains in hospital. I will consider whether it would be . . . appropriate to pass your offer on to her family,' he says, no doubt meaning, 'I don't think trying to buy her loved ones off is the best plan,' but quite clearly not wanting to piss off my father, one of the school's major benefactors.

'But that is something for another day,' Mr McKenzie continues. 'We need to discuss both the future of Smash Balls and, I'm afraid, also the future of Henry and Ophelia at Hamlington Abbey.'

I have my hands pressed together between my knees and am staring at the floor, almost unblinking. Ophelia is looking directly and defiantly at the headmaster. I wish she'd show more deference. Sometimes she utterly fails to read the room, or to play the game.

Father's main concern around all this seems to be that we are not expelled. He says that if that were to happen it would bring shame on the family – generations of Cadwalladers have gone to Hamlington, right back to the sixteenth century or something ridiculous like that. Mr Harwood seemed to think that criminal proceedings could also be possible, though I find that hard to believe because we only ran the party, we didn't sell the drugs. At least that much is true.

'I hope it goes without saying that my children will no longer be running or promoting Smash Balls,' Father says. 'Our entire family is extremely upset about what happened to this young lady, and absolutely appalled that someone decided to ruin an innocent party by selling illegal substances. But out of respect for the poor girl in hospital – and her family, and for fear that something similar could happen again, Henry, Ophelia and I have discussed it and mutually decided that discontinuing the parties would be the right thing to do.'

This is very far from the truth. I love playing host at the parties, and enjoying the small amount of respect and attention Father has offered me since I've actually been able to show a return on his initial investment, which there's no way he would have agreed to if Ophelia hadn't persuaded him. I argued that discontinuing the parties could even make it look like we consider ourselves to blame.

But Father shouted me down. He's recalled his initial outlay and demanded that the parties cease. His right to do this was all written into our initial contract, drawn up by Mr Harwood. The very fact that we had a contract within the family for an amount of money which, to him, is a pittance which would be taken off our eventual inheritance should we fail to show a return on it within two years, probably tells you everything about him that anyone needs to know. I've always known he is a ruthless man, but this weekend, he's shown himself to be more stern and devoid of any human feeling than I ever could have begun to imagine.

Ophelia doesn't care whether the parties continue or not as far as I can tell. All she's interested in is staying in Father's good books – she gets loads of attention wherever she goes looking the way she does, she doesn't have to put on a huge party to make herself feel important. But for me, the balls were my little kingdom. I know it's a bit pathetic, but I enjoyed that.

'I'm glad to hear that,' says Mr McKenzie. 'I agree that that is the right thing to do. We try to move with the times here at Hamlington but, in retrospect, perhaps our tolerance of the Smash Balls and in particular, allowing students to attend this one during termtime, was remiss.'

The room is silent for a few seconds bar the slow, laboured ticking of the grandfather clock.

'We also had another thought,' Father continues. 'Whatever the, erm, outcome for Miss Pennington, we would like to set up a scholarship trust in her name. Henry and Ophelia are very aware of their privileged position in life and of the many advantages this confers, not least an excellent education. The Cadwallader family would like to fund a less fortunate student through their school journey, from the age of eight to eighteen, one each decade, for the next fifty years. It could be called the Pennington scholarship, and perhaps the family or even the young lady herself, assuming that she . . . yes, well, perhaps she or her representative could even play a part in selecting the beneficiary each time. How does that sound?'

Mr McKenzie steeples his fingers. 'That is extremely generous, Mr Cadwallader. I will need to talk to the Pennington family about their feelings about that, assuming that . . . yes. Anyway.'

There is silence again. 'You will also know that we are in discussions with another student, following Ophelia's allegations, as are the police, and his future at the school and whether any criminal action will be taken remain to be decided. As you may know, he is currently denying giving the girl any illegal substances that night.'

Another pause. More ticking.

'I appreciate that Henry and Ophelia have been extremely cooperative in helping us to get to the bottom of this matter. That said, given the severity of the situation, I don't think their involvement with the balls can go entirely unreprimanded. We need to send a message, both internally and externally, that Hamlington Abbey is taking this incident extremely seriously.

'Henry and Ophelia are both exemplary students, expected to go far and, apart from this unfortunate occurrence, they are excellent ambassadors for the school. And the Cadwallader family are valued friends of Hamlington Abbey, as well as being students over many generations, as you well know. So I'm minded to suspend Henry and Ophelia for a period of one week. This will give me time to meet with the governors who, I suspect, especially given your generosity towards the school and with respect to the new scholarship you are proposing, will hopefully agree with me that they should return to the school to continue their studies after that. Thank you for your time today.'

DAY FOUR – Tuesday, 9 a.m.

Henry

I'm not sure how long I am in Ophelia's room – maybe ten minutes, maybe an hour, before I hear a soft knocking on the bathroom door. 'Henry?' It's Julia again. 'Can I come in?'

I swipe at my eyes and stand up – I seem to have slid down to the floor at some point. 'Wait there, Julia. I'll come out now.'

I splash my face, rinse my mouth out with water and dry myself off. I squeeze a dollop of toothpaste out to rub on my teeth and rinse again to try to get the awful taste out. Ophelia's toothbrush is there but I can't bring myself to use it. I feel tears threaten again and squeeze my hands tightly into a fist as I concentrate on holding them back.

Taking a deep breath, I open the door.

'I haven't told anyone what happened or where you are,' Julia says, 'but everyone is asking after you. Mohammed wants to talk to you. I thought I should let you know.'

I wipe at my eyes again.

'Ophelia, is she . . . ?' she asks.

I nod. 'I'm afraid so.' Somehow with a member of staff here, it is easier for me to hold myself together.

Her hand flies to her mouth and her eyes open wide. There is another crash of thunder. 'But what happened?' she asks.

I shake my head. 'I don't know. Perhaps she . . .'

I run through some possibilities in my mind. Perhaps she drank too much. Took too many drugs. Did she even take drugs anymore? I don't know. I didn't think so. At least surely not while she's out here – she wouldn't have brought anything like that with her, surely? Could it have even been suicide? Why would she kill herself?

A thought hits me like a thunderbolt. Did *Ophelia* kill Rob and then kill herself because she was worried about being found out?

No. That doesn't make sense. None of it does. None of it.

'I don't know,' I repeat. Because I *don't* know. But looking at Ophelia, the hideous grimace on her face, whatever it was that killed her was not a nice way to go.

'What . . . will we do now?' Julia asks.

There is another crash of thunder. 'I think . . . so as not to panic the guests, and the other members of staff, we'll leave her here for now.' I close her eyes and fetch a large towel from the bathroom to cover her with. I choke back a sob. 'As soon as the storm blows over, we'll . . . well.'

I can't say arrange to take two bodies back to the mainland. It sounds too ridiculous. What the fuck is happening here?

'I think, if I can rely on you not to tell anyone, Julia, for now it's better if we carry on as normal. I think it's what Ophelia would have wanted.'

May, 1990. Five days after the ball

Xander

'So, I was interviewed by the police last night,' I say. 'They came to school.'

Henry and I are in a café in the local town. Not the one we usually go to, where they know us, and people might listen in. One where we can be anonymous. I don't think either of us wants to be overheard.

He takes a deep drag on his Marlboro Red, holding it between his thumb and forefinger in that way which always sends a stab of lust right through me even though I'm not a smoker. He stubs it out in a disposable aluminium ashtray and then immediately takes another from his monogrammed cigarette case and lights it.

I haven't seen him for a few days, since he's been suspended, and I miss him even more than I imagined

I would. Even in the holidays we usually spend a lot of time together. I quite often stay over at his or he at mine, when he gently ribs me about the 'nouveau' nature of my family home, as he puts it, and takes the piss out of the truckle bed in my room and the wall-to-wall carpet, so different to his dusty old Persian rugs and his four poster bed in which it's rumoured that Napoleon once slept or something.

I know he doesn't feel the same about me, and that nothing will ever happen between us like that, but the simple fact of him being my friend, in my world, having him close, seeing his face, all of those things make the day easier.

He looks up at me in horror. 'Christ. Why did they want to question you? Did the police come to school? Ophelia and I have been suspended. They arrested the dealer guy, didn't they? They spoke to us at home, and they said they might come again if necessary. Why do they need to speak to you as well?'

I shrug, pretending to be much more nonchalant than I actually feel. 'Don't know. It wasn't only me they spoke to. Perhaps it's routine.'

He nods. 'What did they ask?'

'The kind of thing you'd expect, what I did that night, what I drank, if I took anything, if I'd seen Ashley, what she'd done and when. I guess they spent more time with me than most of the others because I spent a lot of time with her that night and because, well, we were seeing each other. Are, I mean.'

'Course, mate. And who else did they speak to?'

'Pretty much everyone. They wanted to talk to anyone from school who had been at the party, try to put together a picture of what happened to Ashley, they say. I guess they can't try to talk to everyone who was at the party because, well, there were so many. So at Hamlington, people who knew – know Ashley,' I correct myself, 'is a good place to start. I suppose.' I take a sip of my coffee which is cold and bitter. 'I don't know how these things work.'

Henry furrows his brow. 'How's she doing? Ashley, I mean.'

I sigh and feel tears threaten. I look at my hands and shake my head. 'I don't know. It's family only at the hospital, they won't let me see her. I went, but they wouldn't let me in. I thought about trying to pretend I was her brother or something but . . . I dunno. It felt wrong to lie on top of everything else.'

I tear off a piece of doughnut and shove it in my mouth. It feels like dust and I struggle to swallow it.

'I've tried to call her mum a couple of times to find out but she . . .' my voice catches in my throat, 'puts the phone down on me. I can only assume that if Ashley had got any worse then someone would have told us at school but . . .'

I wipe away a tear.

'Oh mate,' Henry says. 'I'm sorry. It must be so hard. I know you liked her. Like her. I'm sure . . . she'll pull through.'

I rub my eyes and clear my throat. 'Yeah. Hope so. But the other thing . . . is apparently someone told them they saw me giving her a pill. The police said.'

He frowns. 'And . . . did you?'

'No! I mean, yes, I did, an ibuprofen. She'd hurt her ankle falling off that stupid bull that we thought was such a good idea to get in for the parties.'

'And you've told the police this?'

'Yeah. Of course. But I don't know if they believe me. They kept asking about my clothes, where they are now. I told them I'd taken my DJ to the dry cleaner like I do after any party as it stinks of smoke, plus this time . . . well, it had some pretty gross stuff on after being on the loo floor trying to sort Ashley out and then carrying her and . . . well.'

Henry takes a deep drag of his cigarette and we sit there in silence for a few more seconds than feels entirely comfortable. He stubs it out.

And then I say the thing that's been bothering me incessantly since the ball, the thing which I haven't been able to get out of my head. Maybe if I can share it with someone, I'll feel better.

'Plus . . .' I say hesitantly. Should I say this? I can trust Henry, surely? He's my best mate. 'I can't be 100 per cent sure. It was dark, I was pissed, and I've been having these nightmares where I've accidentally given Ashley the wrong pill and it's all my fault that she's in that hospital bed barely alive and . . .'

Henry shakes his head. 'I don't understand. So you're saying you might have given her the E after all?'

258

I pause. 'I'm ninety-nine per cent sure I didn't. I think her drink was spiked. But not by me.'

'Can you even do that with E?'

'Yeah. The capsule ones with the powder in you probably can. Even the ordinary ones maybe. She was drinking Coke, it's always syrupy and too sweet when they serve it in bars from that nozzle thing. Tastes different every time. She wasn't into drugs. I can't see any other explanation than her being spiked.'

Henry takes out his Zippo and lights yet another cigarette.

'Why would anyone want to do that though?'

I watch him smoke and think about telling him my suspicions – that it was Ophelia, when I stupidly left the drinks with her. But while I'm sure he knows very well that Ophelia is no angel, he worships his sister, and he's never going to thank me for saying something like that about her.

'I don't know,' I say. 'Maybe someone who doesn't like her? Or maybe for a laugh? People do stupid things all the time for no good reason.' I pause. 'Like those bets we use to have, remember? No real reason. Just for fun.'

He grins. 'Yeah. They were fun.'

'They were,' I agree. Somehow that kind of carefree silliness feels like it's from another era. Will we ever do anything like that again? Right now, it feels unlikely.

I take a sip of my coffee and Henry continues to smoke his cigarette in silence for a few minutes, before he asks, 'So what happens next?'

'I have to wait. Wait to see what the police say. Wait to see what the school does. It sounds like there won't be enough evidence to charge me, especially as I'm pretty sure I didn't actually do anything but . . .'

The tears start flowing properly now. I'm so scared. Henry balances his cigarette carefully in the ashtray, moves around the table and sits beside me in silence, his arm around my shoulder as I cry.

DAY FOUR – Tuesday, 9 a.m.

Malia

Breakfast is a bizarre affair. Neither Henry nor Ophelia is anywhere to be seen. Lucy is even paler than she was yesterday and doesn't seem to be able to use her injured arm at all now. Julia, who also looks exhausted and stressed, cuts up Lucy's pancakes for her. She winces with every move as she eats them slowly with a fork held in her right hand.

Araminta clears her throat. 'Mohammed has been in touch with the mainland. Because of the storm, and because, um, there is no life or death emergency, it is considered too dangerous for us to try to cut our trip short, even given the, um, situation. So he and I have discussed the itinerary for today and if you're all in agreement, we're going to go ahead with the spa day today as planned. It seems pointless to simply stay in our rooms when there's nothing we can do to change the sad turn of events. The storm is due to settle later today, so we're hoping, Lucy, we can get you some proper medical attention, as well as, um . . .'

Dealing with Rob's body hangs in the air unsaid.

'And then tomorrow, as we planned, assuming the storm has abated as forecast, we'll be leaving in the morning to travel home,' she continues. 'It would be impossible to bring our travel forward and, as I said, wouldn't change anything anyway so . . . Does that sound OK?'

'Excellent,' Claire agrees. 'I've been looking forward to the spa all week.'

'Indeed,' Araminta says. 'I have a schedule of appointments here,' she hands out thick cream cards which look like classy wedding invitations. My name is written in gold pen, and caviar facial, 10.30 a.m. written underneath.

I turn it over in my hand and look at the back for something to do, relieved that they have chosen a facial treatment rather than a massage for me.

The card is textured and edged with gold. For a resort that prides itself on being so eco, it seems quite wasteful for something which will simply be thrown away.

'The cards are made from fully recycled paper,' Araminta adds, as if reading my mind. I blush. 'The spa has suggested treatments according to the forms you filled in before the trip,' she continues, 'but if there's something else you'd rather have instead, that's fine too – you only have to ask. And there's also the indoor pool, sauna, hammam, sensorial showers and a lovely relaxation room with heated stone beds you can enjoy too. Plus there's the cryotherapy chamber for those who would like a go of that.'

'Not for me,' River says. 'I read that it can freeze your eyeballs if you stay in even a few seconds too long.'

You can smell and hear the spa before you get to it. There is a waft of that typical spa smell which is almost always a variation on the same kind of theme wherever you go, maybe something like rose, lavender, bergamot and a touch of eucalyptus. There is the usual bland, soothing music which must surely have been especially composed for spas as you literally never hear it anywhere else, and nor would you be likely to want to.

The smell gets stronger as the glass doors at the entrance of the spa slide open and I'm greeted by a diminutive staff member I haven't yet met, wearing a version of the hotel uniform with those weird three-quarter length trousers which therapists in all high-end spas seem to wear.

'Good morning, Miss Malia,' she says. The staff at Ketenangan often address us by name and they never get it wrong. It's very impressive. 'I understand you have a treatment booked with us later. Would you like me to show you around, and then you can use the facilities while you wait?'

'That would be lovely, thank you,' I say.

'Excellent. Please come with me.'

First she shows me the changing rooms. 'There is a robe, towel and slippers for you there,' she says, indicating the wall, 'and lockers outside. Then once you are changed, you can go through to the spa. Can I ask that you take off your shoes and put on the slippers first though please? Thank you. You can leave your things here. They will be fine.'

Once I'm in the soft, forest green slippers, we head through to the pool.

Oh wow. Like the restaurant, it is entirely underwater. The water outside is still churning and almost frothing but there is almost nothing between the sea, the blue of the floor tiles and then the pool. A shark looms up close to the glass and then away again. There are several massage jets around the pool, a couple of underwater beds which look like they have jacuzzi jets and also a traditional hot tub bubbling away in the corner.

'The gate is closed today because of the storm,' she explains, 'but normally there is also an outdoor section of this pool so you can go up the steps and swim out into the open air, plus there's a terrace outside too. In the far corner over there,' she adds, indicating the opposite side of the pool, 'you can go through to the sauna and hammam, there's also an ice cave, sensory showers and the relaxation room. If you want to use the cryotherapy chamber, let me know and we can book you a slot. Can I get you a herbal tea or a fruit juice, perhaps?'

'Herbal tea would be lovely, thank you,' I say.

'The house detox blend? It's senna, guarana and ginger.'

'Sounds delicious,' I agree, not that I know what any of those things taste like except ginger.

'Perfect. If you'd like to take a lounger, I'll bring it over when it's ready.'

The facial is absolutely heavenly. The treatment room is lit with scented candles and I think I drift off at several points as the therapist gently rubs, massages and pats. The creams, oils and lotions she is using smell amazing and when she brings me a glass of papaya juice at the end of the session, I feel a little dizzy when I sit up, I am so relaxed.

Afterwards I lie on one of the heated beds in the relaxation room and I am brought a fresh juice on a tray with a little pot of dried fruits. It's still raining, though it looks like the storm is easing slightly, and by now I can make out some of the larger fish in the water, swimming outside the glass walls.

Claire comes in and sits on the lounger next to mine. 'How was your treatment?' she asks.

'Lovely,' I say. 'What are you going to have?'

'I'm having the Ketenangan ritual,' she says. 'Full body massage, ass milk bath and then a facial. Sounds divine.'

I think it's about the first time I've heard her say anything positive since we arrived.

DAY FOUR – Tuesday, 11 a.m.

Henry

I can't even. I can't even. But I must.

I tell Xander what's happened. He doesn't usually have too much input into the running of the hotel itself – his realm is just the turtles. Plus he and Ophelia have never got on, and by mutual, unspoken agreement preferred to keep out of each other's way. But his accommodation is next to ours and I need to tell someone what's happened. Not the more junior staff – it would be inappropriate. I haven't even told Mohammed yet, I'm not entirely sure why. Perhaps because I haven't 100 per cent decided what is best to do about it. So far, to my knowledge at least, only Julia knows about Ophelia, assuming she has kept the news to herself. And instinct somehow tells me it might be better to keep it that way. One person here in the resort was already dead. Two . . . well, no one can write that off as co-incidence, surely? Something is going on here, but the last thing I want to do is cause a panic. Especially while no one can actually leave.

I don't think it's dishonest or unfair not to tell anyone. Because of the storm, there's nothing we can do anyway. Informing the staff or guests right now will serve only to alarm and upset them. I need to take control.

But also, I need a confidant. I'm not usually much good at dealing with anything on my own, and especially not in a crisis. Maybe it's a twin thing, always being used to having someone else to rely on. Or at least being used to having someone close by; admittedly sometimes Ophelia was more of a liability than a support. But she was the leader of the pair of us, there's no denying that. And whatever else we were, we were always friends, and each other's closest ally. Loyal to each other to a fault.

Without Ophelia, Alex – or Xander, as I still think of him – is the nearest thing I have to a friend on the island. And probably, if I'm honest, the closest thing I have to a friend anywhere in the world. Barely spending very long in one place over the last twenty years or so as we set up the hotels, I'm not someone who has ever forged close friendships. And even though Xander and I have certainly had our differences over the years, and there were many years when we didn't speak, we go back a long way. And that counts for a lot.

We were best mates at school. Then all that ball stuff happened. I know we treated Xander terribly. I never wanted to do it, but Ophelia and Father left me no choice. I should have told him at the time how much of a part Ophelia and Father played in all that. But I was so torn, torn between loyalty to my sister and wanting to impress my father, over the loyalty I owed to my best friend. I chose wrongly. And I have always regretted it.

It was Ophelia who suggested that they find Xander's DJ and check the pockets. I could hardly tell the police not to, could I? And then Father . . . all he cared about was keeping us at Hamlington Abbey, and protecting the 'good family name', as usual.

Father had his work cut out protecting the family name that summer, first with the ball and then with what happened with Ophelia afterwards too. As always, Father came out on top. He kept the family secrets. The good name of the Cadwalladers remained unsullied.

But what does all that count for now? Did the 'good family name' make him happy when he was alive? It never seemed to. Does it keep him warm in his stone-cold mausoleum, buried alongside all his ancestors who, chances are, had equally sordid secrets? Did being buttoned-up and miserable his entire life contribute to the heart attack which killed him? Would the success Ophelia and I have made of our business have made him proud? I very much doubt it. Nothing we could do was ever enough. Or most especially, nothing I could do. And now Ophelia is dead. So really, Father, what was it all for?

After school finished, Xander and I lost touch for a long time. He left to go travelling and I went to university.

269

Before the arrival of the internet, it was easy to lose track of someone. But I never stopped feeling bad about what had happened. Never stopped wanting to make amends.

I tried countless times to get in touch. Initially whoever answered the phone at his house simply slammed it down.

After some more time had passed, I'd call his house when I was back for the holidays but his parents always claimed he wasn't there. At the time I didn't know if that was true, or if he simply didn't want to speak to me. It was frustrating. People forget, and young people probably don't even realize, but keeping in touch was different before social media. You might have no idea where anyone was for years on end unless they made the effort to let you know, with a phone call, or even a letter. A letter! Imagine that.

Eventually, I stopped trying. Xander might have moved around, but Cadwallader Castle didn't. He would have known how to find me if he'd wanted to. It was clear that he didn't.

But it continued to niggle. We had been such good friends, he had been so loyal to me, and he had been treated appallingly by my family. Maybe there was more I could have done to help him. Maybe I should have stood up to Father and Ophelia. It might be somewhat of an exaggeration to say that I thought about him every day, but it wasn't all that far off.

The stress ate away at me. I took medication for anxiety, and attended regular therapy, which helped. And many years later, I looked him up. By then, the internet had made it much easier to find people. You no longer needed a private detective or anything fancy like that to find out what someone you had lost touch with was up to. You didn't even have to ask around, or go to the library to look at press cuttings or microfiches. You didn't have to do any more than type a name into a computer screen.

A quick google found that after a few years travelling and volunteering, Xander had returned to the UK and trained as a marine biologist. Looking at his LinkedIn page I felt a stab of shame as I realized that by the time he came back home, I had stopped calling him. So his parents hadn't been lying all those years ago. He probably hadn't been there.

I read through his LinkedIn and a couple of press articles he was mentioned in. One of his main interests was now the conservation of endangered species, especially turtles.

I found an email address – he was listed as a guest lecturer at the University of St Andrews – and got in touch. I fully expected him to ignore me, or to knock me back. I told him that I was planning a new hotel somewhere warm and exotic, and I would love it if he would consider coming onboard.

Our first meeting was in a pub in Henley. He agreed to meet me when he was coming down to visit his parents. I got the impression he wanted to make it clear that he wasn't coming all that way especially to see me, which was fair enough.

I suggested one of the pubs we had favoured as teens because back then the staff didn't care if we were underage. It had changed a lot over the years, of course. The sticky, patterned carpet had been replaced by reclaimed floorboards, and the velour banquettes with a mish mash of vintage wooden chairs and comfy leather sofas. Scampi or chicken and chips in a basket had gone and the menu, scrawled artfully on a chalk board, was now all Beyond Meat burgers and truffle chips. The only beer on offer was made on-site in a microbrewery, and a wide range of organic wines were served by the glass.

We talked about the past, and about his work with turtles in the Maldives from which he'd recently returned in order to deliver a series of lectures at the university.

The Maldives. It seemed like as good a place as any to think about opening our next venue. Xander and the turtles weren't the only reason we went for this place, of course. I had been on the lookout for somewhere to open a year-round hotel for some time. We'd made a great success of our Alpine hotels and I saw no reason at all why the same concept shouldn't translate to somewhere sunny.

So the Maldives had been on my radar for a while, along with some other options, Seychelles, Bali, and a few more. But Xander's forgiveness was important to me, and offering him what he really wanted, his own turtle sanctuary to manage exactly as he wanted, helped ease his forgiveness, I'm sure of it.

It didn't all happen over a few pints that night, of course. Initially he was guarded, hostile even. He said he'd only agreed to meet me out of curiosity, because he was in the area anyway. We'd had a somewhat stilted dinner and parted ways by about 9.30 p.m.

But he'd eventually agreed to meet me again and that time, due to a long conversation I'd had with my therapist about Xander between the two occasions, I apologized for the way my family had treated him. And it turned out, that that was what he had really wanted. Simple recognition that he had been wronged.

'I didn't give Ashley that pill,' he told me. 'I wasn't sure about it as a kid, but the more I thought about it, the more convinced I became. The police and the school needed a scapegoat, and that was me. I was lucky not to serve time.'

I nodded. 'I know. I'm sorry . . . for everything that happened. We should have treated you better. Helped you more. Fought your corner. I'm not entirely sure how, but . . . I feel that strongly.'

Closing time came and went and this time, we moved onto my club. It was 4 a.m. by the time we left, a certain amount of bridge-building done. We hugged as we parted. It was much more than I could have hoped for, and I was determined not to leave it there.

We continued to meet regularly, sometimes as mates for a pint, other times to talk about my work, his work, and how the two could be combined. We commissioned research, had some fun site visits to some incredible places in the process of finding the right island (always funded by me, it was absolutely the least I could do). And eventually we came up with Ketenangan.

Ophelia never wanted him on board. She was quite vocal about it. But this was the one time I stood up to her, put my foot down. Helping Xander in this way, giving him his own turtle sanctuary, it was the best way I could think of to appease my guilty conscience.

But now, Ophelia is gone. There's only me. I'm not sure I can cope.

'Oh God. What an awful thing. I'm so sorry, Henry,' Xander says, my voice cracking as I tell him that Ophelia is dead. He goes to hug me but I put my hand up and move back; I know if he touches me I will cry, and I need to keep it together. 'What . . . how?' he asks.

I shake my head. 'I don't know. She seemed fine last night. A little drunk but, no more than . . . oh God what am I going to do?'

Xander pats my shoulder. 'I think you're right to keep it quiet for now. Nothing we can do till the storm calms down. Then we'll get Lucy sorted, get the police out here, and . . . find out what happened.'

An awful thought pushes its way into my mind. I'm pretty sure Xander has forgiven me for the past, but he never, ever liked Ophelia much, even back when we were teens. He couldn't have . . . no. No. He'd never do that. He wouldn't have it in him, plus he is too loyal to me to do that to my beloved sister.

Isn't he?

274

I *watched closely as the Japanese chef gutted the fish, explaining at great length as he did so exactly what he was doing and why. If you ask me, it was all a bit too theatrical, unnecessarily long and over-dramatized detail. Yeah, yeah, yeah, a fish that can kill you. Whatever. Yawn.*

He was clearly very skilled, as of course he would be, with his Michelin stars, having been brought especially from Japan for the delectation and delight of Ketenangan guests.

I tuned out as various people around the table asked questions and wanged on about what they would and wouldn't eat and why. Like anyone cared. Some of them, Rob especially, were clearly scared. It was pathetic. The man cutting up the fish was a professional and the hotel is a high-class operation. They're hardly going to serve food likely to poison anyone, are they?

There was a moment of drama when Rob played his childish and unfunny joke of pretending to be poisoned. Have to admit, he had me going for a very brief moment. I should have predicted he'd do something like that, in retrospect it seems like exactly the kind of thing he'd do. Absolutely no regard for anyone else. All about him. I felt a bit sorry for the chef – it was rude and I'm sure the incident must have shaken him at least momentarily, fully trained and Michelin-starred or not.

After Rob's little prank, the atmosphere soured rapidly and considerably, and it was clear that no one could wait to get back on the boat. And when they did, I made sure I was last to leave, wearing a disposable plastic glove which I'd nicked from Haruki's workstation earlier, took a pinch of the fugu which was on its way to being correctly and safely disposed of and dropped it into my water bottle.

The chef didn't think of quite everything, did he?

DAY FOUR – Tuesday, 2 p.m.

Henry

I am working on autopilot. My sister is dead. I don't know what I'm going to do.

But this business, and especially this hotel – she loved it. And with her gone, it's all I have now. I've worked too hard on it over the past years, not leaving any time to form a long-term relationship or start a family.

Perhaps I will live to regret that. But I'm sure Ophelia would want me to carry on, to look after the business. We can't have done all this for nothing. I owe it to her to continue. I can't simply lie down and give up, the way I feel like doing right now.

I need to be strong. For her. For me.

I don't understand what happened to her. How can she be dead? She was fine yesterday. A bit pissed, maybe, but I've seen her in far worse states. It was nothing to do with that, I'm sure of it. Something happened. Something else.

And also the way she looked! I choke back a sob. The expression on her face. Horrific. She did not die peacefully. Oh God. I hope she didn't suffer. Was there anything I could have done? Should have noticed? Even if there was, it's clearly too late now.

But whatever it was, even if it was natural causes, we need to hide what has happened from the journalists. I can't have anyone find out. One death . . . well, that was dramatic enough, but two? No way.

I know what journalists are like. If they find out, there'll be stupid sensational headlines saying the resort is cursed, things like that. It's simply not true that all publicity is good publicity, even if we believed that when we were teenagers, running the Smash Balls. We were over the moon when we got in the papers, and ticket sales rocketed. But we were children then. Plus, times have changed and this is very different.

Ketenangan is a luxurious retreat, not a teenage party, nor some restaurant that people try out for a laugh because people on Tripadvisor have reported that the waiters are hilariously rude. There are plenty of luxury resorts for high-net-worth individuals like our clients to choose from – given the choice, they're not going to come to the one which had two deaths in less than twenty-four hours, with dodgy internet to boot. We have some serious damage limitation to do.

Apparently, according to the tech guy, the satellite had somehow got knocked out of alignment and, I assumed, as did he as far as I know, that it had happened by accident.

But now I'm not so sure. Rob . . . well, someone put that ackee in his room. It didn't get there by itself. It could have been a mistake, put there by accident by his butler at a push. Though that would be quite a big push. I've spoken to the butler in question and to the restaurant staff, and any error around this seems unlikely. These guys are fully trained and diligent. I get that if they'd made a mistake, they might not want to admit to it, but I can't imagine it's the kind of mistake they would make. And none of them would have any reason to poison him, surely? So either they are covering their backs, which remains possible I suppose, or someone else put it there. Which to me seems much more likely. Did that person also push Rob in the water? Or did he fall, as at least one person has suggested?

And now Ophelia. Oh God. I don't understand what's happening here. I feel like I don't understand anything anymore.

I look out the window where I can see that the storm is finally waning.

The journalists are due to leave tomorrow. They'll all be gone. I'll be able to breathe again. We'll be able to regroup, work out how to deal with all this. Have a crisis comms meeting. Probably delay the opening. But eventually, hopefully, be able to return to some semblance of normal.

Although the idea of that seems impossible without Ophelia.

May, 1990. Nine days after the ball

Xander

'Thank you for coming to see me today,' says Mr McKenzie. 'I only wish it was in happier circumstances.'

I nod, knowing that if I speak, I will probably cry. Again. I have cried a lot over the last few days. I know what he's going to say, and I don't want to hear it.

'I understand that you were in a relationship with Ashley Pennington,' he continues.

Were in a relationship. Is that just a figure of speech he's using as she's not at school at the moment or . . .

I manage to mumble, 'Yes sir,' while looking at the ground.

'An announcement will be made to the school in assembly later today,' he continues, his voice low and sombre, 'but I'm sorry to tell you that Ashley's family made the difficult decision to switch off her life support

281

system today, after doctors confirmed that she was never going to recover from the injuries caused by the drugs she took. Or, as her family believe, the drugs which were given to her without her knowledge.'

I look at my hands and screw my eyes up tight but there is no way to stop the tears coming. Mr McKenzie isn't exactly the kind of headmaster you'd want to cry in front of but there's nothing I can do about that right now.

My fault. It's all my fault. Even if I didn't give her the pill, if I hadn't had sex with Ophelia that time, if Ophelia hadn't been jealous of Ashley because of all that, none of this would have happened. She probably wouldn't have spiked Ashley's drink. It must have been her. Must have been. But as far as I can tell, I might as well have done it myself. It may not have been my hand which put the pill in her drink, but the outcome is the same. Ashley is dead, and it's all because of me.

I don't even like Ophelia. I never even fancied her, not really. Someone touching my dick is always going to be exciting because I'm seventeen years old and it's not like it exactly happens very often but given the choice, I'm not sure I actually fancy girls at all. I liked Ashley a lot, and I tried to like her in *that* way, but Henry was usually all I could think about, and it was him I thought about when I kissed her. Ashley was sweet and kind and absolutely did not deserve any of this to happen to her. I liked her, but mainly I asked her to be my girlfriend because I know it's unlikely that Dad would want a gay son. And Henry wouldn't want to hang out with me if he knew how much I think about how it would feel to touch him in the way I want to.

This is all my fault.

I am not listening to Mr McKenzie because I don't care what happens to me now. I don't care about anything.

'Alexander? Did you hear me? I think it's best that, given the circumstances, you go home for a few days at least. You will need time to . . . grieve. I will ask my secretary to call your parents to come and collect you. And now is not the time, but in light of all that has happened, at some point we will have to discuss your future at the school too.'

As you would expect from a high-end resort, Ketenangan has an excellent website – you can tell as soon as you open it that they spent a fortune. There will have been high-end agencies involved, focus groups and it's been translated into several languages by native speakers, as befits a hotel of its stature. Every little detail will have been scrutinized and pored over I'm sure, from the colours and fonts right down to the stupid turtle logo which is everywhere.

They are very proud of their restaurants here on Ketenangan, of their menus, and of their 'zero miles' concept. Much of the food served is sourced from within the Maldives and items that can't be come from as close by as they can possibly manage. In theory, anyway.

The restaurants are indeed excellent, the chefs skilled, the quality of the ingredients top notch, and the ecological credentials of not bringing in things from too far away clearly extremely laudable.

For some items, though, this is much easier to achieve than for others. Fish and seafood – there's obviously a plentiful, varied and exotic supply right on the resort's doorstep, most of which is extremely suited to high-end dining. So that's easy. The hotel also offers various excursions where clients can catch and even cook their own, as we did. Again, no surprise there. It's not exactly an original concept, but it's one that tourists seem to like.

Dairy is a little trickier – there are no cows or sheep in the Maldives, so no Maldivian cheese! And high-end clients expect high-end products, so most of the cheese comes from France. Ketenangan prides itself on its cheeseboard – on many of the islands, you'll only be offered a couple of options of fairly unexciting varieties. Here, the cheeses are all sourced from small, artisanal makers, so boutique and exclusive that the waiters can pretty much tell you the name of the cow that produced the milk the cheese was made from, as well as the cheesemaker's wife's star sign. A lot of the wine is from organic French vineyards, plus there are also Italian and New World wines to keep almost everyone happy. So the zero miles idea, while a nice one, doesn't bear very close scrutiny.

Looking at fruit, vegetables and herbs, though, we're back on track. Again there is quite a range that is available locally, and the hotel has its own garden where it grows as much as possible – avocado, mango, papaya, lime, chilli, bananas and plenty more. All good stuff and no carbon miles involved at all. Even the waste from the fruit is mulched and composted and goes back into the ground to nourish the next round of plants.

All of this is detailed on the website, along with lovely pictures of the hotel gardens with the local staff tending them, and even 'fun facts' about the various plants and in some cases, nutritional information. Clients like to know what they are eating and where it comes from, or at least whoever designed the website seems to think they do.

But as well as the native plants, the head gardener here likes to experiment with introducing other plants which are less typical, some of which the chef has requested especially because he likes to include them in his dishes, to make his restaurant different from the others on the islands. Again, all of these fruit and veg are carefully detailed on the website, along with their reasons for them being grown here, with a lot of wanging on about how great care is taken in doing so not to upset the local ecosystem yada yada yada. Yawn.

One of these plants is ackee. Ackee is native to west Africa and looks a little like a lychee. I believe one of the chefs who helped set up the kitchen at the outset came from Jamaica, and it was his idea to grow ackee here – a USP for the resort. Ackee grows year-round in many African countries and is a popular ingredient, especially in Jamaica where ackee and saltfish is the official national dish. You can fry it, put it in curries or add to soups. It's cheap, flexible and easy to prepare. It's full of vitamins and is cited as offering all sorts of health benefits. No wonder it's popular – what's not to like?

However, like fugu, it's important you know how to prepare it and do it properly, otherwise – who knew? – it can be very poisonous. So poisonous, in fact, that in certain countries, such as America, you can only get it in tins, because it's already been cooked and is safe. You wouldn't find it raw there. It's not grown commercially and it's illegal to import it.

It can be safe to eat raw, and in some countries, is often eaten that way. Which is usually fine, as long as you know what you're doing. Ackee needs to be ripe when it's eaten. It's when it's unripe that you run into problems.

If you wait for the fruit to ripen and open on the tree before you pick or eat it, it will probably be safe, even consumed raw. At Ketenangan, as it says on the website, not only do they ensure the fruit is ripe before it is picked, but it is always cooked too for extra safety. Belt and braces and all that.

So obviously I didn't do any of that when I picked my ackee for Rob. I went for a walk in the garden, picked a few unripe fruit which hadn't even started to open from the tree, and separated out the pods and seeds. Now all I needed to do was get Rob to eat it.

The doors here are not the kind you can easily break in to and the system logs every time a room door is open. Apparently it's something to do with helping the staff be more discreet as they go about their duties, only turning up to make beds when the rooms are unoccupied, so that the clients are never disturbed. So when the group were having drinks on the terrace after coming back from the dive trip, the tide was low and I knew exactly where that scumbag was, I briefly excused myself, took the unripe fruits I'd collected earlier, dropped down into the water from my room and waded round to his, climbed out and let myself in through his terrace doors which had been, unsurprisingly, left unlocked and added my fruit to his platter. They look a little like lychees, though they don't taste anything like them, more like a nut, apparently. I went back the same way, drying my legs off before anyone saw me.

Jamaican vomiting sickness is caused by an enzyme in the raw ackee and usually comes on six hours to two

287

days after you've eaten it. In the process of doing my extensive pre-trip research and having seen the website's boasts about ackee on the island, I already knew the details of what it could do well before I left. My plan had clearly worked, Rob had eaten the ackee, and that's why he was looking so ropey that day at breakfast, though he probably simply thought he'd drunk too much the night before.

It causes vomiting, which then stops, well before the poison is actually likely to be fatal. If you get treatment then, in a hospital, with intravenous fluids, you'd normally be fine, unless you're extremely unlucky.

But Rob obviously had no idea he'd eaten poison and probably decided he'd be better simply sleeping it off. Thinking he'd simply overdone it the night before and was suffering the after-effects, he'd probably have been embarrassed to make a fuss about not feeling too good, especially as he wasn't exactly in anyone's good books after his stupid prank with the fugu.

Eating unripe ackee won't always kill you. If you're a healthy adult, even if you don't get treatment, chances are it will just make you very, very sick. I wanted him to suffer, of course, but that wasn't going to be quite enough for me. When I popped back to his room the same way to check on him, shortly after the group got back from the quad biking the next day, he was still alive, though very weak and somewhat delirious, delirious enough not to notice that I'd come in through the terrace doors rather than actually knocking on his door. And as far as the high-tech system is concerned, his front door wouldn't have been opened since that morning. So if any terrible accident were to befall him, it would very much look like it must have been his own fault.

I suggested to Rob that getting out onto the terrace into the fresh air would make him feel better. He didn't notice it had started to rain. He could barely walk, hanging on to me as I lowered him down into a chair. I left him there briefly while I went back inside to reply to a message sent by his butler earlier in the day, saying that he didn't need anything and that he would rather be left alone.

He sat there on the terrace in the pouring rain, slumped over, not moving. Barely even aware of where he was, it seemed.

So I went back outside and pushed him in the water. The tide was only a little higher but he was clearly too weak to save himself. I sat on the edge of the terrace and kept my feet on his shoulders just in case he tried to get out but it wasn't really necessary, he barely moved. Once I was certain the deed was done I waded back the same way I'd come. I was already soaked through anyway from the rain and I'm good in the water. Unlike poor Rob.

I would say rest in peace, but I wouldn't mean it.

DAY FOUR – Tuesday, 8 p.m.

Henry

'Ophelia sends her apologies, she has a migraine and needs to lie down in the dark,' I tell the journalists at dinner. I had considered not going to eat with them this evening and making an excuse to stay in my room. I realize now that I can barely function at the best of times without Ophelia, and knowing that I will never see her again . . . it's almost too much to bear.

But bear it I must. I need to make the effort. She would want me to. This was the favourite of her hotels yet; she never really liked the cold. Setting up the first hotels in ski resorts was my idea. Ophelia was always much happier in the sun. I must make a go of it. Save face. These journalists must not know that there has been another terrible death on this luxurious, get-away-from-it-all island.

291

Fortunately Mohammed is leading the conversation tonight, talking about the hotel's eco-credentials and some of our plans for the future here as if nothing untoward has happened since they all arrived. To their credit, the group is at least making a pretence of listening and taking an interest.

I can see in their faces though, they are all more than ready to leave. Looking forward to tomorrow when they can get off the island. It's hardly surprising, given the circumstances. The dishes we are being served are beautifully presented as always, and no doubt delicious, but everyone is picking at them gingerly and while I am trying my best to look like I'm eating, my stomach is in knots and I can barely bring myself to swallow this best-of-everything food.

'I realize the trip has not turned out exactly as we hoped,' I say, as Mohammed pauses momentarily in his marketing spiel. For God's sake, Henry. Not only a non-sequitur, but possibly the biggest understatement of the year. Do better, I tell myself. 'But I hope that, well, apart from . . .' I trail off. This is ridiculous. What can I say? Nothing can make this alright. 'I hope, perhaps, you will come back another time when things are normal and . . . I hope you can take away at least some impression of how beautiful the place is from your visit.'

'Of course we can!' Araminta cries, but even she sounds less enthusiastic than usual. Somewhat desperate. And why wouldn't she? She must be as keen to get away from here as anyone else. 'None of this is anyone's fault and nor could it have been predicted,' she continues. 'The storm. What happened to poor Rob. We don't know yet, obviously, but chances are it would have happened, he would have . . . even if he'd been at home.'

She looks at me with such an earnest expression I feel like crying. It's unlikely he'd have been accidentally eating unripe ackee if he was at home, isn't it? And I don't know where he lives but I doubt it's somewhere where he can easily fall or be pushed into the sea. But as far as Araminta is concerned, the most likely scenario is he died of a heart attack or of some other natural cause. So I nod sagely in agreement.

'You've set the place up very nicely,' Claire says, forking in another mouthful of whatever fish it is we're eating this evening, I wasn't listening when Fadi described it. 'And given the circumstances, you've looked after us very well. I liked the spa especially. But I was a little disappointed not to have enough time to have a go in the cryotherapy chamber. I thought we'd have had more time in the spa, to be honest.'

Fuck's sake. Always something to complain about. She had pretty much the entire day to spend in the spa today, why didn't she ask about this earlier? I'm about to launch into some platitude about how there'll always be next time when Araminta pipes up, 'I'm sure you could have a go after dinner, couldn't she? Henry?'

What? I dab at my mouth with a napkin. 'Well, I'm afraid that might be a little difficult,' I counter. 'While normally our spa runs twenty-four hours a day, as this is a soft opening and with there currently only being your small group in the resort, we haven't quite finished recruiting our staff, so it's not currently open overnight, and there'd be no one to—'

'But you could show her, Henry!' Araminta interjects, uncharacteristically pushy. This is surely not what we pay the PR agency for, is it? I get that she's supposed to give the journalists what they want, make sure they have a good time and see the hotel in the best possible light but . . . At the end of the day I'm still in charge here. Aren't I?

'I know that installing the chamber was your idea,' Araminta continues, 'and that you learnt how to operate it when it arrived because you were so keen to have one on the island, and start benefiting from it straight away while you were here so much during the set up. Isn't that right?'

Fuck. We do indeed have the only full cryochamber in the Maldives. And it *was* my idea to get it after I read that a whole load of footballers use them as part of their training and rehabilitation. I became a bit obsessed by the idea, I had to have one. And it did turn out to be a good decision. In fact, I like it so much that I'm planning to get them installed in all our other hotels too.

According to Ophelia, God rest her soul, instead of buying a Ferrari or a motorbike like any normal bloke on the cusp of their fifties, I made my mid-life crisis a drive to get fit instead. Since the chamber arrived on the island, I have been using it at least three times a week when I am here, which has been most of the time for the last few months. I guess marketing and PR must have passed that on.

'Yes. That's right,' I agree, reluctantly. 'But it's not something I'd generally do immediately after dinner and I don't know if . . .'

'I really, really would like to see how it works, Henry,' Claire insists. 'If you don't mind.'

I do mind. But it seems like I don't have a choice.

June, 1990

Funeral held for 17-year-old drugs death Hamlington Abbey student

The funeral of Ashley Pennington, who died after taking Ecstasy at a party at Tentingdon Hall largely attended by privately educated teens, was held today.

Mourners dressed in white for the short service and carried white helium balloons, which were released into the air as the white coffin was lowered in the ground.

As well as traditional hymns 'Amazing Grace' and 'The Lord's My Shepherd', 'Nothing Compares 2U' and Simply Red's 'If You Don't Know Me By Now' were also played during the service.

Following an investigation, a seventeen-year-old boy, who cannot be named for legal reasons, was arrested on suspicion of spiking the girl's drink, when a dinner jacket he was wearing, retrieved by police from a dry-cleaning shop, was found to contain traces of MDMA in the pockets. He was later released without charge, and has been suspended from the £7,000 a year school.

Meanwhile eighteen-year-old Robert Hall, who attends Drummonds Academy, a private London day school, was arrested and charged after being found with a large quantity of MDMA, also known as Ecstasy, at the party. He will appear in court on a charge of possession of a class A drug with intent to supply next month.

Ashley's mother Linda Pennington, 37, who, in a cruel twist was serving drinks at the ball, said, 'The light has gone out of our lives. Ashley's sister Jade and I will never come to terms with what has happened.

'I had told Ashley I didn't want her to go to this party. She was a good girl, but she was also a teenager who wanted to fit in with her friends. I don't blame her for going to the party. Girls will do what girls want to do.

'However, I firmly believe that she would not have willingly taken that drug. Her father died of a drugs overdose when Ashley was a baby, and I have never kept that a secret from her, or from anyone else. I myself am a reformed addict. Drugs were a frequent subject of discussion in our home and she fully understood the dangers.

'While it is of some small comfort that the young man who was selling drugs at the party is facing criminal charges, I am disappointed that no one has yet been prosecuted for spiking my daughter's drink. I, however, will not rest until anyone involved in my daughter's death has been punished for taking away my pride and joy, and ending the life of a young girl, full of promise, before it had even begun.'

DAY FOUR – Tuesday, 10 p.m.

Henry

'The cryotherapy chamber operates at around -135 degrees Celsius,' I say, mechanically, parroting what I read in the promotional brochure and what I was told in the training session I had when it was installed. I insisted on being in on the training, as Araminta rightly said, as I wanted to be able to use it as and when without having to bother one of the staff with showing me what to do each time.

Claire is dressed in simple blue shorts and T-shirts especially designed for the chamber, cotton only as anything else would freeze. On her feet she is wearing socks and slippers and I'm holding the large, super-insulated mittens she will need to protect her fingers. 'It offers a wide range of benefits – reduced inflammation, easing of pain, better blood circulation, improved mood and sleep, an increase in metabolism, higher white blood cell count and many other things besides. In fact, it's pretty good all round really.'

Running through the benefits like this reminds me why I wanted this thing and, since I've been using it two or three times a week, I *have* been feeling fitter.

Claire nods and then frowns. 'It does sound impressive. But I hadn't realized it operated at quite such a low temperature! I thought it would be more like one of those giant freezers you get in restaurants. Can it really be safe?'

'Absolutely safe. There are certain people who shouldn't use it, including people with very high blood pressure, pregnant women or people with heart conditions, but as long as you're reasonably fit and healthy, it's all good.'

I'd got her to fill in the usual form with its tick boxes and disclaimers, in which she confirmed she had no major health issues. It *is* safe, but there's no point in taking unnecessary risks.

'You only go in for a few minutes,' I continue, 'I'd suggest two as you're a beginner, I usually do three myself. And then when you come out, you have to go on the exercise bike for about ten minutes to warm your core up again. You'll feel amazing, I promise. It's about the best thing I've ever bought.'

She nods again. 'And what's the maximum possible length of time you can stay in for?'

'No more than four minutes is recommended.'

'And what would happen if you stayed in longer?'

'Well, you mustn't, it's as simple as that.' It's actually pretty gruesome what happens if you stay in too long, they ran through it in the training to emphasize the importance of using it correctly. But that's not something I'd want to talk about with a client. Stay too much longer than four minutes and you lose consciousness. Eight minutes in, you're probably dead.

'OK. Got it,' she says. 'Will you go first to show me?' she adds, in an irritating little-girl voice.

Fuck's sake. I didn't really want to do this at all but . . . what the client wants, the client gets. And in all honesty, given everything that's happened today, it probably is exactly what I need. 'OK,' I agree. 'Just give me a minute to get changed.'

I get into the chamber and set the timer, jigging up and down and walking around in circles in the small box, a little like a reverse sauna, to keep everything moving the way you are meant to. I feel my mood improve as the endorphins rise and actually, as I suspected, this is exactly what I need this evening to help me cope with everything that's going on.

The timer beeps, one minute.

I give Claire a thumbs up through the window and she gives me one back, with a smile. Pace, pace, pace. Poor Ophelia. But I will think about her later. I can cope. I am strong. I can do this. I can manage without her. It will be OK. I will make the hotel great. Perhaps I could rename it in her honour?

Another beep. Two minutes. I wave at Claire and she waves back. It will all be OK. I can do it. Mohammed is an excellent manager. Somewhat wasted in a small place like this. He probably won't stay forever. But Xander will help me. I can promote him. He could be executive director or something. He'd like that. We were always a good team back in the day. He can still look after the turtles too. We can afford more staff for the sanctuary. I'm sure we can.

Beeeep. Three minutes. Time up. I go to open the door.

It's stuck. I pull it again. Something is holding it closed. I try to call out to Claire but she is no longer there. I look for the emergency button but there isn't one, the equipment isn't designed to be used alone.

I pull at the door again, and again, and again. I go to bang on the glass but it doesn't matter. It's all OK. Everything will be OK. It'll be fine. It will all work out. It'll be . . .

DAY FIVE – Wednesday, 4.30 a.m

Malia

'Miss Malia? Are you awake?'

Adhara has let herself in and is standing by my bed with a small tray, which she sets down on my bedside table. 'I brought you some breakfast,' she says softly. 'As it is such an early start, I thought you wouldn't want to eat too much. So there is your usual latte, orange juice, freshly squeezed of course, yoghurt and fruit. But if you would like anything more, let me know and I can bring it straight away. We have a chef on standby.'

I sit up, rub my eyes and glance down at the tray. As usual, it is exquisite. The latte with the turtle logo and this time, a sprinkle of edible glitter. The fruit topped with flowers and the yoghurt in a tiny turtle-shaped dish with a little silver spoon. The orange juice in a crystal shot glass.

'No, thank you, this looks perfect.'

She gives a little nod. 'I will leave you to have break-fast, and then, if you like, I can come and pack for you?'

I shake my head. 'No thank you, that's OK. I've already done most of it, there's only a few other bits and pieces to put away.'

We are leaving today. It's going to be weird going home to my somewhat dingy little flat in a not-very-exciting suburb of outer London, getting back to ordinary things again like going to the supermarket, doing the dishes and cooking my boring little repertoire of meals for one.

'As you wish,' she says. 'The sea plane leaves at 5.30 a.m. to take you to the mainland for the early flight. Someone will come to collect your bags before-hand. In the meantime, if you need anything, you can ask me via the app as usual.'

'Thank you.' Adhara gives a little bow and leaves the room.

I get out of bed, wrap myself in my robe and slide open the terrace doors. It is still dark, but it is warm, the wind has dropped and it's finally stopped raining. I take the tray and bring it outside, placing it on the table by the outdoor sofa. It's still a little damp but my robe is so thick and absorbent I don't imagine I'll even feel it.

I sip the latte and look out over the water, where, unless I'm imagining it, I can see a few specks of those bioluminescent creatures we saw on that beach.

Can that really have been only three days ago? So much has happened. Lucy injured. Rob dead. A huge amount to think about.

I wonder what has happened to Rob's body. Have they already taken it away? I realize I don't actually know anything about him really – his website I looked at before I left very much stuck to the professional side of things. Does he have a family? Children, even? Will anyone grieve for him?

I didn't know him for long, and if I'm honest, I didn't like him much, but even so, I resolve to find out about his funeral when I am back, and try to go. I'm sure Araminta will be able to let me know about it. She'll have next of kin details, I imagine.

I eat the fruit and yoghurt and head inside for a shower.

At 5.15 a.m., as instructed, I go to the jetty. Araminta is already there in full makeup, looking slightly less perky than normal probably due to the early hour, but immaculately turned out as always nonetheless. River is in tracksuit bottoms and a slouchy hoodie which, even though it looks casual, I happen to know from the brand, one of his collaborators, costs several hundred pounds. He's staring out over the water.

'Malia, excellent, there you are!' Araminta exclaims, though thankfully at a more gentle level than normal. Adhara steps forward to hand me a tote bag with the turtle logo. 'Water and snacks for your journey, Miss Malia, plus a few souvenirs of your trip,' she says. 'It has been a pleasure to look after you this week, and I hope you have enjoyed your stay.'

'Thank you,' I say, taking the bag and slinging it over my shoulder. I'm desperate to have a look what's inside the bag, but I realize that would probably seem rude.

Araminta glances at her watch and frowns. 'Oh dear, I do hope the others hurry up,' she says.

Lucy arrives, followed by Julia carrying her case and bag. 'Sorry I'm a few minutes late,' she says. 'It's still taking me ages to get dressed.' She inclines her head towards her sling.

Araminta pulls a sympathetic face. 'Of course. You poor thing. And you definitely you don't want to see if you can get your shoulder seen to in Male before the long flight back? I'm sure your travel insurance would cover it.'

She shakes her head. 'No. Thank you. I've taken some more painkillers and it's really not that bad. With everything that's gone on I'd rather get home now.'

I can hardly blame her. Araminta glances at her watch again. 'Oh dear I do hope . . . ah, there you are!' she cries, as Claire slouches up, hair tied up in the ponytail, wearing basically a low-rent version of what River is wearing, but not nearly so well.

'I wish they'd arrange these transfers for a more reasonable time,' she grumbles. 'I feel like I've only had about two minutes' sleep.'

'Ah well, you can sleep on the plane!' Araminta replies. 'Right, now that everyone is here, shall we go? I know Henry and Ophelia would have liked to have said goodbye in person – but given the early hour, I'm sure you can forgive them for not doing so this time!'

Given their attentiveness during the rest of the trip it does seem a little odd. But I guess there are always limits.

I make a mental reminder to myself to send an email to them both to say thank you personally. In spite of everything, it has been pretty amazing.

As the sea plane takes us back to the mainland, I look out as the sun rises over the azure sea. It's stunning. I've never been anywhere like this before in my life. I imagine it's likely I never will again. I feel tears well as I think of Rob's twisted grimace as he loomed above us in the underwater restaurant.

Now that we're almost back online, that communication can be reopened and people can finally get onto and off the island again, hopefully they can find out what happened to him.

After stealing the fugu that night, I had been waiting for my chance. There are easier ways to murder people, of course, but it seemed fitting to kill Opheiia with reference to her ostentation. I mean, poisonous sea creatures on the menu! What is the point? What's wrong with a nice simple fillet of white fish, perhaps with a drizzle of basil oil or something if you're being fancy?

I'd kept a tiny bit of the innards in my water bottle and tucked the poison away at the back of a drawer once we got back to make sure none of the somewhat overzealous housekeeping staff took it upon themselves to wash the bottle out.

The chef that night, in between pontificating about how skilled and excellent he was, had told the group that you only needed a tiny amount of the poison from fugu to be fatal. The amount which would fit on a pinhead, I think he said? Something like that. So when Ophelia came to my door, I figured that rinsing a glass, tipping the fugu in, sloshing it around and then chucking it down the loo should leave more than enough poison in the glass to be effective. I came out of the bathroom, stood at the bar and poured the wine in to the glass before handing it to her.

She'd already had quite a lot of wine that night, but drank it all down anyway. And then after she left, I threw the glass into the sea.

November, 1990

Ophelia

The sun is streaming through the window when I open my eyes. I have that usual few seconds on waking of forgetting that everything is weird and strange now before reality crashes back in on me.

I sit up in bed. It is a beautiful room, strewn with furs and sheepskins – the kind of room I'd be delighted with for a skiing holiday. I can see snow outside the window, but I'm not in a ski resort. I'm in the middle of nowhere, simply here to be looked after, 'take the air,' like I'm some kind of Victorian invalid, and be kept out of the way. Not long now though. Just a couple more days, they think, though the exact dates are a little uncertain.

Elena knocks softly on the door and brings in my breakfast on a tray. 'How are you doing, Ophelia?'

she asks, her English immaculate but with a slight Swiss accent. 'Feeling OK? Is there anything I can get you?'

'I'm fine,' I snap, tears unexpectedly coming to my eyes. I've totally had enough of this. 'Can't wait to get out of this place. Get back to normal life.'

Elena nods. 'I know. Won't be long now. After that you can get back home and get on with things.'

I bite my lip. 'Can't wait,' I mutter, accepting the tray.

It was Father's idea that I came here. I ignored the problem for as long as I could, too long, until it was too late to do anything about it.

It had never occurred to me that I might get pregnant. It somehow seemed like the kind of thing which only happened to other people.

And it's not like I'd even had sex that often – not nearly as often as I'd made out to Thalia and Danute anyway. Yes, I liked to flirt, let the boys touch me, and sometimes I'd let them take it further, but mainly I didn't. The fun had gone out of it by then, so unless I really felt up for it, often I didn't bother to see it through. Mainly, I liked the chase. It's not like teenage boys are ever very good at it, is it?

That time with Xander, for example, total virgin, as I'd expected. And even though at the time he was notionally going out with that scholarship girl, the one who died, I'm pretty sure he's gay. The way he moons around Henry. Ridiculous. Henry knows it too, though he pretends he doesn't, because he likes to keep Xander at his beck and call. Or at least I think that's it. I don't know.

Xander was often at Cadwallader Castle at week-ends, he loved coming over. I don't think it was even a social climbing thing with him, like it is with some people who like to hang out with us there. I think it was all about Henry. I know all boys have mates they're stupidly close to, but there was always something different about the way Xander was with my brother. Mostly, I pretty much ignored Xander when he was round and left him and Henry to get on with their ball organizing stuff; the less I had to do with it, the better, except when it suited me.

But I was bored that weekend, and looking for something to do. Looking to have some fun.

'I know,' I'd said to Henry. 'Let's see who can touch Xander's dick first. Bet you twenty pound I win.' I loved getting Henry into bets with me. I pretty much always won. I didn't do it for the money. I did it because it was fun, to see how far I could push him. See what I could get him to do.

He gave me a withering look. 'Don't be disgusting. You're vile, Ophelia. I'm not touching anyone's dick, least of all Xander's. There's no way I'm getting involved in anything like that.'

'He'd love it if you did though,' I teased.

He tutted. 'Don't be gross. No he wouldn't. He's going out with a girl, Ashley, I think her name is, in case you hadn't noticed.'

I shrugged. 'She's a cover. Unless he's bi, maybe, I guess. Haven't you seen how he looks at you?'

Henry laughed. 'He looks at me in a totally normal way. We're mates. That's all. He is not interested in the contents of my pants in any shape or form.'

'If you say so,' I said, sarcastically.

'I absolutely do say so,' he replied. 'I also think, though, that he's a good bloke who wouldn't want you sniffing around him anyway. He's got a girlfriend and he's not that type.'

'*All* blokes are that type, given the chance,' I countered. 'Even the ones like Xander who are mainly gay.' I paused. 'Bet if you leave us alone for a couple of hours, I could prove it.'

He rolled his eyes. 'Fine. Whatever makes you happy, Ophelia. I think you're wrong, but I'll happily take your twenty pounds.'

Of course I wasn't wrong. And even though he was a crap shag and I had no interest in repeating the experience, it still pissed me off that afterwards he wanted to pretend it hadn't happened, and all he was bothered about was whether I'd tell Henry and that his precious girlfriend didn't find out.

What was wrong with me? I wondered. I was prettier, thinner, richer, had better clothes than her, so why would he be more interested in someone like her than someone like me? I didn't get it. It was offensive and disrespectful.

Stupid bitch. I was still annoyed about it by the May Ball, a few months later. So when the opportunity to put the pill in her drink was offered to me basically on a plate, I did it for a laugh. I thought it would be fun to have Xander see his prissy, strait-laced girlfriend in a different light. Who knew, he might even thank me for it. She'd probably be more up for it when she was off her head.

I didn't expect her to die. I didn't expect him to be expelled. And I definitely didn't expect to get pregnant.

Because I usually basically starved myself to stay thin, I hardly ever had periods and so I never particularly noticed that they weren't coming. Then it was summer, school had finished, so I was out a lot, partying, drinking, and assumed that was why I'd put on a bit of weight.

By the time I'd realized what was happening, it was too late to do anything about it.

Telling Father was the worst thing. He's never made any secret of the fact that I'm his favourite child. Not that he's ever said it, of course, but we all know it. All three of us. Mum died a long time ago. I don't remember her, but I've seen pictures. According to legend, she was everything to him, and I look just like her.

He actually cried when I told him. I had never seen him cry.

I told him I didn't know who the father of the baby was, and that was the truth. It was better that way anyway – if there had been a father he knew about, I was quite sure he would kill him. Literally kill him.

So yes, it may have been Xander, but there were a couple of other possibilities too, at least one of whom I wouldn't even be able to put a name to.

I considered claiming I'd been raped, but that would have meant either involving the police or, more likely,

Father trying to take justice into his own hands. And while I was annoyed with the way Xander had treated me, I didn't want things to go that far. Especially as Ashley, well, even if her death wasn't my fault exactly, I had played my part. This wasn't the time to be drawing any extra attention to myself.

So while Father wasn't exactly delighted at the news of his only daughter having had sex with more than one boy, as always, his main concern was for the good family name. An illegitimate child being his daughter's first-born when she was barely out of school was quite clearly not the image he sought for the Cadwalladers.

And as for me . . . I certainly wasn't ready to be a mother. There was so much I still wanted to do. Parties, travelling, maybe studying. Not nappies and school runs. Not now, not yet, probably not ever. I didn't ever see myself as a mother – my body being contorted out of shape, scarred forever with stretch marks, my lovely boobs belonging to a baby, being expected to put someone else before myself the whole time. No thank you.

Mr Harwood was called in, as usual, not only the Cadwallader solicitor but also the general family fixer. He would arrange everything, he said. He would find a nice family who would be grateful for the baby. Who would bring it up as their own. No one would ever know. In the meantime, he knew a discreet place in Switzerland where I could be looked after when my changing body could no longer be easily disguised simply by voluminous clothes, until the baby was born and its new parents came to collect it. We would tell everyone I was travelling, having a gap year. I had just finished school, there was no reason for anyone to doubt this version of events.

I agreed because really, what else could I do? I didn't want anyone knowing about it, or even seeing me as I got fat and ugly. I didn't want a baby, and I didn't want to be a mother. It was too late for the other option. This seemed to be the best way out. Afterwards, I would get a personal trainer, get my body back and get on with my life as if nothing had happened. It would be fine.

The pains started in the middle of the night. First, cramping. This is OK, I thought. I can cope with this. What's all the fuss about?

It was a little later than 2 a.m. but I rang my buzzer even so, I thought I should let someone know what was happening. The night nurse put her head around the door.

'Yes, Ophelia?'

'I think it's starting,' I said.

She came in and smiled, kindly, stroking my forehead. 'Ah. That's exciting! How are you feeling? Can I get you anything?'

I shook my head. 'No. I'm OK.'

'Good. Maybe try to get some more rest then, if you can. As a first timer, you might be in for the long haul, I'm afraid. Give me a buzz again if you need anything or even if you just want some company.'

I lay down again and tried to go back to sleep. But it was impossible.

317

Being in denial and with my head pretty much in the sand, I hadn't read much about labour or birth. I didn't really want to know. It would hurt though, that much I knew.

Suddenly, after months of simply ignoring the situation and then more months of trying my hardest to not think about what was coming, it was happening. There was no getting away from it. And I was scared. I squeezed my eyes tight and tried to shut out the intrusive thoughts, images I'd seen in films of women crying out in labour running through my head, as well as that somewhat traumatizing film they once showed us at school in their laughable, and somewhat pathetic, attempt at sex education in an effort to stop us ever wanting to have sex, probably.

I lay awake, wincing, intermittently crying, not from the pain, but from fear and self-pity. I felt so alone. I didn't want to do this. I should have paid more attention. Not had sex with Xander or those other boys simply for something to do. At least insisted they used condoms. Noticed I was pregnant in time to do something about it. So many things I could have done. And now there was no way out. It was too late. I had to go through with it, like it or not.

By the time my breakfast was brought in at 8 a.m., the pains had got worse, and I felt like I might throw up if I tried to eat.

'How long will this go on?' I asked.

Elena inclined her head. 'Difficult to say. It varies so much. All you can do is see how it goes, and we'll do our best to keep you as comfortable as possible.'

I felt a sudden wave of panic. I wasn't ready for this. Why hadn't I asked more questions? Maybe I should have listened when they tried to tell me how it would all go. Taken them up on the private and bespoke antenatal classes they suggested for me, instead of spending my time here simply walking, reading and watching old videos. But I didn't want to hear about it. It was better not to know. I wasn't good at dealing with pain at the best of times, and certainly not for several hours at a stretch.

'And when will we go to the hospital?' I asked. 'How far away is that?'

She squeezed my hand. 'We're hoping to not have to do that. We have everything we need for you and the baby here.'

I felt a stab of alarm. 'What? Here? Aren't babies normally born in hospital? What if something goes wrong?'

Elena stroked my hair. 'You're young, you're healthy, we've been monitoring you both carefully and everything seems fine. Chances are your labour and the birth will all go smoothly. It wasn't that long ago that all women laboured at home.'

'But it's 1990!' I shouted. 'No one does that anymore!' Another cramp came, harder this time. 'Please, take me to hospital. I can't do this here. I'm scared.'

I curled into the best approximation of a foetal position I could manage given my bump and Elena rubbed my lower back. 'Plenty of women give birth outside of hospital,' she said. Her voice was low and soothing but nothing she said was making me feel any better. 'It's a natural process. You'll be absolutely fine. Me and the other midwives will make sure of it.'

I wriggled away from her. Another cramp, this one making me cry out. I started crying. 'Please, it's really hurting now. Take me to hospital. Here,' I picked my Rolex up from the bedside table and tried to hand it to her. 'Have this. It's yours. It's worth thousands. I'll tell Father I lost it. You can keep it if you take me to hospital. Please.'

She took the watch from me and placed it gently back on the table. Her expression became more stern, though I thought I saw a trace of something else in it as well. Empathy? Pity, even?

She cleared her throat and looked away from me. 'Ophelia. I don't want your watch. But I'm afraid your father insisted that we keep you here if at all possible, for reasons of privacy, as well as your own wellbeing,' she said, fussing with some pillows at the head of my bed and gently guiding me into a more upright position to recline against them. 'And we have a full team on hand, not only midwives, a doctor too. You'll actually get much more care and attention here. The only thing we can't do is carry out a caesarean. Should that become necessary, we have permission to take you to hospital, of course. We also have our own fully equipped ambulance. But in all likelihood, that won't be necessary and you will be much more comfortable here while your baby arrives, I promise you.'

Another cramp, this one feels like someone is pushing a poker through me. 'It hurts though!' I scream. 'It really hurts!'

She strokes my hair again. 'I know, my darling. It does hurt. I'll get you some gas and air – we'll see how you get on with that. It takes the edge off. I'll be right back. Take deep breaths, and try not to worry.'

Present

British national held after three deaths on paradise island

A British national is being held on suspicion of murder on the island of Ketenangan in the Maldives.

The unnamed person was arrested after hotel owner Henry Cadwallader, 49, was found frozen to death in a cryotherapy chamber as spa staff arrived for work at the upmarket Henphelia Hotels resort on Wednesday.

Co-owner Ophelia Cadwallader, 49, was also found dead in her room. A third person, believed to be a journalist from the UK, died earlier in the week in suspicious circumstances, according to reports.

The suspect is being held in custody as investigations continue.

November, 1990

Ophelia

The pain was like nothing I had ever known. I literally felt like I was going to die. Surely something hurting this much couldn't be normal? Surely something was wrong? Surely the midwives weren't understanding how much agony I was in as they reassured that everything was fine and that I was doing brilliantly. How could something 'natural' feel like this?

They were kind, the women that attended me, but I also hated them. Hated that they couldn't stop my pain. But even more, I hated my father for putting me here, in this awful place, shut away. Hated whichever boy it was who got me in this situation. Why didn't they take responsibility? But most of all, I hated myself. I had done this. It was all my doing.

And then, just when I thought I couldn't bear any more, that I would beg the midwives to kill me so that I didn't have to endure this any longer, or throw myself out of the window to get away from this seemingly never-ending pain, with one final cramp which felt like a giant was squeezing me in the fist of his enormous hand and then trying to tear me in half, something slid out of me onto the bed. The midwife picked up the thing from the bed which looked like an alien covered in gunk and slime and there was a tiny cry, almost like a kitten mewling.

A baby, I realized, almost delirious with relief that the pain had gone and it hadn't killed me as I was convinced it would. My baby.

'It's a girl,' the midwife told me, grinning from ear to ear. 'A beautiful baby girl.'

They did something with giant scissors, I didn't want to look, wrapped her in a blanket and passed her to me.

'You did wonderfully, Ophelia,' she said. 'Meet your baby daughter.'

It had already been decided that I was not going to keep the baby. I was eighteen years old, my whole life ahead of me. Not to mention the shame it would bring on the family, which was Father's key worry. As far as anyone knew, I was on a year out, having deferred my university course on a whim. Because that's the kind of thing I did – party girl Ophelia, unpredictable, out for a good time. My friends thought I was doing a ski season in Val d'Isère. And then some worthy volunteering somewhere, looking after animals or maybe orphaned children, I forget – maybe Costa Rica? And working as crew on a yacht.

And I *would* be doing some of that. The ski season hadn't quite started yet, there was still time. Father has some friends who will give me a job in their hotel, even if I get there later than the rest of the staff. But somehow the excitement of it all seemed to have diminished since the baby was born.

I wasn't even remotely prepared for how I would feel. Those perfect tiny fingernails which grasped my finger. The softness of the soles of her feet which had never walked on anything. The little eyelashes that fluttered as I gave her a bottle. The tiny strawberry birthmark on her ankle.

I only had her with me for one night. Even though I was exhausted from the labour I stayed awake, watching her as she slept. She was wrapped up tightly in a blanket with a little white bonnet on her head. I kept her in bed with me until I felt sleepy, and was worried I might roll on her, crush her. She was so tiny and delicate. So then I put her in the little bassinet next to me to keep her safe, but still I barely slept. I didn't want to miss a minute of her. Not a second.

I knew I wasn't going to be allowed to name her, but in my head I christened her even so.

'Beatrice,' I whispered to her. 'I'm going to call you Beatrice.'

Father came to see me the next morning. He glanced at the baby, kissed my forehead and sat down next to the bed.

Tears were streaming down my cheeks. I hadn't been able to stop crying since I woke up after the short, fitful sleep I had managed.

'Ophelia, try to compose yourself,' Father said. 'I understand from the midwives that everything went well, and that you and the child are both in good health. That's really all that matters here.'

I wiped my nose on the back of my hand and saw Father wince. He handed me a tissue and I blew my nose noisily. I ignored his expression of disgust.

'Ophelia, please. None of this silliness. The new parents of the baby are here to meet her. They've been desperate for a child for many years, and have ample means to support her. Mr Harwood has thoroughly vetted them and feels they can be relied upon to be discreet. She will be well loved, cared for and provided for. This arrangement is the best thing for her, as well as for you. I realize it might not seem so now, but you are very young, and in time, you will come to realize that this is the correct course of action.'

I started to sob.

Father sighed. 'Ophelia. All you are doing is making this harder for yourself. It's like ripping off a plaster. Best to get it over with quickly.'

'I don't want to,' I choked out.

'Don't want to what?' he snapped.

'Don't want to let her go. I've changed my mind. I want to keep her,' I wailed.

Father sighed again. 'Don't be silly. You're only a child yourself. You have your whole life ahead of you.

A ski season, some travelling, university, and after that, who knows? You can't do any of that with a baby in tow. It's unconscionable.'

'I don't care,' I snivelled. 'I've changed my mind. I won't do it. I want to keep her.'

I flinched as Father's face darkened and he stood up. He had never hit me, but he was an imposing and frightening figure who Henry and I were always too scared of to disobey. This was the first time in my life I could think of that I'd actually even attempted to stand up to him.

'You are an adult, although only just,' he said, evenly. 'So I can't force you to give this baby away. But the papers are signed. You would be severely letting down a couple who are desperate for this child.'

The room was silent apart from my sobs. Was I supposed to care what some random couple I'd never met wanted? Wasn't being with my own daughter more important?

'I can't make you do this against your will,' he reiterated. 'But you must know that, should you decide to keep this baby and thus bring indelible shame on the family, I will no longer regard you as my daughter, and you will never see a penny from me.' He put his face close to mine. 'And I imagine it goes without saying, neither will your bastard offspring,' he added, his voice dark and full of venom.

'But . . . but . . .' I protested.

Father sat back down and looked out of the window instead of at me for around a minute while I continued to cry.

'Ophelia,' he said eventually, turning his head back towards me. 'This has always been your problem. You only ever think about the here and now. You never look at the bigger picture. And, I regret to say, that you only ever consider yourself, and what is best for you.'

I shook my head. This wasn't only about me. This was also about my baby. Wasn't it?

'You have a choice now,' he continued, his voice still low and measured. 'You can keep this baby, and ruin two lives – hers and yours – as you scrape through life, probably always struggling, without two pennies to rub together.

'Or, you can let her go. Give her to the couple waiting downstairs who will take her home to the warm and comfortable nursery they've already decorated for her. You can give both them and her a wonderful gift. Then you can get up, have a shower, get dressed, and get on with your life. If you like, we can even discuss that idea you had for opening a chain of hotels with Henry. I might be open to investing. It's your decision, Ophelia, but I think you know what you need to do.'

Claire

It was all Araminta's idea originally, or Jen, as I had known her, when she was still at Hamlington Abbey.

She was a great friend to Ashley. Her only true friend at that school, as I found out later.

I'd been so excited when Ashley was offered a fully funded place – there was no way I could have ever have afforded to send her somewhere like that. I thought it was an incredible opportunity for her, not only to experience the best education that money can buy, but also to be mixing with all the right people. Because everyone knows that's what's really important, isn't it? It's not what you know, it's *who* you know.

If I had my time again, I would have done things differently, of course. I knew Ashley didn't *love* the school, but she kept quite how miserable it was making

329

her from me. How badly out of place she felt there. How friendless she was, apart from Jen.

Would I have listened if she'd told me how much she hated it? I like to think so. But if I'm really honest with myself, I may not have done. Her being able to attend Hamlington seemed like such a gift to me. Such a world away from anything I'd ever known. I never wanted anything but the best for Ashley and in sending her to one of the most prestigious schools in the country, that's what I thought she was getting.

If only I'd known. If she'd never gone to that school, she wouldn't have gone to that awful party, and she'd probably still be alive today. Kids at our local comp, like the one her sister Jade went to, they didn't go to events like that. They wouldn't have wanted to, they knew they wouldn't have been welcome. I saw what those public school kids were like when I worked the bar at the ball, ironically enough to be able to afford Ashley's uniform. Stuck up and entitled little shits, the lot of them.

But back to Jen. When Ashley was at Hamlington, Jen would often come round to ours, stay over. Sometimes she'd be with us for long weekends or even the shorter holidays because her parents were abroad and there wasn't enough time for her to get out there and back, or they were staying somewhere unsuitable for her to visit, or the flight was too expensive.

After Ashley died, Jen and I became close. By then Jade had moved away from home, and her way of dealing with the loss of her sister was to simply not talk about her. To act like nothing had happened. To almost erase Ashley from her life, pretend she hadn't ever existed. And though I found that upsetting, I felt that I had to respect it. Jade had her own life to lead. If that was how she wanted to play things, I had to allow her to do that.

Jen, though, she dealt with the whole thing very differently. Jen loved to talk about Ashley. And because her parents were so far away, I think she started to see me as a kind of surrogate mother figure. After Ashley died she'd come over regularly and we'd do the kinds of things together that I used to do with my own daughter. Simple things, watch a film, go shopping maybe, paint each other's nails, nothing special or fancy. Sometimes I'd get out old photo albums and we'd look through them, reminiscing about Ashley. About her goodness. Her vitality. Her intelligence. Her kindness. And the terrible injustice of her not being able to live the rest of her life. The cruelty of it. The waste.

Jen, like me, was sure that Ashley didn't willingly take drugs that night. No doubt there are plenty of mothers who might say that about their own son or daughter, and be wrong. No one wants to think about their child taking illegal substances, do they? Every mother wants to believe the best of their baby.

I know that no teenager tells their parents absolutely everything, I'm not that naïve. But with my background as an ex-addict, I'm convinced Ashley had been put off drugs for life. I'd shown her pictures of myself at my worst, told her about the nights I'd spent in horrific squats, the rancid men I'd let do things to me in exchange for a hit. How I'd seen her father die with a needle in his arm. I was graphic about it, no detail spared. I wanted her to know.

She still could have gone ahead though, experimented, of course; that would always have been a possibility. She probably wouldn't have told me if she'd taken anything, I get that. But she'd have had no reason to lie to *Jen*. They told each other everything, and Jen agreed with me, Ashley was completely anti-drugs.

We are sure Ashley's drink was spiked. Over the years, usually as we bonded over a bottle of wine or two, we started getting together a list of the people who were to blame for her death. First, Rob Hall, the dealer at the party. I made it my business to find out who he was and what happened to him. Arrested and charged, but his punishment was little more than a slap on the wrist. He was done for possession with intent to supply, there wasn't enough evidence to make a charge of manslaughter stick. His youth, previous good record and, no doubt, rich daddy meant he got off with a fine and suspended sentence. He deserved to be punished. People like him are a scourge on society, harming and even killing others just to put some extra cash in their pocket. He was responsible for Ashley's death and for all I know, may have been responsible for others too, or at least for their potential spiral into addiction. He absolutely definitely deserved to die – no question in my mind at all. I knew what it was like to be a drug addict, and I wouldn't wish that on anyone. Drug dealers are scum, end of.

Secondly, Henry and Ophelia, obviously, also needed to be punished, for many reasons. For not caring that drugs were being sold at the parties they were running and being more interested in the profits, but mainly for not even offering Ashley the most basic level of care on the night she died. Most people would treat a dog better than they treated my Ashley. Jen saw what happened – they did as good as nothing, dithering around for ages, more bothered about getting found out for cutting corners and their fun being spoilt than they were that my darling daughter, my baby, was dying. It was Jen who had to call the ambulance. The Cadwallader twins didn't even care enough about my daughter to interrupt their partying.

And then, of course, they lied. They told the school they knew nothing about the drugs, about what went on at their parties. But *of course* they knew. How could they not know? If it had been any family other than the Cadwalladers, my betting is, things would have been investigated more closely. For all I know, maybe the father slipped someone at the police a sweetener to make sure things went their way. He certainly did at the school.

And finally, there was Alexander. Ashley's so-called boyfriend. He tried to call me repeatedly after Ashley died, but I refused to take his calls. Traces of drugs were found in his pockets and someone saw him giving her a pill that night. He probably gave her the substance that killed her, even though he denied it. He lied, said he did nothing more than give her a painkiller. And when she fell ill, he was much more worried about covering his own arse than about getting Ashley the help she needed, according to Jen. He found her unconscious on the floor but instead of calling an ambulance like any normal person would, he carried her all the way through the party and up to the VIP area. If less time had been wasted, maybe Ashley could have been saved, who knows? None of the three of them had bothered to arrange a first aid station – surely essential at an event of that size – yet another way in which they failed my daughter.

Alexander was expelled from school, but so what? The school year was pretty much over by then anyway; he still got to take his exams, as far as I understand. And then his rich daddy sent him off to volunteer abroad, the kind of thing only those with money have a realistic chance of doing, and he ended up doing something worthy with turtles. Happy as a clam, no doubt.

It wasn't the same for Jen. She was so distraught at Ashley's death and the guilt she felt about whether she could have done more to help her, she had a breakdown and missed her A levels. When she had recovered, she recommenced her studies and even went through uni, a few years later than her contemporaries, but some of the best years of her life were wasted while she caught up. She's never really forgiven herself for what happened to Ashley, even though it quite clearly wasn't her fault, and that's affected her mental health quite significantly over the years, off and on. There have been suicide attempts, and even a spell on a psychiatric ward. Things have been far from easy for her.

Meantime, as these four rich kids, Henry, Ophelia, Rob and Alexander, were all getting on with their lives, enjoying themselves, my little girl was rotting in the ground.

Taking revenge wasn't a plan Jen and I sat down and concocted over an evening. Far from it. It grew and gestated over a long, long time. Festered, even, you might say.

Jen would hear news of what some of them were up to from alumni newsletters sent by the school, and now and again we would see a piece about the Cadwallader family in the paper, what they were doing, and their hotel openings. Then, as the internet emerged and grew, it became easier and easier to keep track of them all, their wins and their successes. Kids like those grow into adults who don't often find themselves dealing with disappointment. And we both became angrier and angrier.

Araminta, as Jen was legally called by then, had already landed herself a job in PR. She had felt so belittled and punished for her lower-middle class background at Hamlington Abbey that once she left, after she finally got her A levels and before she started university, she took a new name to match her by now cut-glass accent. Jen Smith was gone, and Araminta Fernsby-Smythe was born. She'd changed her hair, ditched the glasses and lost a couple of stone. She looked like a totally different person.

It wasn't hard to find out which PR agency was looking after Henry and Ophelia's Henphelia hotel group, and when a job for an account manager there came up, Jen/Araminta applied, and she got it.

Even ignoring the fact that this brought us closer to our targets, I was really pleased for her. Before, she'd been working in pharmaceutical PR, so this was quite a change. There are lots of perks to working in luxury travel – dining in high-end restaurants as you schmooze clients, events in amazing venues where you'd never normally get to put your head around the door, and that's even before you get to the trips to the incredible holiday destinations. I totally understand that it's not always a walk in the park – that some clients can be arses and some journalists can be wankers – honestly – some of the stories Jen tells! But every few months she was off somewhere exotic, checking out a new resort the agency might have taken on to find the best angles to sell into the press, or accompanying a group somewhere they'd also experience the best of the local tourist attractions, jumping all the queues, eating in the smartest restaurants. Generally living the life of Riley.

It was actually one time when she was telling me about some of the shenanigans that the journalists get up to which gave us the idea for what we could do once the Cadwalladers' new resort opened. The lies that some of them had told to get on these lavish, all-expenses-paid trips! The freelancers who would claim to have a commission from a magazine or newspaper which would mysteriously fall down later. Some would fib about who they worked for. And that's even before you get to the kind of things that would happen when they were away on these trips. The demands they made. In and out of each other's bedrooms. Missing flights. Getting falling-down drunk. Stealing valuable items from hotels and restaurants. All sorts of things going on like you wouldn't believe.

Setting it all up took a good few years. We played the long game. Araminta made sure she was working on the Henphelia Hotels account as soon as she joined the agency, a good couple of years at least before their new opening in the Maldives. Even before the launch, she was sending out press releases about the luxury suites, the amazing restaurants, the chefs they'd brought on board, the turtle sanctuary. All that and more.

It was clear that they would want to organize a press trip for the soft launch, and we knew that this could be our big chance. Apparently, hotel owners quite regularly make an appearance for journalists on trips to their properties, so it wasn't hard for Jen to ensure that both Henry and Ophelia would be there. The Cadwalladers pride themselves on being hands-on in the running of the hotels (at least in the media) and on the hotel group being family-run. As it turned out, Henry and Ophelia had planned to be at the opening press trip anyway, and were both already spending quite a lot of time in the resort during the set up, especially Henry.

Jen knew the resort inside out before it opened. She made several site visits during the build, telling the marketing people that it was easier for her to get journalists excited about the resort the more she knew about it. So she was aware of the arrival of the cryotherapy

337

chamber, the personalized dive suits and the quad bike excursions. The guest fugu chef was actually originally her idea, though Ophelia later credited it to herself. Ironic, really, given what eventually happened.

Meantime, instead of accepting the Cadwallader's offensive offer to set up a scholarship in Ashley's name when she died – there was no way I wanted to inflict that awful school on anyone else – I asked that the funds were instead used to establish a charitable foundation to help rehabilitate young drug users, with the condition that no one in their family had any input beyond the original donation, and I have spent my time since Ashley's death fundraising and managing that. I learnt skills I never knew I had on the job and it's been immensely rewarding. I have never been the public face of it though – we have an ex-addict boy band member who acts as our ambassador, and does it brilliantly.

'I can't leave dealing with everything on the island all to you though,' I'd told Jen. 'I want to be there. Look them in the eye. Play my part in their downfall.'

So we'd hatched a plan.

While Jen was always expected to do what she called 'due diligence' about the journalists she invited on trips, she had also told me that occasionally people slipped through the net, and either weren't exactly who they said they were, or didn't end up delivering the coverage they'd promised.

Some travel clients would insist on any freelancers proving a commission in the form of something like an email from the publication they were writing for, stating that they would be publishing an article along with details of how many words and how many pictures etcetera. But the vast majority didn't do this, and would simply trust that the PR had done their job properly, and was working with journalists that they either knew and trusted, or ones for whom they had thoroughly checked out their credentials.

When we were thinking about how we could wangle a place for me on the trip, I remembered a story Jen had told me in the past about a journalist she'd heard about who had claimed several bogus commissions to luxury resorts all around the world. By the time anyone realized the commissions were complete fabrication, he was dead. It turned out he'd been diagnosed with terminal cancer, felt he had nothing to lose, and thought he deserved some free holidays before he finally checked out.

We'd also discussed how Jen and her clients go about ascertaining whether a journalist is legit before inviting them on a trip which might sometimes be worth thousands. Apparently, if it's not a journalist they already know, the first thing they would do is have a look at their online presence, especially if they are a freelancer.

'We don't exactly do a deep dive though,' she'd told me. 'To be honest, it wouldn't be that hard for almost anyone to get a place on a trip with a little bit of effort.'

And this is where our idea started. We decided that I needed to travel under a fake name. It was unlikely that Henry or Ophelia would remember my name from all those years ago, even if they had even ever known it, particularly as they had seemed to care so little about what had happened. But we felt it was a risk that could easily be eliminated, and so was well worth doing. Plus, in case anyone cottoned on to what we were up to, it would be easier for me to disappear afterwards.

We bought a fake passport first. I'd thought the dark net was only for criminals but no, apparently anyone can use it. And just like that, I became Claire Dixon. Perfect.

Once we'd got that sorted, we built a website. It's not like in the old days when you needed to be a computer whizz to do it and know about things like coding; just about anyone can do it now, which was lucky, as it wasn't exactly the kind of thing we would have wanted to outsource. You don't need any special skills, just patience really. It's kind of like building with blocks, only online. Once I'd got the hang of it, I quite enjoyed it.

We invented a good career for me, using some real magazines in obscure places around the world, where we figured it was unlikely anyone who looked at the site would know anybody working at the publication. We deliberately mostly chose ones which are no longer running for extra safety. Jen dug out various old pieces of copy (as articles are called by journalists, she said), changed them around, downloaded some photos from online libraries, made PDFs and put my name on them. They would serve as 'cuttings' – we didn't need too many. We added a few fake references and testimonials from made-up people at the various magazines I'd 'worked for'.

It was brilliant – it all looked really convincing to me.

'The site might not bear very close scrutiny,' Jen said, 'but it's unlikely the client or anyone else will look at it and, even if they do, it will only be a quick glance. There's no way they'll contact any of the magazines we've said you've worked for or anything like that. And we'll take it straight down after the trip. If anyone asks, which they won't, we'll say you've retired.'

Jen had told me about some of the journalists she'd met on trips who basically complain about everything even though they're in the lap of luxury with everything possible being done to ensure they have a great time. I thought it would be fun to make that my persona. A diva, never happy with anything. Almost the exact opposite of my true self.

'The, erm, older ladies tend to be the worst for that kind of thing,' she'd said. 'Always showing off about where else they've been and how everything was better back in the day. And then there are also the ones who think everyone fancies them and flirt with any man who looks their way. It's embarrassing for everyone. On one trip I had, one woman in her sixties decided not to come back with us because she'd apparently fallen in love with the twenty-five-year-old waiter. Next time I saw her she was being interviewed on breakfast TV after he'd married her and run off with all her money.'

I was so excited about it all – the trip, the role play, the luxurious destination which I'd never be able to afford myself; everything about it sounded amazing. But best of all, we were going out there to pay Henry,

Ophelia and Alexander back for what they did to my darling girl.

And then we had another brilliant idea. We would get the man who provided the drugs which killed my baby to come out there too. Get rid of them all in one fell swoop. It was going to be amazing.

Araminta

It was me spending far more time than was healthy jealously obsessing over Rob and all the exotic press trips he was going on which originally gave me the idea of moving into travel PR.

After my breakdown, finally getting my A levels, missing out on the Oxbridge place I'd originally been slated for but eventually getting a degree at a mediocre university, I started working in PR almost immediately, but for boring, dull things ranging from pharmaceuticals to photocopiers.

By around the mid-2000s, as more and more publications were coming online, ex drug dealer Rob Hall was a kind of *bon viveur* about town, writing sneering columns for a couple of the lad mags, and also travel articles – taking trips to luxurious and exotic places.

They were painful for me to read, but I couldn't help it, like probing a bad tooth. Seeing him doing so well for himself and going to these amazing places quite clearly on someone else's dime made me furious. Ashley never got to do anything like that. And I would never be able to afford it. Unless I got a job which would take me to those kind of places without needing to pay for it.

So I got myself a job where I could do exactly that. Though by the time I got my first job in travel for Amazing Places PR, Rob, along with the lad mags, seemed to be disappearing from the journalism scene. A bit more internet research and some other features that he'd written suggested that he'd had a period of ill-health, possibly alcohol related. And from his LinkedIn page which I viewed from a colleague's computer so that he wouldn't know I had been checking him out, it looked like he had moved on to importing wine, though he still wrote the odd piece, largely when publications wanted something retro about lad culture or similar. And when I was tasked with organizing the Ketenangan trip for Henry and Ophelia, I got in touch.

I had to be persistent. He didn't reply to my first few emails, and then he said that he was out of the game and didn't think it was something he could pitch. I nearly cried with frustration.

I needed to get him on the trip, but I also needed to make sure there was no paper trail. It was important that no one knew that I had gone out of my way to persuade him to come. So I arranged to meet him for dinner in a restaurant which was newly opened and was near-impossible to get in to unless you were an A-list celebrity, had booked several months in advance and had several hundred pounds available to spunk on one meal, or were looking after their PR and pretending you were taking an important food critic to dine there, like I was. I thought the invitation would tempt him out and luckily, I was right. I put on a low-cut dress, did my hair and makeup, and prepared my spiel.

He arrived before me, and was already seated at the table when I arrived. He was pretty much what I expected, a fatter, older, craggier version of his byline picture, like most journalists are. I knew from the old press reports that he was only a year older than me, but anyone looking at us would think it was more like ten. I look after myself, admittedly, and am not ashamed to admit I've had a bit of work. It's important in my game.

I had to steel myself not to physically recoil as he stood up as I arrived at the table and shook my hand, barely even trying to conceal his lecherous look which travelled up and down my gym-toned body, sheathed in a tight black dress. Ugh.

'Rob! Thank you for coming,' I said, as a waiter pulled back my seat and gently pushed it back in for me as I sat down, before covering my lap with a white napkin with a flourish. I ordered a bottle of wine – I needed Rob to have a good night and leave him wanting to spend more time in my company. Plus, I could do with a few glasses myself to get through this evening with this abhorrent man who had helped to kill my best friend and stolen what should have been some of the best years of my life.

We read the menus in silence and then placed our orders – I noticed that Rob opted for the most expensive things on the menu, but whatever. I kept my face in my usual 'whatever you want is absolutely no problem' expression; it's not like I cared anyway as obviously the client was picking up the tab.

We made small talk about our journeys, our day, what we'd been up to lately. I was barely listening as our starters arrived, our main courses, and finally, dessert. It felt like a very long evening. He wasn't good company and I had no interest in what he'd been doing or how he felt about anything. All I cared about was getting him to come on to this trip.

'So, down to business,' I said, leaning in a little more to give him a better view of my surgically enhanced cleavage and toying with the stem of my wine glass suggestively. 'The Maldives trip I emailed you about. I think with your experience and profile you'd be an ideal fit. It'll be a really good one – incredible food, diving, quad biking, all the usual stuff. And no expense spared, none of the nonsense you get sometimes on trips about one glass of wine only with dinner and empty minibars. These hotel owners want their guests to have a good time.'

He sat back in his chair, his expression inscrutable. I held my breath as I briefly wondered if he would make the connection between the balls where he sold drugs and the hotel, but it seemed unlikely. I hadn't put it in my release. Why would he even have taken in who owns the hotel? It's more than likely he didn't even know or care who ran the balls all those years ago either. He was at a different school and while, to someone like me as a naïve teenager, Henry and Ophelia seemed almost on a par with the people I was reading about in *More!* magazine celebrity-wise, with the benefit of hindsight I can see that they weren't as important and famous as I thought they were, or indeed that they made themselves out to be.

I wasn't worried about them recognizing Rob – he was just a random boy who attended a school slightly less exclusive than ours and sold drugs in a dark corner. He's literally twice the size he was as a teenaged dealer, pure fat, no muscle. Balding. I saw him briefly in court, and at Ashley's inquest, and there's no way I would have put the two together.

It's very likely he never even met Henry or Ophelia – those parties were huge and I'm sure she would have got someone else to actually hand over the money and collect her pills. She wouldn't have got her hands dirty with something like that. She may have even sourced her drugs elsewhere – I have no idea.

Rob took a large slug of wine and nodded at the waiter in brief acknowledgement as he took away his cleared plate.

'I'm flattered that you're so keen that I come,' he said, 'but to be honest I'm not sure where I'd pitch it. I'm a bit out of the game these days – I'm not doing stuff for Condé Nast or the national travel sections or any of those places that these kind of resorts usually want anymore. Most of the mags I used to work for have closed.'

'Yep. I get that. But . . . even though clients always say they only want coverage in high-end glossies, sometimes they have to accept that that's not what they're going to get. And while the resort is beautiful, the nationals have already done the Maldives to death, and in the current climate are often more interested in covering destinations which are more affordable. And between you and me . . .' I lean in and see his eyes flick downwards to my chest again for fuck's sake, 'it's been pretty hard work getting people to come on this trip at all. It's too long, it's the wrong time of year, the freelancers can't get a commission, the staffers can't take that much time out of the office.'

He takes another large gulp of wine and looks at me intently.

'If you were to come along . . . you'd be doing me a favour,' I continue. 'The client won't be pleased if I don't get enough bums on those plane seats and, well, my job doesn't exactly feel secure at the moment so . . .'

I sit back, look down at him and then look up at him through my eyelashes, head tilted down. I even bite my bottom lip. All extremely cliched stuff, but I can see him weakening.

'Well, I'm sorry to hear all that, Araminta, and I'd love to help, of course,' he says, wiping his hands on his napkin and throwing it on to the table in a scrunched ball. 'But like I said, I don't have any contacts in any of the kind of publications they'd go for anymore and you know what editors are like, they use the same old stable of freelancers and it's impossible to even get a foot in the door so . . .'

I lean towards him. Time for the big guns. 'Rob,' I interrupt, my voice low and confidential. 'Tell you what. We've had a nice time tonight, haven't we? I'd love it if you came on the trip. Give us some time to . . . get to know each other better.'

He leers. He actually leers. It's disgusting. But I just about manage to keep my cool.

'I'll have a chat with some of the editors I know,' I continue. 'The ones I work with regularly. I'm sure I can find one to take a piece from someone of your calibre. If you can make time in your diary, I can get you on the trip. I'll tell you who you're writing for nearer the time.' I pause, twiddling a lock of hair around one of my fingers. 'Something online. Or a membership mag. I'm sure I can sort something out. Nice trip for you, gold star for me, extra coverage for the client. Winners all round.'

He nods. 'Well. If you're sure, and, like, if it helps you out . . . yeah, why not?'

I smile at him, swallowing down my revulsion. 'Excellent. I'm glad we understand each other. I'll be in touch.'

And that was that. A few days later, thanks to me he had a couple of fake commissions and I booked his plane ticket.

He probably couldn't believe his luck.

*

I knew that Henry and Ophelia wouldn't look too closely at who I was bringing on the trip. I'd worked with them for a few years by now, even though I have rarely met them in person, and they trusted me. I held my breath the first time we met, frightened that they might remember me, and I was relieved and entirely unsurprised that there wasn't even a glimmer of recognition. As well as looking very different to how I did as a dumpy 17-year-old schoolgirl, I was never even remotely on their radar back then. They were only interested in themselves and their own circle, someone like me as I was then would barely have registered.

There *was* one surprising thing that came up while I was booking the trip though. Ophelia sent me an email about an influencer she wanted to come. Neither of them ever bothered with anything like that usually, they leave it up to me and the rest of the team. I looked her up – Malia somebody – and didn't understand why Ophelia wanted her there. Malia was a part-timer who had a day job in a library, didn't have very many followers, and her whole schtick seemed to be about being ordinary and relatable. But ordinary and relatable people don't tend to be able to afford to go to a luxury resort in the Maldives and, even if they did, there are plenty of other influencers much like her but with larger followings who would have been a much better fit as far as I could see.

I suggested a few of them but Ophelia said no, she'd really like this particular girl to come, along with some convoluted nonsense about how she thought she was going to be the next big thing.

I couldn't see it myself, but Ophelia was the boss, so I made sure Malia was invited, and of course she jumped at the chance, bless her. She'd barely done more than the odd spa and restaurant review before.

It was only later that I started to have my suspicions as to why she'd been asked along, and why Ophelia had been so insistent about it. And then the truth came out.

Influencer revealed as heir to
the Cadwallader family fortune

Following the deaths of Ophelia Cadwallader and her twin brother Henry, the heir to the family's fortune has finally been found.

Librarian and influencer Malia Tate, 33, from Gloucestershire, is set to inherit Cadwallader Castle, along with the Henphelia Hotel chain, and other assets believed to be worth several million pounds.

A forensic examination of Ms Cadwallader's computer found that one year ago she had employed a private detective to trace her daughter, born in secret when she was just eighteen years old and privately adopted shortly afterwards.

DNA samples comparing the two have since confirmed the match.

'Of course it was a huge shock,' Ms Tate told reporters. 'I had a comfortable, middle-class upbringing and had no idea I was related to one of the richest families in the country, or even that I was adopted until I was contacted on behalf of the Cadwallader estate.'

Malia's adoptive father died last year, and her mother resides in a nursing home, suffering from Alzheimer's. An investigation has been launched into the illegal adoption, but it is believed to be unlikely that any charges will be brought.

'I wish my parents, as I continue to think of the people who brought me up, had told me the truth,' Malia continued. 'As things stand, I don't even know who my biological father is or was. But I bear the couple that brought me up no ill-will, and I am forever grateful to them for taking me on and giving me the happy childhood that I had.'

'When I was invited on the inaugural press and influencer trip to Ketenangan,' Malia continued, 'I was very surprised, but I thought I'd just been lucky. The PR who organized the trip has since told me that Ophelia asked for me especially. I will, sadly, never know her reasons. Perhaps she was going to tell me she was my mother. Perhaps she wanted no more than to have a look at me out of simple curiosity. But if she was going to reveal herself to me, she was killed before she got the chance.'

Neither Ms or Mr Cadwallader were in long-term relationships, and their mirror wills, drawn up by the same family solicitor before his retirement, left the entirety of their estate to each other.

Ms Cadwallader added a codicil to hers that in the event of both their deaths, her daughter should be traced and inherit.

Probate is ongoing and it is believed that the will is currently being contested by at least one distant relative of the Cadwallader family.

Meantime, the hotel chain continues to be run by managers and trustees, until the beneficiary of the will can be confirmed.

Six months later

Malia

'Hey look, the results are back!' I say, holding the letter out to show River.

The envelope is marked 'DNA TO GO'.

I know what it is. This envelope might hold the secrets to my parentage, to links to other family who I've never known.

Or it might tell me nothing at all.

I had never been told that I was adopted. And when I found out that Ophelia was my mother, almost the first question I had was, of course, who was my father?

It took an age to get hold of my birth certificate, because there was so much secrecy around my adoption and because a lot of the admin seemed to have been fudged, but when I eventually managed to track it down, it came back as 'father unknown'. My adoptive father was already dead, and even if my adoptive mother ever knew, she certainly wouldn't be able to tell me much now. Most of the time, she barely even recognizes me when I visit.

I tracked down the Cadwallader family solicitor Mr Harwood, who clearly thinks I'm well beneath him and the Cadwallader family he knew, and has no interest in talking to me. Though I imagine chances are, he doesn't know who my father was either. For all I know, Ophelia, or my mother as I am trying and failing to think of her, may not ever have known.

River puts his arms around me and nuzzles my neck. I love it when he does that.

We kept in touch after the Ketenangan trip, messaging each other on Insta because it was comforting to speak to someone who'd been through the whole thing too. I hadn't realized quite how traumatized by the whole thing I was until I got back, when I'd find myself bursting into tears for no reason, sometimes at really inconvenient times, and other days, just not wanting to get out of bed. I even had to take time off work – fortunately, they were really understanding about it.

I found I wanted to talk about it, but not with my usual friends. With someone who was there, who understood. Like River. We started meeting up for the odd coffee, then drinks, then one night, after quite a few drinks, we ended up coming back to mine and having sex and since then we've pretty much been a couple. Our followers love us even more as a pair, we've both gained masses and we do loads of collabs. There's the odd troll, sure, saying River must only be with someone like me for the money, when he could have anyone he likes, but whatever. They're just jealous. I know he's with me for me, I don't care what they think. We got together before all that stuff about me being Ophelia's daughter came out anyway.

And he was such a huge support with all that. I don't know how I'd have done it without him. It's pretty weird to be told you've gone from barely having a penny to your name to being probably one of the richest people in the country.

It was River who suggested I try DNA TO GO. 'It may come to nothing,' he'd said, 'But it's worth a go. If whoever your father is has ever been interested in finding out about his heritage, he may be on there. If he's never registered, then he won't be, but you've got nothing to lose. And you never know, there might even be some undiscovered half siblings or cousins knocking around. Maybe Henry had kids he didn't know about. Maybe Ophelia had another secret baby. You might not be the only one!'

I laughed, but it was a little hollow. Wouldn't siblings complicate things even more?

The probate thing is still rumbling on. The will is clear – Ophelia wanted me traced and her estate left to me – and there are no other direct descendants of either Henry or Ophelia, at least none that anyone knows of. But there are various second cousins twice removed who say that the castle has been in the Cadwallader family since the twelfth century or something like that and it shouldn't be going to some random like me, although not in so many words.

I'm *not* a random though. I am a Cadwallader, whether they like it or not, and indeed, whether I like it or not. And I'm not entirely sure how I feel about it yet. I've always been quite happy with my lot, simple and unexceptional as it is. And while a castle and riches might sound like a dream come true, it's also kind of overwhelming. If it does all come to me, I'll no doubt need a team of advisors, accountants, hotel managers and all sorts. I'm thirty-three years old and work in a library, I don't know how to deal with any of that. And that's even before you get to the things that the Cadwalladers have done over the years. Slave trafficking is just the start of it. I'm not sure it's a family I can be proud to be part of.

Since all this happened, some of the papers have decided to take a deep dive into things that happened in the past. Not only covering up my birth, but also, it sounds like, making sure the death of that poor girl who died at one of their balls before I was born was brushed under the carpet. Awful.

However, I am a Cadwallader, whether I like it or not. And if I inherit their fortune, I intend to turn things around. I can see now that Henry at least was trying to do that in his small way, but I intend to do much more. Charitable foundations. Education programmes for underprivileged children. I wouldn't know how to set up any of these things, but I'm determined to try to make some of the wrongs of the past right.

'Well, let's see then,' River says. 'Let's find out. Open it.'

I hold my breath and tear it open.

There's a list of a few names, tagged with things like less than one per cent shared DNA, fourth to sixth cousin.

And then there's one that leaps out at me.

Fifty per cent match.

Alexander Chadwick, Maldives.

Claire

Part of me thought it was a shame to kill Henry that way, in the cryotherapy chamber. Too quick. In an ideal world, I would have liked him to suffer more. After what, I imagine, would have been a fairly fleeting few minutes of panic, as far as I understand, when you die of hypothermia, there's a feeling of euphoria before you die. I didn't want him to experience that. Hopefully the ridiculously low temperature the chamber is set at means that there wouldn't have been time for that euphoria. I hope it hurt. I hope he felt his eyeballs freeze and his lungs seize up from the cold.

I mean, really though, he deserved it. Not only for what happened years back, but for being so vain and stupid as to submit himself to such a ridiculous treatment willingly. It's so typical of his type – sums up everything about him. I mean, who puts themselves in a box at sub-arctic temperatures just for fun? Utterly ridiculous. He deserved everything he got. There's no way you'd catch me in something like that. I mean, I would have gone in if I'd absolutely had to, but I'd have come out within a few seconds, claiming claustrophobia or something like that.

Thing is, by then I was getting desperate. We were going to be leaving the next day, and Henry was still alive. That wasn't part of the plan. After Jen's messing around with the diving equipment failed, we had to think fast. I took the fugu and poisoned Ophelia without too much problem, but couldn't find a suitable time to get to Henry in a way he wouldn't notice. It was much easier with Ophelia as she spent so much of her time pissed. So in the end it didn't matter too much that Jen's hobbling of the quad bike didn't go quite to plan, and she certainly played a blinder with Rob and the ackee.

One plus, though, about the diving sabotage failing, is that Henry got to see his sister die. Ophelia was such a cold-hearted bitch I doubt she'd have cared that much about Henry's demise had the deaths happened the other way round. At least he saw her after she'd been poisoned, and he had a good few hours of suffering, knowing that she was dead. My only regret is that I didn't have time to tell him it was us who killed her, and why. Oh well. I thought about opening the door of the chamber to give him the big reveal, but it was too risky. He could have overpowered me and escaped. And obviously the

362

temperature needed to stay low, otherwise it wouldn't have worked at all.

Once I knew Henry was dead, I unblocked the door and switched the machine off. Henry was accustomed to using the machine and I imagine he'd happily use it unattended, even though I'm quite sure you'd be warned not to. People like him are so arrogant, think they're invincible, that nothing can touch them. I could have left the machine on, and then when he was found dead in the morning by some unfortunate cleaner or spa worker, their first thought would, I imagine, have been that it was a tragic accident, or even suicide following the death of his beloved sister.

But no. That wasn't what we wanted. Even though we were leaving the island, we weren't quite finished. There was still someone else who needed to suffer. Who needed to be made to pay.

It was hard, meeting him for the first time at the turtle sanctuary. I couldn't bring myself to talk to him, or look him in the eye, I felt such hatred towards him.

I emailed the local police from an anonymous account especially set up for the purpose to let them know where to find the 'trophies' that Jen had planted – in Alexander's filing cabinet on turtle island. They found them and he was arrested. I'm pretty confident he'll be found guilty.

Justice will finally be done for my Ashley.

British man in court following three deaths at luxury Maldives resort

Alexander Chadwick, 48, originally from Caversham, Berkshire, has appeared in court in Male charged with the murders of hoteliers Henry and Ophelia Cadwallader, and British journalist and wine importer Rob Hall.

During a recent press trip arranged to celebrate the opening of the ultra-luxe Ketenangan resort in the Maldives, Mr Hall was found floating in the water above the island's underwater restaurant. A post-mortem found the cause of death to be drowning, while a toxicology report revealed that he had recently ingested highly poisonous unripe ackee.

Ms Cadwallader's death was found to have been caused by fugu poisoning. While the notoriously potentially poisonous Japanese delicacy fugu had been served to the group of journalists and influencers a few days earlier without incident, Ms Cadwallader was not present at the meal, or even on the island when it was served, and it is not known how she came to ingest the poison. Mr Cadwallader was found dead in the resort's cryotherapy chamber.

Items belonging to all three victims – Ms Cadwallader's sunglasses, Mr Cadwallader's electronic cigarette and a baseball cap belonging to

Mr Hall were found in a filing cabinet in the defendant's offices, trophies taken from the victims, according to the prosecution.

The prosecution has requested psychiatric evaluation for Mr Chadwick, suggesting that the collecting of souvenirs from the deceased could be indicative of psychopathic or sociopathic tendencies. Prosecuting counsel added that it was possible that Mr Chadwick had been seeking revenge against the Cadwallader twins and Mr Hall over a drugs-related crime he felt he had been wrongly accused of while still at school.

Mr Chadwick's defence barrister argued that all evidence given at the trial was purely circumstantial, and that there was no concrete proof that Mr Chadwick had taken the items, administered the poisons, or caused Mr Cadwallader to become trapped in the cryotherapy chamber.

He added that all three deceased had ongoing distressing personal issues, and it was possible that any one of them, or indeed all of them, could have deliberately taken their own lives.

The hearing was adjourned for legal argument around the necessity of psychiatric evaluation of the defendant.

Acknowledgements

First thanks as always to my brilliant agent Gaia Banks for all the advice, reading of terrible half-drafts and general handholding. Thanks to everyone at HarperCollins who I still feel it is a privilege to work with, four (!) books in, especially Kate Bradley, Fliss Denham and Meg Le Huquet.

Thank you to the people of Huvafen Fushi who were so welcoming during my visit – I knew the Maldives would be wonderful but my stay absolutely exceeded my expectations. Special thanks to marine biologist Hamid, dive instructor Antonina and marketing and communications manager Ankita Thakur for answering all my endless questions about poisonous sea creatures, potential diving accidents and how the communication and transport work in the islands. As well as being one of the most beautiful places I've been lucky enough to visit on my press trips, it also felt like one of the safest, and I have taken substantial liberties for reasons of fiction in cutting the island off in the book. Thanks also to butler Yoonus for looking after me so well, and to Charlie Dyer for facilitating the trip.

Thank you to River Scott-Tyler for your generous bid in the Book Fuel auction to name a character. Hope you like him!

Thanks to beta readers Hannah Parry, Sarah Clarke and Fran Bevan, your input was invaluable.

As usual thanks to my online friends who have been involved in several aspects of the book, including helping to name the island, donating their surnames to characters (quite a few made it in this time), pedantic discussions of grammar points (everyone seems to love those!), as well as generally keeping me entertained. Special thanks to the Savvies, the D20s and the Witches.

Thank you to the crime writing community for being such fabulous and supportive people – it was so exciting to finally meet some of you this year and I'm really looking forward to doing much more of that in the future. Special thanks to those who have read and endorsed the previous books – every single one is appreciated. Even more thanks of course to Phoebe Morgan for bringing me to HarperCollins, as well as for all the support along the way.

As ever thanks to Alex for your general support, keeping the house running while I'm doing my important lady authoring, for reading drafts of this book (twice!), and always listening when I am boring on about my plot issues and character motivations. I know

I am very lucky. Thanks to Toby and Livi for always making me proud, as well as lending your childhood toys' names to turtles in this book.

And finally, thank you to the bloggers, bookstagrammers and readers! I am so grateful for your support and enthusiasm for the books, and I'm always delighted to hear from you through the usual channels.

If you enjoyed *The Island*, don't miss out on
Catherine Cooper's other gripping thrillers . . .

Four friends. One luxury getaway. The perfect murder.

French Alps, 1998

Two young men ski into a blizzard . . . but only
one returns.

20 years later

Four people connected to the missing man find
themselves in that same resort. Each has a secret.
Two may have blood on their hands. One is a
killer-in-waiting.

Someone knows what really happened that day.

And somebody will pay.

They thought it was perfect. They were wrong . . .

A couple on the brink
A body on the lawn
Welcome to...

THE
CHATEAU

CATHERINE COOPER
THE *SUNDAY TIMES* BESTSELLER

A luxurious chateau

Aura and Nick don't talk about what happened in England. They've bought a chateau in France to make a fresh start, and their kids need them to stay together – whatever it costs.

A couple on the brink

The expat community is welcoming, but when a neighbour is murdered at a lavish party, Aura and Nick don't know who to trust.

A secret that is bound to come out . . .

Someone knows exactly why they really came to the chateau. And someone is going to give them what they deserve.

A glamorous ship. A missing woman.
A holiday to DIE for . . .

A glamorous ship

During a New Year's Eve party on a large,
luxurious cruise ship in the Caribbean, the ship's
dancer, Lola, goes missing.

Everyone on board has something to hide

Two weeks later, the ship is out of service, laid
up far from land with no more than a skeleton
crew on board. And then more people start
disappearing . . .

No one is safe

Why are the crew being harmed?
Who is responsible? And who will be next?